ANNE DEW

Squirrels in The Roof

Published by Curlew Books, Colchester

Second edition

ISBN
978-0-95707-880-2

Printed by Think Ink, Ipswich, Suffolk

Squirrels in The Roof

My thanks to editors Dimitri Murray and Jennifer Castle for their valuable help and guidance and to Robin for the layout of the book.

Dedicated to Bodo and Madge.

Chapter One

Two houses. One on the Thames and one on the Spree. Big houses. Old houses. With one big problem. How do you go about keeping what isn't yours when spiritually and by reason of occupancy, ancestry and the simple fact that it's your home, it should be yours? Possession is nine-tenths of the law but try telling Kitty that as she sits at her long table in her long front room (much too spacious for a soon to be octogenarian but that's another story) bonding the shard of porcelain to the plate wedged in a bed of plasticine in front of her. She has already made a trial run by fitting the pieces together with Scotch tape and numbering them with post-its. Now the moment has come to apply the adhesive, five parts AY103 (Epotek 301) to one part HY956, which she has mixed on her palette with a small spoon and left to partially set for an hour.

Kitty in her kitchen mixing her potions, adding titanium dioxide powder to counteract the effect of yellowing, the whiff of peroxide, Araldite, the tang of oil paint, all pervading and mingling with last night's fish supper. The fish lady comes once a fortnight in her van from Hull and, if Kitty is out, slips a pound of haddock on the hook in the porch where it is inaccessible to cats, squirrels and marauding foxes.

The shard locks into place and the bird amputated of legs and wing is restored upon its perch of flowering cherry. Kitty appraises the join, and sees where a little of the adhesive will have to be lifted with a double-edged razor blade once it is dry. She will have to sand, repaint and glaze it. Applying Chintex is a delicate task. It has a tendency to form air bubbles. But Kitty isn't worried about that now. She leaves the plate resting on its bed of plasticine, a sunburst poised upon a dark cloud.

Cumuli are gathering in the west, above the chestnuts on the ait they roll, plumed dark as ink. Outside her window, beyond the voluptuous peace roses, the Thames barely moves, a pool of mercury, sluggish. Kitty gives it hardly a glance. She leaves that to others.

Even the young woman had forgotten for a moment the damage to her Chelsea plate, 1756 or thereabouts she'd been told, and had gone to the window to view the front lawn freshly mown leading to the white picket gate and the towpath, grass fronded and below it the river, wide hipped as it takes the curve before narrowing again at Teddington. One of the last stretches of rural Kingston. 'You could be in the country. Imagine, only twenty minutes to Waterloo. It must be worth a fortune. Two million at least!'

Kitty hasn't had the house valued. Numbers worry her. Instead she points out the damp on the wall where the drainpipe burst five summers ago and still hasn't been repaired and the stains on the green carpet, worn to the yellow of lichen and tells anyone who will listen that there is an underground stream which rises in time of flood and turns the floor to sponge. 'The house will have to be pulled down. The wiring hasn't been touched since 1938. And as for the plumbing....' The pipes boom like an ocean going liner blasting off a head of steam when there's an airlock. It's as if by some quirk of the compass, the QE2 has docked below Teddington Lock and is now sending out a distress signal.

That's what a tug of the lavatory chain does if the house is feeling bullish. If it wants to roar rather than settle back amid the lilac, humoured by the tickle of bats and butterflies, the nesting birds and the squawk of the herons. If it is feeling benign, Kitty can get on with her china restoring and her classes and forget about the precariousness of her existence on the river's edge, in her rural backwater a mile downstream from the shopping malls and nightclubs of Kingston.

The plate isn't Chelsea. Kitty had been suspicious of the Raised Anchor mark, something about it not quite right, and the absence of moons was always a giveaway, those circles of transparency when you hold the object against the light. Chelsea Moons. There had been no hint even of an eclipse, but Kitty had decided not to mention it. The young woman, 'please call me Amanda,' was upset enough so why rub salt in the wounds? Besides, was the plate worth any less emotionally, just because it was baked in a kiln in China some hundred years later? People put too much value on provenance.

Kitty doesn't own the house. People assumed that she did and when she said, 'I'm only the tenant. I'm looking after it for an old friend who's in a nursing home,' there was usually a pause. So not the dotty old spinster sitting on a fortune, then?

Wrong on all accounts where Kitty is concerned. Her husband Alfred had died of Alzheimers fourteen years ago and she'd nursed him through his violent outbursts. And his wanderings. He would climb out the window at night and be found hours later in the Ham Lands, his face and hands lacerated by brambles. Once he'd got as far as the Grand Union Canal at Brentford, eight miles away, a man of seventy nine in filthy pyjamas trying to board one of the barges. Heaven knows what he'd been thinking. Where had his mind gone? What had spirited it away and replaced it with this blankness? Kitty would stroke his cheek and look into his eyes that were the *bleu turquin* of a Sèvres vase, and she would talk to him about the past. About their son Derrick, killed in Malaya during the Emergency, a soldier of twenty one who'd gone into the jungle one day and never come back. It had comforted Kitty to speak so freely about him for it was something she'd never been able to do when Alfred was of sound mind. The subject had become taboo over the years, a wound that had built up scar tissue and been calloused by feelings of separation.

After Derrick's death, Alfred had become a spiritualist. But Kitty couldn't bring herself to make public her grief. She was a private person and putting her feelings on display made her feel vulnerable and somehow cheated. Nor could she suspend belief like Alfred did. She wanted so much for Derrick to walk through her door and to hold his long boned body against hers. Nothing but his physical presence would do, so what was the point of trying to commune with a ghost? Kitty didn't believe that the dead could be roused in a tiny airless chapel and identify themselves to a stranger as the letter D with brown eyes.

Derrick's had been hazel. Didn't Alfred remember anything? She'd got so mad with him. They'd rowed all the time until it had been so exhausting that they'd stopped mentioning Derrick for fear of unleashing more demons. So much recrimination. Leave him to rest between them, an unspoken presence until Kitty dies and takes his memory with her. Kitty has no vision of the astral plain that Alfred had spoken about.

But Elsie did. She was a believer. She and Alfred attending services in the spiritual chapel on Villiers Road, its foundation stone engraved with the name of its benefactor, Sir Arthur Conan Doyle. That is how they had met.

But then Elsie had loved Derrick too. She had known him when he was a little boy. Elsie - now... she really is sitting on a fortune. Here's this house by the river and another at Farnham which she inherited from her grandmother. That was sold ten years ago and a housing estate stands on the site now. But Elsie didn't make a fortune. She promised it to the first developer who came to her door with an offer (a young man who reminded her of Derrick) and Elsie never went back on her word, not even when she was told she could have doubled the price.

After her second stroke she moved to Fircroft which cost half of what they were asking for at the five star nursing home she'd set her heart on up at Kingston Hill with its state-of-the-art facilities, on call medical staff and fees of four thousand a month.

Kitty has made that quick calculation over and over. That's forty-eight thousand a year, enough to provide for a family, no, a whole village in Africa for an entire life time. Kitty clutches her throat and shakes her head at the thought. Who says all lives have equal value?

Yesterday, after Kitty had washed the Chelsea plate with warm water and ammonia and left it to dry on a lint free cloth, she had climbed into her Nissan Micra automatic and driven over the bridge to Teddington to see Elsie. To check up on her landlady, her benefactor. Every Friday without fail. On the passenger seat is a pack of three Marks and Spencer's individual trifles, a cherry Genoa cake and some snapshots Kitty has picked up that morning from Jessop's photo shop.

You would think after a year of telling Elsie the same White Lie that it would roll off Kitty's tongue as smoothly as jelly and cream. A matter of survival, is what Kitty says to herself to make it more palatable.

And when she sees Elsie with her face all misaligned from her stroke and the touch of rouge added by a cheerful young carer that adds to the impression of a dressed corpse, like Lenin, Kitty thinks, her darling Elsie hanging on by a thread that coils tight around Kitty's throat, her voice trembles. 'Elsie darling,' Kitty says in her piping voice, 'you're looking well. What a pretty dress.'

She smooths Elsie's lap where the bony knees protrude under the silk skirt and smiles into her friend's eyes, for since her stroke Elsie has lost the use of her right side and it is a matter of interpretation, the darkening and lightening of the eyes, the interlocking fingers, that give Kitty to understand that she is welcome.

Kitty pushes Elsie in her wheelchair onto the terrace and they sit blinking into the sunlight like a pair of old cats and Kitty begins to give Elsie the latest gossip; the new neighbour who drives her yellow Ferrari to the shops that are just five minutes away. 'There's a young man living with her but I don't think it's her son.' Kitty had peered out the window one evening and seen the Ferrari parked in the front garden with a shapely leg sticking out the window and a man's bare bottom mooning the windscreen.

'Bob and Sylvia have just come back from China. They said it was wonderful but very crowded. Oh, and there's talk of putting double yellow lines along Water Lane but the Calloways, you remember them, mother and daughter divorced, big settlement, who take in strays? They put the high fence up to stop the dogs from escaping, well they're against all forms of restriction. Richard, the lawyer at number 107 is calling a residents meeting in the pavilion next week but I don't know whether I'll go.' Kitty's voice falters. Elsie has closed her eyes. Maybe she's asleep, or just bored? She doesn't know the people Kitty's talking about. It's been all change at Water Lane since she left. The past is her comfort zone now.

'And Freddy....'

Elsie opens her eyes. The welfare of her beloved Yorkie whom she left in Kitty's care when she moved to Fircroft is the only thing that interests her. Let the wealthy young professionals snap up the properties and convert them into million pound homes, it's of no consequence to Elsie. It's

Freddy, her companion of the last six years with his failing kidney and weak bladder (forget the underground river beneath the carpet, those stains pong in hot weather) who sets her speech falteringly into motion. Slurred yet coherent enough for Kitty who has been waiting for just such a moment. That is why she is here. To make her report. To pull out the latest batch of pictures and perpetuate the White Lie.

She selects four of the best. Freddy at the window, Freddy in the garden. Freddy beady eyed above the mint bed, that pointy snout, those tiny teeth sharp as a piranha's barred in what Elsie will interpret as a smile. Freddy at the back of the vast lawn, a small straggly dot of dusty oily hair, fringe yanked into a waterspout and tied with a strip of blue ribbon. Kitty had given them barely a glance when she'd gone to collect them from the photo shop but now with horror she notices that her best friend Adele, who had been helping her with the shoot, had propped Freddy against the wooden cross marking his grave. Freddy within and without.

'He's doing well,' Kitty enthuses, sticking her thumb over the offending corner. 'I'm giving him the course of vitamins the vet advised. Oh, he's frisky for his age and I still tootle down the towpath with him as far as the gym.'

Maria, one of the Polish care workers employed in the home treads across the lawn with the ankles of a young gazelle. 'How are you doing?' she asks, beaming at the two elderly ladies. She knows Kitty now, recognising the high cheekbones and wide face that is more Polish looking than English. Kitty's complexion is like a crushed magnolia petal, her hair like corn stubble after rain.

'Hallo, Maria,' she replies.

'Ah you have more pictures of little dog. You show me, please?'

'So cute,' Maria enthuses, wrinkling her nose as she slips them out of Elsie's lap. 'My mother has little dog also. I don't know name in English.'

She slides the photographs between her hands but Kitty notices that it is the ellipse of lawn and the house poised at its cusp, the backdrop of river where a sailing boat idles, that is the focus of Maria's attention. Freddy could be a garden ornament. He could be the base of a stone birdbath or a dead mutt brought vividly to life by the expertise of a Surrey taxidermist for all Maria cares. Which is the truth. The counterpoint to the White Lie.

Kitty had driven all the way to the Devil's Punchbowl with Freddy packed in ice in the picnic box on the back seat, a sheaf of photos in her bag to give Mrs Brindley a feel for his personality. She had told Kitty on the telephone that it was important to try and encapsulate the spirit of the animal. She didn't just mount and be done with it.

Kitty felt as if she had travelled across all of Surrey trying to follow Mrs Brindley's directions and it had been such a hot day. When she finally found the flint cottage which was on the edge of a Forestry Commission's pine plantation, the ice had melted and poor Freddie was already starting to smell. Mrs Brindley had appeared in her floral smock and with a pair of muscular tattooed arms had plucked Freddy from his box and examined him under a strong light.

'Old age, was it?' she'd asked.

'I suppose it was,' Kitty had replied, 'I was taking him down the towpath for his morning walk when he suddenly keeled over.'

She was still in a state of shock. Mrs Brindley had removed a twig from Freddy's stiff coat and brushed the earth off his paws. 'I'd already buried him,' Kitty explained. 'It was my first reaction...'

'And then you couldn't part with your little sweetheart,' Mrs Brindley had said kindly. 'Mind you, with the digital age most people are content with a DVD. There isn't much call for mounting pets in this day and age. My best business is in birds, for decorative purposes. I pop them under bell jars for instant Victoriana and sell them to antique shops in Guildford.'

Freddy had been laid to rest in the deep freeze amongst the road kill pheasants, stoats and badgers. There had been the peppering of grit as he'd been lowered inside and Kitty had sunk into a chair, stricken by the memory of Freddy dropping dead in front of her. Just a few seconds earlier he had been baring his fangs at the ducks on the bank and cocking his leg over the ankles of a dozing fisherman. Business as usual. She must have looked horrified for the man had come hurrying over but all Kitty could remember was the dark stain on his trousers and thinking whether she should offer to pay for his dry cleaning.

Elsie loves the photographs and Kitty says she will frame the best one and add it to Elsie's collection that she keeps on top of the walnut cabinet she brought with her from Seething Wells. The rest of Elsie's furniture, the good pieces of rosewood and mahogany, the kidney shaped chairs, the chiffonier and French sideboard with its gilded cherub cornices and most of the china, are still in the house exactly where Elsie left them. Kitty has not moved a thing except her table which she got Rosario the gardener to bring down when she took over the house.

For three months Kitty had stayed put in her flat upstairs; a small unheated bathroom and kitchen but a large front room, (Elsie's parent's old bedroom) shabby, cold in winter when the wind blows through the dormer windows and cuts your ankles to shreds, but more than compensated for by the view. And the unrelenting light that picks out the hairline crack in a creamware teapot. Kitty had muffled herself up in winter and thrown open the windows in summer. It could be like a sauna in July living under the roof.

Kitty had never complained. She had been eternally grateful to Elsie for giving her a home where she could mend china and at the same time slowly pick up the pieces of her life. She hadn't wanted to stay in her old flat with its memories of Alfred and when her landlord put up the rent it was a good excuse to move on.

Kitty saw her restoration of a Derby vase as a watershed; remodelling and gilding a lost handle and retouching the chipped panel of polychrome flowers with a deftness that had always been there but had been neglected during the years of nursing Alfred. Kitty had always had a gift for handling colour and applying texture and had had no trouble recognising the Chelsea as a copy. A master like O'Neale would never have delivered such a poor representation of roses and forget-me-nots.

Her vision is still good, incredibly so, for a woman of almost eighty. Kitty attributes this to her Highland mother's winter diet of salted herrings and potatoes when she was growing up with her three brothers in rural Surrey. No cataracts. Stronger glasses though. But no tremor in her hands. Not like her best friend Adele who often can't hold a teacup for spilling it. She has been a regular member of Kitty's china class since its inception in 1978 and still attends most Mondays for the company if nothing else.

Just this weariness that rolls over Kitty when she's stressed. She feels it coming on now as Elsie peers lovingly at Freddy's snapshots. It's as if God has reached up for the light switch and turned it off.

And it is at moments like this that Kitty is tempted to tell Elsie the truth about Freddy and have done with it. Elsie is sure to find out sooner or later and it's better coming from Kitty than that nephew of hers who will only distort the White Lie and make it his truth. Which isn't what Kitty wants at all.

Jason had begun turning up unexpectedly at Seething Wells after Elsie moved into Fircroft. That was when Freddy was still alive. He'd stand in the kitchen, arms folded across his chest as though he were already the proprietor, and Kitty could tell by the way his eyes wriggled like a pair of tadpoles in his big round face that he was already sizing up the place and making plans. Kitty had turned to pour him a cup of tea one day and caught him making little jabs at Freddy with his boot. He was allergic to dogs he told her and Freddy knew it of course and played up to it, making forays at his ankles and trying to hump his bulging calf muscle if Jason didn't watch out.

He was a health professional, Jason had told Kitty, but when she had shown him the deep cut on her finger (what with the abundance of sharp knives, toothpicks and razor blades, Kitty's table after one of her classes resembled the aftermath of a cannibalistic feast) Jason had suggested she go along to A&E and have it stitched. He wasn't a doctor, he was in management in the NHS, running research projects. *Funding* was a word that popped up a lot in conversation with Jason, and Kitty suspected that she too had become a project and that Jason had already decided she should become self-funding as soon as possible.

'Aunt Elsie's not in for the long haul,' he'd said to Kitty when they had met at the nursing home after Elsie's last stroke. Kitty had conjured up this image of a jumbo jet and replied absently, 'No, I suppose not,' which had seemed to cheer Jason up.

'Without sounding insensitive, I think it's time we dusted off those contingency plans,' he'd said. And as Jason was expecting an answer Kitty had replied, 'Yes, you're right,' before putting it out of her mind. The future was already behind you when you were knocking eighty.

When Jason learned that it was Elsie's express wish that Kitty stay in the house and look after Freddy, Fircroft having a strict no pets policy, he had not been happy. 'How old is the dog?' he kept asking. 'Six,' Kitty had said and then thinking about the implications she'd consulted Adele and they'd come to the unanimous decision that Freddy should, like Zsa Zsa Gabor, simply lose a couple of years. So when Jason asked to be reminded, Kitty said, 'Um, four. Yes, that's right, born in Gwent. He's a Welsh Yorkie with a long pedigree.'

For a while there was talk of Jason adopting Freddy and taking him back to his wife Marion who was also a health professional. But what to do about the window panes rattling and the china chinking on the shelf whenever Jason had a sneezing fit? He tried a whole range of anti-allergen products but they only seemed to aggravate his condition.

And when Marion turned up with the basket to take Freddy back with her for a trial run, Freddy had wriggled out of her grasp and raced round and round the house, cocking his leg on every piece of furniture and tearing backwards and forwards into the garden and yapping his head off at the jogger on the towpath and making such a scene that Marion had tugged at her navy jacket, the one with the shoulder pads removed, and made a hasty retreat up the garden path.

After that embarrassing incident, Kitty was to glance out her kitchen window sometimes and catch Jason and Marion cruising past in their BMW but they never called in. And after one of those sightings, Kitty always made a point of having Rosario dead head the roses and give the lawn an extra trim, for she knew that Jason was looking for the slightest excuse to get rid of her, and an untidy hedge might be viewed by some as symptomatic of a general decline in other areas where Kitty was just fine thank you very much.

The same could not be said for Elsie, poor thing. Sometimes Kitty thought it was only her tales of Freddy's derring do that were keeping her alive. The morning Freddy slipped his lead and joined the Tao Kwon Do class at the Adult Education Centre always got a smile. Oh, and the day Kitty had found him lying on the carpet in Fran's up the road watching a racy film with her on the DVD player.

But for how much longer could she keep up the deception?

When she returned from Fircroft, she poured herself a whisky and went into the porch. Across the river on the ait the trees were a blur of yellow green. Spring was the harbinger of new life but in Kitty's experience it also quickened the pace of Death. Alfred had passed away in March and so had several of her friends. The promise of warmth and blossom helped them to struggle through the rigours of winter but as the days grew lighter they were often too spent to enjoy it.

Elsie had struck Kitty as very frail. Her skin exuded a dry papery smell and her eyes were so milky that it was a miracle she could see at all. And yet, in spite of everything, Freddy's photographs always managed to spark that tiny portion of her brain where memory remained untarnished.

Kitty kept Freddy in the porch, away from the mice that used the skirting boards in the front room as the M1. He was also a deterrent to the opportunist when the French doors were left open. Mrs Brindley had done an excellent job, cocking his head at an alert angle, pricking his ears and giving him the hint of a snarl that was designed to make anyone think twice about overstepping the boundaries between the front lawn and the towpath.

Kitty was comforted by Freddy's presence and not just for reasons of safety. Like one of the ravens at the Tower, the Yorkie was both a symbol of permanence as well as uncertainty. So far she'd been lucky. Her secret was safe with 'the girls' from her china class; they knew what was at stake and she was always careful to keep Freddy out of sight when she had visitors. She had thought of getting another dog - all Yorkies looked more or less the same to Kitty, and she was sure that Elsie would never spot the difference, but it went against the rules of fair play to forfeit what little there was of the real Freddy to an impostor. Freddy might not be able to yap and go walkies but in essence he was still the dog that Elsie had known and loved.

The sun was glancing off his glass eye and for a moment Kitty was almost fooled into believing he'd come back to life; revitalised by a play of the light and her wishful thinking. She scooped him up, mindful of his dusty smell that weakened the waft of winter verbena outside the door, and squeezed his hard body underneath its silvery coat.

'Well Freddy, what's going to happen to us?' she said, holding him up to her face and giving him a wiggle as if he were a toddler. 'What, indeed?'

Something had fallen onto the floor and peering down she saw that one of Freddy's claws had fallen off. It was a reminder, if Kitty needed one, that even a stuffed animal came with a sell by date and recourse to needle, thread and superglue would one day not be enough to patch together the ravages caused by damp, moths and her own guilty conscience.

Chapter Two

Not even Jason and Marion at their most passive-aggressive had worried Kitty as much as the sight of Elsie hunched in on herself that day at Fircroft. It had seemed to Kitty that Elsie was already negotiating with the spirit world for her place on the celestial plane, her time on earth being almost done. Elsie had told Kitty that animals did not possess souls and, although she would see Freddy before she passed on to a higher level, he would never be allowed to join her.

'It's Freddy that's keeping her alive,' Kitty told the china class when they turned up on Monday. Thc twins Milly and Molly driving down from Guildford in the Rover and treading the path to her door in their rubber soled Eccos, a flurry of pastels and knife pleats and Yardley lavender water. Then Doreen, motoring in from Godalming in her 1976 Mercedes coupé, the year of her divorce from Alan when nothing but a kick in the engine and a blast of exhaust would dispel the misery of his adultery with Billy Vane, a New Romantic who had worn ruffled shirts and tight black leather and hung out at Camden Lock in a haze of Afghan Gold. Bosco, the huge Portuguese with a face cratered with the smallpox he'd caught as a child in Macau, came puffing up the path with a parrot under his arm. 'Capodimonte' he wheezed, brandishing the bird above his head in triumph.

'More Casa Pupo if you ask me,' Sylvia had murmured from the kitchen where, with a tea towel wrapped around her waist, she had been the first to arrive and had taken charge of the coffee making.

'One broken beak,' Bosco said, placing the cockatoo on the table and flopping into a chair. He pulled out a handkerchief and mopped his brow. 'I bought it on e-bay for five pounds.'

Kitty picked it up and said, 'I think we can fashion a new bill from some modelling wax.'

'You need to see the Will,' Sylvia said bringing in the cafetiere. She had been a woman of business before her retirement, a buyer for a large London department store, travelling the world for novelties and gifts. 'You have to find out whether Elsie has left you anything, Kitty. It's no good pussy footing. You must be totally informed of your position before the old girl snuffs it.'

'She's right,' Molly and Milly chorused. 'You can't assume anything in this day and age.'

'And Jason will have no compunction in seeing you off,' Sylvia warned, bustling across the room, wren like, dressed in a blue costume with a pearl brooch pinned to the lapel. She had been responsible for hundreds and thousands of pounds in her old job. Taking risks, assessing the taste of her customers and realising early on that tat outsold style and quality a hundredfold. Anything with animals. Nudes were good business too.

'Talk to Elsie before it's too late.'

Kitty had always believed that left alone, things usually took care of themselves and even the best laid plans could not guarantee a satisfactory outcome. Life was like the Thames outside her window. It began with a sprightly gurgle in the chalky hills of Oxfordshire but as it grew bolder it was straight jacketed into weirs and forced through tortuous locks with disastrous results. The water table had risen in some areas and flooding was now an annual event.

'We forget the bigger picture at our peril,' she had warned, to which Sylvia had retorted, 'In your case Kitty, if you don't manage your situation and quickly, you will be staring at the walls of sheltered housing on the Bembridge Estate.'

Sylvia owned a detached house in New Malden where she had lived with her mother until her death in 1997. Sylvia had never married. 'All the best men went in the War,' she had told Kitty without bitterness. There had been a few liaisons during her travels. A married man in Singapore whom she'd grown fond of but he wouldn't leave his wife, and then as she'd got older she had come to the conclusion that most men were selfish and only looking for someone to take care of them, and that wasn't her thing after mother.

Bosco turned his melancholic face towards Sylvia, his black eyes like melted liquorice and asked whether there was any reference to a parrot in one of her books. Kitty had gone over to the shelf and taken down the volume of World Ceramics, grateful for the diversion. Sylvia could be so intense at times.

'Is Elsie still paying the bills?'

Sylvia was sanding a jug after filling in the crack with plaster of Paris and a little polyvinyl acetate emulsion. Her grey hair, neatly coiffed in a gentle bouffant and then lacquered, did not move as her head bobbed

'I believe she is.'

Sylvia dropped the twist of sandpaper onto the table. 'You mean you don't know? Oh, dear. Have you a standing order for the council tax? What about the gas and electricity?'

Kitty was rummaging through her drawer for a piece of wax to give to Bosco who had been waiting impatiently for her to get on with the modelling. No Capodimonte featuring a cockatoo, no sign of a parrot at all. 'Why don't you study the parakeets on the tree outside?' Molly had suggested. 'I counted over thirty the last time I was here.'

'Parakeets aren't cockatoos,' Bosco had replied testily.

'But they're taking over. They're squeezing out the

local wildlife and killing the trees,' Milly said, pale on pale, her face and hair like a head of wild parsley.

'Sylvia's right. Get something in writing, dear,' Doreen advised. 'Thank God I did that with Alan. This was long before prenups, but as I was earning so little as a concert pianist, it was Alan who had the idea of making provision for me should anything go wrong. I think he already knew he swung both ways and once he'd made up his mind what end of the pendulum he was on I was given my settlement. It was guilt money, of course.'

The china class had heard this story too often to look interested and there was an audible intake of breath from the others as Doreen toyed with the idea of giving her marital history another airing.

'If I hear how Billy Vane ruined Doreen's life just one more time, I'll say something I'll regret,' Sylvia was heard to hiss when she was washing up. She was feeling testy on that particular Monday after her plan to finish her Victorian doll's head had been thwarted.

For days she had been practising drawing on sheets of paper to achieve just the right expression; forceful yet not boastful, knowing your own worth while still retaining an air of detachment. Then the colouring; red madder genuine for the cheeks, burnt umber for eyebrows and a mixture of Indian red and burnt sienna for the lips. Painting on a face had brought back memories of getting ready for dances during the war.

And then, just as Sylvia had been set to go, Kitty remembered that she'd knocked the airbrush off its cradle and broken it. There was a man in Bromley who kept spare parts but Kitty had mislaid his number and then forgotten.

'What you need is a lodger,' Milly piped, 'Someone quiet, with money, like a Japanese student.'

Molly screwed up her mouth and glanced at Milly.

'But the Japanese are so cruel.'

'Just a thought, but it would help to pay the bills in case they're gathering on the horizon.'

'The agreement was that Elsie took care of everything as long as I stayed and looked after Freddy,' Kitty protested.

'Yes, but Freddy's not here,' Sylvia said quietly. 'I mean, we pretend he is but let's not fool ourselves. Remember Kitty, Jason knows the life expectancy of a Yorkie. He's young, he can afford to wait.'

Kitty hated this kind of grilling. Her friends were bursting with *Schadenfreude* for they were proof that shoring up the bank produced a comfortable retirement. Sylvia had two private pension schemes and Doreen was forever commenting on the FTSE and her investments. Milly and Molly were just as bad, banging on about equities and gilt edged. Only Bosco seemed to match Kitty for financial incompetence, his dourness and Portuguese fatalism, (he had the hand of Fatima as his door knocker) making them unconscious allies, although their relationship was becoming increasingly strained this morning as Kitty failed to lay her hands on the modelling wax.

On the table the cockatoo cast a cynical eye on the proceedings, his porcelain feathers metaphorically ruffled by the sense of unease that had settled over Kitty thanks to her friends' prodding.

And here was Molly opening the cupboard to stare at the bewildering array of art materials stored therein to ask where she could lay her hands on the Chintex and Doreen reminding Molly to dig out the sepiolite while she was there and Milly and Sylvia engrossed in their own theory about climate change, 'Scaremongering. I haven't forgotten the winter of 1942 or the hot summers of 1948 and 1977. The weather's always been unpredictable and as for this Il Nino. An ill wind cooked up by those environmentalists to justify their huge salaries. I read in the paper.....'

And they were off again using Elsie's house in Water Lane as Speaker's Corner, their voices quivering in the beams that criss crossed the ceiling in a riot of woodworm and dry rot and penetrating as far as the back porch where on the road behind the hedge of syringa and budding hebe, a dark BMW stopped to survey the two cars parked in the drive before continuing slowly on its way.

* * * * *

Kitty was secretly relieved when the class left early, Milly's worry about traffic on the Hogsback being the precursor for a general exodus. A rather grumpy class that day, Kitty observed as she followed them to the door and onto the path. Not much had been achieved in the way of china mending, her failure to locate the modelling wax being compounded by the discovery that she had run out of Chintex, although she could have sworn she'd bought new supplies from the King's Road only last week.

'If that's the case then where have you put it?' Molly had demanded, trying hard not to sound frustrated, but it was a round trip of sixty miles from Guildford to Kingston and she had planned on glazing and baking her shepherdess and returning it to the top of the TV console where it had stood before Milly's cat had knocked it over. Molly was not an animal lover and Milly collected strays just to spite her.

In fact, she found it quite an ordeal having to eat her lunch in the porch under the glittering eye of Elsie's stuffed dog, although no one else seemed to mind. Bosco, whether aware of her queasiness or not, always gave Freddy a pat before dipping into his KFC bucket and pulling out a quantity of jumbo sized chicken legs and thighs, all pumped full of hormones, for no chicken in Molly's experience ever grew to those proportions. And she had seen Bosco using Freddy as a napkin, wiping his greasy fingers on his coat when no one was looking. Not that Molly cared. But Bosco never seemed to wash his hands and she had noticed two silvery hairs trailing from the cockatoo's comb in a smear of grease when she'd inspected the bird after lunch.

On the way home Molly said to Milly that she couldn't see the point of keeping Freddy if the only purpose was to take a few snapshots to show Elsie. 'Elsie's almost blind, it could be any dog. And he's starting to smell.'

Milly stroked the little castle pastille burner in her lap. It had taken her weeks to replace the missing flowers; moulding the kaolin putty into petals and, after they had dried, bonding them with Araldite onto the pink turret. After the third layer of aureolin yellow and white paint and a coat of plain glaze, Kitty had commented that she couldn't have done better herself. Praise indeed for someone famous in china circles for her restoration of a Bustelli Columbine. Kitty had spent hours researching the archives for the specifications. Once she found a project that interested her she could be relentless. 'Although,' as she had said at the time, 'whatever anyone says, the Columbine's arm is still missing and all I have done is recreate an illusion of wholeness.'

Kitty's thoughts were all over the place that afternoon as she carried the teacups into the kitchen. Everything her friends had said was true. She had to take her situation seriously and not live under the delusion that something would turn up when she needed it, like a knight at the door of Milly's little pastille castle come to rescue his princess.

A commotion on Water Lane brought her reluctantly back to the present and with a sinking heart she saw the BMW in her driveway and an expanse of pink flesh and a turnip top as Jason's head emerged from the driver's window. He was not looking her way but at the other BMW pulled up alongside and now there was another man on the road as tall and broad as Jason only double his age; Jason meeting his *Doppelgänger* in some futuristic experiment, the man's silvery hair stark against his light blue shirt. They were engaged in a standoff, Jason hands on hips and the other shaking his head and prodding his temple with his forefinger which struck Kitty as peculiarly foreign, like an extra in a Fellini film.

She was about to close the door and disappear upstairs when Adele called her from the path. 'Am I too late? Oh dear, I forgot what day it was and I've brought angel cake for our tea. Help me ducky will you, I've got all this shopping, heaven knows why when Gordon bless him is never at home but I buy in case. Everything all right Kitty dear? You look a little peaky.'

Adele with her angel hair fluffing about her long face that was painted in shades of blue and crimson, her mascara spluttering about grey eyes. She embraced Kitty in a twirl of her turquoise duster coat.

'What is Jason doing having an altercation in your driveway? Why don't you shoo him away? It's your home, darling.'

'Is it?' Kitty murmured as both men now turned their attention to the house.

'A pen?' Kitty cocked an ear and peered at Jason, his face pink with pique. 'Have you got a pen,' he repeated loudly. 'We need to exchange addresses, except this joker here doesn't appear to have one.'

'I am between homes,' the stranger said. 'Sorry.'

'You'll have plenty to be sorry about once I've done with you matey,' Jason muttered under his breath. He exuded a brutish smell of male deodorant and peppermints. Kitty went to fetch a pen.

'Such a fuss. I only touched his mirror.'

The stranger had followed her into the front room and

for all his size Kitty thought he looked shrunken by bewilderment. ‘Not even a scratch.’

‘Oh, Jason's a bureaucrat,’ Kitty said, ‘he should work in Brussels.’

‘I said I was prepared to pay for this invisible scratch but he refuses.’

Kitty detected a foreign accent but she didn't ask.

In the kitchen she heard Adele flutter, ‘So how are you Jason? How is the NHS nowadays? The last time I visited a friend in Kingston Hospital there was an auxiliary heating up her porridge and he was almost as old as she was. That can't be right, surely? But I suppose with all the cuts it's what we've come to expect, isn't it? A dog gets better treatment than an old person nowadays.’

Kitty could almost hear Jason's thought processes, the clicking into gear as his brain transmitted the fact that Freddy had not yet made a kamikaze attack on his ankles. No hysterical yapping came from the garden. There was no scratching of claws at the kitchen door or sonorous growls. Only the buzzing of Kitty's ears. And now Jason had got it.

‘Dog sick or something? Where is he?’

‘Oh, I don't know, out somewhere gallivanting I suppose.’ Adele's attempt to be flirtatious had no effect on Jason.

‘She lets him wander the towpath by himself, does she? Isn't she worried he'll get lost or fall in the river?’

In the front room, the stranger reached for the pen Kitty was clutching in her hand but she was too preoccupied to notice. Was there time to pluck Freddy from the porch and conceal him in the verbena? She could try and bluff it out if only she could think of something convincing to say.

‘This is yours?’ the man's voice made her jump. She had forgotten he was still there and blinked at him. He was standing at the table peering at Bosco's cockatoo.

From the kitchen Jason said, ‘Where's Kitty? I think

we need to talk about this. It's not what was agreed in the contract.'

'You are so close to the river. You don't realise from the road.'

The man had followed Kitty into the porch and easing past her was now admiring the view from the gate.

Kitty grabbed Freddy just as Jason came marching into the room and pushed him into the stranger's arms.

Jason saw Freddy's ears cocked above the man's shoulder and said, 'Put that flaming animal down,' and the stranger, thinking it was a joke, growled and made to lunge at Jason as if Freddy were a glove puppet.

Jason made a hasty retreat to the kitchen. 'He's allergic to dog hairs,' Kitty explained. The stranger looked at the stiff and battered Freddy and then at Kitty's shocked expression and nodded. 'I see.'

* * * * *

'A house on the Spree?'

'Yes, not far from Berlin. You have heard of the Spreewald, famous for its gherkins? This reminds me of my family house.'

Kitty had a confusion of images. 'Gherkins? Ah. Pickled cucumbers.'

'The Spreewald is a series of small islands.'

Adele tripped onto the lawn with the angel cake. 'A pity to let it go to waste now that Jason's gone.'

It was rare to have a man of such distinction occupying Elsie's garden seat. Bosco was big too, an overlapping mound of chins and belly, a currant bun of a man, an ooze of flesh that was soft and congenial compared to this firmly upright German who had the grey eyes of water and a scar from temple to chin. Kitty offered him the plate and

Armin plucked a slice with tapered fingers where the nails were buffed and pink as shells. He brushed a few yellow crumbs from his lap and reaching into his breast pocket produced a snakeskin wallet and from that a visiting card.

Kitty read, 'Armin von Hassendorf. CEO World Trade Agency, Palm Beach, Florida, USA.' There is an e-mail and web address, mobile and landline and a PO box number.

'World trade?'

'Sugar from the West Indies. Steel from India. Wood from Canada,' and they picked up the trace of a New World accent.

'I am here for a couple of days. I have been working out of Miami, setting up my new organisation.'

The women nodded approvingly, investing Armin with the silvery allure of a sleek cat.

'Your family is in Miami, Mr von Hassendorf?' Adele posed with the teapot, head coquettishly to one side. At seventy nine she was the youngest of the china class but with a memory that stretched back to the Bloomsbury Set. Her parents had rented a flat opposite the British Museum and her mother had been a friend of Virginia Woolf. Adele could never make sense of the books but the cloaks, velvets and vivid jewellery she wears are a reminder of those days; rakish, bohemian although she was never an advocate of free love. 'It's my Catholic upbringing, you see.'

'I'm divorced.'

'And do you have children?'

Kitty shot Adele a look. She was starting to pry but if she was making Armin von Hassendorf uncomfortable there was no indication of it when Kitty stole a glance at him.

'I have a son, Alexander. He lives in San Francisco but I'm hoping he'll move to Germany once we have the house. My great aunt died last week.'

'And you have inherited it? Lucky you!' Adele exclaimed.

'Me and my cousin, both,' he replied but Kitty thought she detected a lack of enthusiasm in Mr von Hassendorf's voice and was reminded how the mention of close relatives often brought a dark cloud to the most silver of linings. 'But you are lucky too,' Armin said stretching his arms to embrace the river and the bosky ait in front of them.

'Ah, but Kitty isn't going to inherit.' Adele shifted the bangles up her arm and left them to tumble in a discordant jangle about her slender wrists.

'I am only the tenant,' Kitty explained. 'The lady who owns Seething Wells is in a nursing home and I'll have to move out when she dies.'

'Oh darling,' Adele cried, 'It doesn't bear thinking about.'

She turned to Armin and said, 'Kitty is a highly respected china restorer. She's done everything; Ming, Worcester, Sèvres, Dresden. It would be unbearable to see her go.'

'My house on the Spree has eighteenth century furniture, paintings and porcelain, all of it catalogued by the socialist regime when it was in power. Everything was to be given to the museum but now that's history.' Armin gave the wisp of a smile. He had a deep, mesmeric voice.

'And you are off to Berlin to take possession?' Adele said enthusiastically. She loved a happy ending. Too much misery nowadays. She never watches the news, or opens a paper and prefers to believe that every person who crosses her path has been sent there for a purpose. This was newsworthy enough for Adele.

And Armin von Hassendorf, CEO of World Trade Agency, the bottom button of his shirt clinging by a thread to betray his domestic poverty, the wife and homemaker now divorced or dead? Adele seethed with curiosity but she preferred the delicious state of speculation.

Mr von Hassendorf does not look cared for. He does not look loved, is what she will tell Kitty when they are alone.

* * * * *

During the course of that afternoon a silver BMW could be seen parked in several places in the Hounslow area and anyone lingering by the shelves of Mr Kipling cakes, white sliced bread, tins of spaghetti rings and baked beans that make up the staple fare of the corner shop, will not have failed to notice the tall distinguished man talking to one of the Singhs, Patels, or Rahmans who run these family enterprises. In many of these tiny worlds of business Armin was already a well established figure, arriving with his James Bond briefcase, that of the coded locks that spring open once the digits are correctly aligned, to remove his catalogues from Deli World and House of Chocolate. But he had not been seen for a while.

Fan the glossy pages and smell the *Wurst*, peppered, garlicky, eyed with fat, its colour heightened to the unnatural pink of a porn still, there the blond waxy cheeses blue veined under their milky cheeks, the lumpfish caviar and smoked eel, the potato and bread dumplings like pubescent breasts. Vikram, one of Armin's best customers inserted a finger and the catalogue fell open on the counter, rustling the flanks of chocolate bars. Armin reached inside his jacket for his red notebook and flicked the ballpoint ready for action.

Vikram had noticed an influx of Poles into the area and wanted to expand his small deli selection. He moved the tray of samosas prepared by his wife that morning to one side and studied the pictures that Armin had found for him in Deli World; the platters of pickled marrows, pumpkin, red cabbage, sauerkraut in wine or brine. Armin produced a sample from his case and, placing it on the counter, prised open the gold top to let the aroma of vinegar and dill mingle with the smell of floorboards, damp and cardboard, the whiff of cardamom and packaged cakes, newsprint and sickly milk chocolate.

'Try one,' Armin urged and Vikram took a toothpick from one of the samosas and inserted it into the crisp green gherkin.

'Best German quality. From the Spreewald,' Armin said and his grey eyes flooded with emotion as Vikram took a cautious bite, the sweet and sour bursting into his mouth as the cucumber yielded under his white teeth.

Chapter Three

Kitty saw the cloud rising above the chestnuts on the ait. It was damson coloured and the rumblings from its belly trembled the walls and clinked the china on the shelves. As it approached it grew meaner and soon it was spitting hailstones as big as golf balls. Kitty watched with amazement at first. The sky like night and on the ground ice; a landscape transformed to a negative. The hail bounced across the lawn and flattened the flowerbeds. It rolled over the grassy dyke and down into the river and foamed in the weir at Teddington Lock. All about her the house rang with the clattering of the storm and shivered in the sulphur of its breath. Then the hail stopped and the rain began.

Rain that Bosco remembered from the Far East he would tell them, when his father was an officer in Macau with the Zoaves. Rain that came with horizontal gusts that blew the wet through the cracks in Kitty's roof and swelled the underground streams. The torrents bucked against the concrete floor and slathered the joists where the rust was eating at the skeleton of the house. A house built of steel and lashed together with concrete plates that were reverting to sand.

Prod a sharp instrument into the outer wall and the cement will crumble like honeycomb. Kitty's very own gingerbread house becoming soggier by the minute. Water rippled over the roof like an incoming tide and, finding the exit holes of squirrels, the chewed-through fabric above the guttering and in the eaves, it dribbled into the loft, a place

Kitty never ventured, quickly turning puddles into ponds that found outlets in the light fixtures and began to pour first through Kitty's kitchen and then into Elsie's below.

Kitty grabbed every container she could find from pudding basins and buckets to Elsie's old tin bath and watched as the ceiling tiles turned brown and loosened. The whole ceiling was on the move, shifting and jostling like styropor blocks in the river's eddies.

'I really thought the house was going to tumble down about my ears!' she will say to the china class when they meet the following Monday. And there was enough evidence of it even after five days of consecutive sunshine; the cardboard stepping stones across the soggy carpet, the streaky walls that had the texture of worn sandpaper, the flickering neon strip in the kitchen and front room from where the water had cascaded and which Sylvia cheerfully called a death trap. 'Don't touch those switches Kitty, or you'll be burned to a frazzle.'

But Kitty already had, that very same evening once the storm had passed and Lee had bunged up the holes in the roof with cement. 'It's temporary,' he'd said, crouched by the chimney stack, his upper body covered in tattoos so that Kitty could have mistaken him for a scribble if she hadn't known it was the young man next door. Trish offering Lee to her like a gift when Kitty had come hurrying into her garden in a distressed state. 'I'll ask Lee to take a look,' she'd said, tottering from the garden on her four inch wedges from where she'd been bewailing the damage to her Ferrari parked between the salvia beds. 'It's going to cost me a bloody fortune.'

And for a moment Kitty had forgotten about the imminent collapse of her home as she'd stared in shocked fascination at the moon landscape that was Trish's car. Trish fingering the dents, oblivious to the rain flattening her bleached hair to wet straw and making her clothes cling to her in unflattering outlines of blubber; spitting like a mermaid while the raindrops had made little puddles in the hailstone craters. But she had seen how upset Kitty was and had yelled for Lee and he'd come out smelling smoky sweet from the cigarette between his fingers and after passing it to Trish he'd shimmied up the pear tree and onto Kitty's roof.

'It was like watching Johnny Weissmueller,' Kitty said, reminded of the German who had come to her rescue the other day.

'You're going to need a new roof,' Lee had told her, the rain streaming off him and making his tattoos flicker like a moving picture.

Kitty had swooped the umbrella over him, giving Lee shelter while he had sucked in his cheeks, estimating the cost of tiles by the square meter. 'You're talking two grand at least.'

'Two thousand,' Kitty gasped.

'When did you last have the place rewired?'

Kitty didn't know but Elsie had told her once that her mother had been a dab hand with a hammer.

Lee had swept the rain from his big shoulders. 'Sell up and buy yourself a nice little bungalow somewhere is my advice. You'd have enough left over to keep you sitting pretty for the rest of your life. Winter on the Costas...'

It had seemed unfair to dampen Lee's enthusiasm by telling him the facts of her situation and, besides, by then Kitty could hardly speak for weariness. It was the creeping exhaustion she always experienced when her security was threatened, a mental anguish far more debilitating than hurrying backwards and forwards across the lawn or sitting up until the early hours baking a Chintex glaze in the oven. But later that evening with the timpani of raindrops in the saucepans reduced to the occasional drip she had pulled on an old jumper and an extra pair of socks and gone to her table to mould a new beak for Bosco's cockatoo.

'Two thousand pounds!' Kitty can do without Adele's theatrics, the rolling of the eyeballs and the open crimson mouth put on in haste without her glasses that morning and shaping now into a grimace.

They are carrying chairs into the front garden while the others assemble the picnic in the kitchen.

'But you haven't got that kind of money,' Adele continues as if Kitty needs reminding.

'Lee said he could patch it up for me and he'd charge me only for materials,' Kitty says.

'You know I'd dearly love to help.' Adele flops into a deckchair, looking wistful.

'And I wouldn't hear of it,' Kitty concludes.

Adele plucks at the lilac pashmina and flings it over the chair. The sun is out and it is hot.

'So humiliating but Gordon's resting at the moment. The job at Scunthorpe didn't materialise, they chose the boyfriend of the director instead, oh everything always boils down to sex, Kitty, the trading of favours, which can mean the difference between three months in Dangerous Corner or the bric-a-brac stall.'

Adele had brought with her a Parian figure with a hand missing that Gordon had found in a junkshop while up north and Kitty, thinking it might be a copy of Innocence from the Copeland Factory, had busied herself for most of the morning trying to find a reference to it in one of her books. Sylvia had muttered that it wasn't on and they all had work that needed attention, Adele and by inference her layabout son monopolising Kitty and abusing her sweet nature.

Then Bosco had bonded the cockatoo's beak upside down, purposely or not, no one could be sure, but it was enough to alert Kitty to the fact that she had been neglecting her class, an application of Nitromors on Bosco's epoxy resin being about enough to restore equilibrium.

It had seemed a good moment to stop for lunch.

'You're going to have to do something Kitty or you'll be on tenterhooks each time there's a downpour. You'll be like Noah with his Ark half built.'

Kitty indulged herself for a moment and thought about the creatures assembling at her gate; the squirrels in the roof, the foxes that share her supper leftovers from Wiltshire Farms, the badgers that trundle the towpath at night, the tawny owl, heron, Canada geese, coot, moorhen, green and goldfinch, pipit, wren, woodpecker both yellow and spotted, blackbird, song thrush, robin, flycatcher, sparrow, dunnock, the tits, great, blue, coal and longtailed and wagtail, grey and yellow, the kingfisher and phoenix like shag, the parakeets that fly over the house in flocks of fifty or more screeching like squeaky toys, fantailed the softest green to turquoise. Not to mention the migratory swift and sand martin, the redwing and fieldfare. And what about the hedgehogs, voles and mice with their big transparent ears and liquidy eyes, the rat who scowls under the potting shed and darts out to vacuum up the dropped seeds from the bird table, the pipistrelles that flit between the firs on those first soft evenings in April? The neighbourhood pets. Kitty is quite dizzy. The house is more than the sum of its parts, it is a big heart pulsating to the rhythm of nature and she cannot bear the thought of it ever stopping.

'I have a little saved,' she said.

'Which you might need for your old age,' Adele replied, as though they are women in their forties who have just discovered their first wrinkle.

'Elsie's not to know about this. Jason will find out and it will be the excuse he's looking for. The house is unsafe. He'll have it condemned.'

Like a prisoner to the gallows, Kitty thought and she felt the rope tighten about her throat and the trap door tremble beneath her feet and uttered an elongated, 'Oh,' for her glance had alighted on Freddy standing sentinel in the porch and there was something not quite right. Something about the angle of his body that sent her out of her chair to wrestle him from the tangle of umbrellas, chipped plates, books and back numbers of Saga Magazine which had supported him during his solitary watch.

'Oh my goodness, Kitty!'

Adele clapped her hands to her mouth in horror, for Freddy's left leg was no more and the stump was leaking mice droppings like an hourglass.

* * * * *

Two houses. One on the Thames that is beyond restoration as Kitty has already discovered, its life span almost spent, for there is little that can be done if the skeleton is crumbling and the carapace is worn and falling away. Three score years and ten is not long for a house, but this was an experiment, a builder's mix of steel, sand and folly that ignored the damp from the river and the underlying clay that baked in summer and became a mire in winter; a house that did not move with the times like wood that can be tarred and bricks that can be replaced and repointed. A prefab, Lee had called it.

The other house is on the Spree.

It is Armin von Hassendorf's house, or at least half of it will be his, if his reading of the situation is correct and he will inherit together with his younger cousin Karl, the three storey family home with its painted ceilings and circular staircases that wind like corkscrews past landings reflected in leaded lights and intimate stuccowork. Enter the cobbled courtyard from the two massive wooden doors at street level (doors that were built to withstand a siege if not the Russians) and for a moment you are airlocked like an astronaut between the past and the future. Armin anticipates the future will bring him riches.

So much Armin had gathered from his cousin but it is nearly two years since they last met. Trudy was still alive then and driving up to the Baltic in her Trabi to spend August in the State guest house on Ruegen, back in private hands after reunification, but which had seen her coming there since the sixties. For forty years Trudy had pulled on her elasticised one piece and taken her daily dip in the tideless sea, irrespective of weather or political climate. She had called herself, proudly, *Deutsch Nationalist* owing no allegiance to the horrors of the past, just a statement of her roots founded in a Germany so far east that it no longer exists.

Trudy never talked about her years in the underground hospital, tending the wounded sent back from the Russian front. She remained *stumm* to a past trapped like the fly frozen in resin that she had plucked one day from the white sand on her walk along the beach.

A year before her death Trudy had gone into a home. Karl had written that she was too frail to look after herself, retreating in winter to the room with the coal fed *Kachelofen* where she slept and ate, the soot settling in the skirts of the Meissen shepherdesses and smearing the damask of the eighteen century chairs. Its fumes had turned the walls the rheumy colour of smoked haddock and made a sepia portrait of the painted ceilings. It was Karl's wife Crystal who had found a suitable place; a sanatorium where the socialist elite had once recuperated under crystal chandeliers with en suite facilities behind a drab facade that resembled one of the crumbling blocks of the proletariat. Now it had been given a makeover for well to do *Wessies*.

Trudy was in the best of hands, Karl had written to Armin's post box number in Miami. They visited her most weekends, driving the two hundred and fifty kilometres from their big house on the Weser to sit in the Bauhaus chair by

Trudy's bedside; Crystal dressed like a fifties revival, lustrous brown hair kiss-curled about a broad Russian face, rearranging the begonias on the windowsill while Karl talked through Trudy to reach the heart of his as yet undescribed ambitions.

Sometimes when the weather was fine they would walk about the garden with Trudy leaning heavily on Karl's arm and in confused moments she would urge him to take back with him a small memento; a Lalique vase, a fourteenth century pestle and mortar, a piece of art nouveau jewellery finely worked in square cut diamonds and gold. 'It's all going to the *Staatsmuseum*,' she would mumble, eyes suddenly defiant, 'everything has been labelled and catalogued. It will all disappear once I'm gone.'

Karl squeezes his aunt's withered arm. 'Socialism is dead,' he reminds her. It is all one Germany now and everything is secure. He is seeing to that.

Even before the Wall came down Karl and Crystal would make little shopping trips to Trudy, travelling in the SL type Mercedes to the house in Berlin and bringing with them gifts of Dallmayr Coffee, Liptons orange pekoe and Scottish shortbread. During those brief stopovers, their permit expired at midnight, they rarely left empty handed. Their house on the Weser is evidence of Trudy's largesse and Crystal's guile; the early Meissen pots, the Marcolini cups and saucers, the fifteenth century apothecary jars hidden under the passenger seat and, in the case of the emerald earrings, thumbed into the *Kalbsleberwurst* sandwiches that Trudy insisted they take with them for the long journey back to Bremen.

It is a fact that at Crystal's first airing of the von Hassendorf's emeralds at the Hamburg State Opera some weeks later, a morsel of congealed paté could still be seen clinging to one of the platinum claws.

When Karl telephoned Armin to tell him that Trudy

had passed away peacefully that night, it had caught Armin at a crossroads in his life. He had been living in England until a year ago when his divorce and lacklustre business had sent him in search of new horizons. He had decided to go back to America, a country he had always considered lucky for him, in the hope of recapturing some of his old panache. He had been seconded to the USAF while in the German air force and trained to fly the Starfighter, a plane with such a poor safety record that it was referred to by colleagues as the flying coffin. Armin had emerged physically unscathed from the experience but the loss of a good friend while on a training mission over Arizona had convinced him to quit while he was still ahead. He did not know what psychological scars he still carried, nor did it trouble him to find out. What had remained was the belief that America offered more than its fair share of second chances and his arrival in Miami some twelve months ago had found him full of hope that his fortunes were about to change.

And so it had proved for within a week he had met Patty Holzen in a shopping mall in West Palm Beach while sampling some new lines from a health food shop called the Sunshine Fruit Basket. Food and sex had been a potent mix in Armin's life and this was to be no exception. Down to his last hundred dollars and sleeping on his old pal Otto's floor, the promise of a free meal had been irresistible (foraging was second nature to Armin after surviving the war rooting for beetroot in the fields around Berlin) and he had been making inroads into the apricots and cranberries when a woman's voice at his shoulder had asked whether they were sun dried.

Patty had been intrigued at finding such a distinguished looking man (her first impression was of Gunther Sachs post BB) unreservedly helping himself to the specials. Armin on his part had been flattered by the attention of a frosted blond in her early fifties (a very generous assessment), platinum edged like so many Miami matrons, but in Patty's case quite genuine. He had replied 'I have no idea but I'm hoping to find out.' Which had struck Patty Holzen as hysterically funny.

Soon she was inviting Armin to her home in Palm Beach and giving him the keys to her white Impala for drives along the hibiscus hedged roads on the estate. After a few mojitos under Florida's tropical skies Armin had collected his belongings from Otto's floor and moved into Villa Carmina where he quickly established himself as Patty's lover, driver and devourer of the crusts from her four seasons pizza takeouts. He learned that Patty had recently been widowed, her late husband, Irwin, a manufacturer from New Jersey having finally succumbed to the double whammy of clogged arteries and Viagra. 'He loved steak. He loved meat. He was a great lover of life, period,' was Patty's epithet for the man with whom she had shared her life for almost a quarter century.

There was no doubt that Patty was the best thing that had happened to Armin since his divorce. She was generous and affectionate and, most importantly, she let him dream his big dreams without interfering. She liked powerful men. She had been married to one for twenty four years and, although she didn't understand how Armin made his money, she never bothered to ask. She liked the fact that there was no frantic rush in the morning and no working late into the night. Armin had time for her. Occasionally he went downtown to see his lawyer friend Otto, a buddy from his Starfighter days and they talked business although what kind of business, Patty was never sure. World Trade Agency sounded impressive and she was just happy that it gave her Prussian aristocrat the freedom to spend quality time with her at the pool while she swam her daily half mile and popped the pills and potions that kept her looking ten years younger than the date on her birth certificate. She was Armin's senior by two years but never let it be known.

One thing Patty didn't want was another Irwin on her hands. She had seen what too much cholesterol could do and she enforced a strict regime on Armin. No fatty foods. Definitely no red meat. When she caught him munching on a Big Mac one day she went berserk and Armin learned to restrict his carnivorous appetite to business lunches with Otto where plans for World Trade Agency were discussed over platters of Argentinian T-bone.

What Patty failed to understand was that Armin's relationship with food was as much psychological as a need to fill a gap. It went all the way back to pre-war Berlin when Trudy in her Astrakhan hat and fur coat had taken her favourite nephew to sample the sticky *Bienenstich* and sugar crusted *Schweinsohren,* the *Obst Torten* and *Kaesekuchen*, the *Sandkuchen, Sahnehoernchen, Berliner and Amerikaner* displayed in the windows of the *Konditoreien* on the Friedrichstrasse.

Trudy was rarely in Armin's thoughts and yet, each time he evaded Patty and indulged his fancy for a Krispy Kreme in a downtown coffee shop, he was unconsciously connecting with an age so far removed from now, it could have been another lifetime away.

So when Karl phoned to say Trudy had died and would be laid to rest in the family plot in the cemetery, it was almost as if Armin had been expecting it. 'I'm coming,' he told Karl, even though he would have to borrow the air fare from Otto to get there.

Armin turns on the shower and the water drums on his hunched shoulders and crinkles his toes and fingers and he thinks about the journey he is soon to make to a Berlin that has been transformed since he left it many years ago. His cousin had suggested they stay in the house. 'There have been some changes,' he says when Armin queries the arrangements, for weren't most of the rooms so damp and decaying that Trudy had abandoned them for the soot filled salon on the first floor? Karl does not elaborate. He is in full flow and will have no interruption. 'Listen to me,' he says and Armin can see that wagging forefinger and the chipped ice eyes behind the heavy lids, 'Listen to me... We couldn't leave the house as it was. Once Trudy went into the home we had to make some improvements.'

'And the Will?'

'Let's wait until you get here.'

Karl is tetchy, perhaps because it is two o'clock in the morning in Berlin and he and Crystal have been on their feet since paying their last respects to Trudy in the chapel of rest earlier that day. It is Karl and Crystal who have selected the coffin from the middle range of veneered woods and elected to have bunches of scilla decorate the chapel, flowers that Crystal and their daughter Julia will gather from the long garden of Trudy's house where they drift in waves of brilliant blue under the fruit trees and sprouting roses. They were Trudy's favourite; harbingers of spring after the bitter Berlin winter and a reminder of her beloved Baltic and the soft blue waters of the summer to come.

Chapter Four

Armin spent his first night in London sleeping in VJ's BMW in the car park opposite the tennis courts at Ham. He needed to save what little money he had for Berlin and the quiet reaches of the Thames and the BMW's cushioned upholstery had turned out to be a surprisingly comfortable and cheap alternative to an hotel.

He had been woken in the early morning by the hollow plop of a tennis ball and the spectacle of two players determined to thrash each other into submission. He guessed they had jobs in finance or sales and it was a way of working off the stress. He didn't envy them the hassle. He had lost some of his drive after the glycol scandal when a shipload of white wine he'd imported had been impounded at Miami docks. Antifreeze, an effective sweetener for the tartness of European grapes, had been found in samples and the consignment subsequently destroyed. He had never fully recovered from the blow. It had been instrumental in Angela leaving him and once the house was gone there had been no reason to hang around.

He was grateful to VJ for the loan of his car. They were old business associates from his Thames Fine Food days when Armin had sold Riesling from the Rhine and Nahe valleys and VJ had been one of his best promoters. VJ who had been born in Mauritius had a ‘try anything’ attitude common to many immigrants and had been only too willing to stock Armin's goods on his shelves. Over the years VJ had gone from strength to strength and now owned three retail outlets and four properties in the Wembley area. It was down to hard work and not much play; an ethic that was lost on VJ's son who preferred to hang out with a group of friends, bangla music blaring from his souped up silver BMW as he cruised the streets of Hounslow.

Reclining in the passenger seat with his coat pulled up to his chin, the darkling brick of Ham House just visible between the budding limes, Armin had been too groggy to consider the irony of his situation. A week ago he had been offering Patty succour in the Kingsize, pumping himself up for the finale with the help of the little blue pills that she kept in a camellia scented drawer. Later, they had shared a candlelit takeout from Patty's favourite pizzeria and Armin had made a point of not commenting on her infuriating habit of eating only the olive and mozzarella topping.

A farewell dinner was not the occasion for a grumpy lecture on waste to someone who in desperation had chewed his leather bootstraps in the winter of 1944. But he did mention while staring meaningfully at the litter of crusts and pizza base that in the last war more people had died from eating poisonous fungi than from starvation. Patty had refilled his glass of pinot grigio and said, 'That's what I love about you, *Schatz*, you're so full of bullshit innuendo.'

In the morning she had driven him to the airport and he'd looked out across the flat horizon where a solitary palm tree had bristled against the sky like a lavatory brush and made a solemn promise not to return until he had something more substantial in the bag.

'You ring me as soon as you know how much the good *Tante* has left you,' Patty had murmured before kissing him on the mouth. 'I can't wait to visit the house, if it's all you say it is.'

'And more!' he'd said.

Patty and Palm Beach were not inseparable and, if business suddenly perked up after an injection of cash, then he saw plenty of opportunities for himself and Patty to enjoy the house. Patty had a collection of furs in cold storage and a Berlin winter was the ideal setting for her to show them off. They would go to concerts and drink hot chocolate in one of those interesting little cafés in Spandau. Patty had clutched his arm, her liver spotted hands gloved in white crochet and said, 'We're good together *Liebling*, don't keep me waiting too long.'

Armin had decided to spend two days in London, not for sentimental reasons, (he rarely looked back which in retrospect was a bad idea. Armin ought to have visited Trudy more) but to put out feelers among the business community who had made up his customer base when he was still running Fine Foods and had represented House of Chocolate and Deli World.

He was surprised how much had changed since he'd last been here. Some shops had been taken over by a new wave of immigrants; Sri Lankans and the more enterprising Poles who understood the significance of pickled gherkins in dill for a horde of homesick new arrivals. Standing in a shop in Ealing that had once belonged to his friend Nilesh, he had nodded approvingly at the gleaming array of pickled cucumbers, sliced marrows, beetroots, the borsch soup and packets of ready mix dumplings as the dark haired girl with the skin of light honey had counted out a dozen smoked sprats that were the speckled gold and sepia of an old print of Bansin. Not one for nostalgia, but he had been reminded of family meals in his grandmother's house and the servant girl carrying in the white tureen brimming with the grainy cream of potato soup.

He had kept the sprats for later and then eaten them in the dark of the car park before easing back in the passenger seat and falling asleep.

The next day he had gone to Hounslow and hooked up with VJ who had taken him for a curry and talked business between the syncopated trill of two mobile phones and the appearance at their table of an Armenian with contacts in the oil and gas industry. VJ had bought him a drink, his face all smiles but watchful and then left them to take a call outside, his conversation a mix of French, English and Tamil that drifted into the restaurant from the street each time the door opened.

Armin had shuffled through his wallet and plucked the freshly minted business card with the words World Trade Agency, CEO Armin von Hassendorf, Palm Beach, Florida, USA embossed in gold lettering upon it. His head office was in Miami, he told the thick set man in the leather jacket sitting opposite, his stumpy fingers ringed with gold. The Armenian had no business card and was not forthcoming with a name.

In the afternoon he drove to Harlesden only to discover that another customer, Good Times, had become a Tesco Express. The dry cleaners next door told him that Sarvesh and family had emigrated to Canada and were now running a motel. But further down the high street he met up with familiar faces and before long had promised to pass on their requests to Deli World, his impulse to trade overriding the fact that the new rep on the block would not take kindly to Armin's part time hustling on his behalf.

But his instinct for commerce had sent him searching for a ballpoint in an inside pocket, 'Good choice,' he'd intoned, unwittingly echoing the words of the cocktail waitress in Cuba Libra the Miami bar where he'd ordered two mojitos on his first date with Patty. That same evening she had driven him in the Impala back to Palm Beach, a lonely widow incredulous that in all the bars in all the world the daughter of a Prussian officer should find her soulmate in this latino jungle.

It was at moments like this, sat in a Croatian café with a Brazilian football match on Sky and a slivovitz warming his belly, that Armin touched base with his ambition to build a company that would straddle all five continents. Export surplus grain to places where it was in short supply, sell sugar for steel, aloe vera to rich countries to boost the economies of the poor. Roses from Kenya in return for computers. Spare engine parts to be traded for spices. The combinations were endless. He already had friends in Africa and India waiting for the go ahead. Waiter, another slivovitz! All he needed was collateral.

He tried to picture Trudy's house on the banks of the Spree. In his imagination it was now five storeys high and crammed with precious items. He remembered a seventeenth century cabinet fashioned in satin and pear wood and an ormolu clock enhanced by Meissen figurines. Rooms with exquisite paintings emerged through the pleasant fog of the schnapps. He had seen them with his own eyes, grimed by the accumulated soot from decades of communist winters but still there, intact and just waiting for the restorer's sable brush.

How much is the house worth? A million. Two million euros, Two million dollars US? Or even more. Armin's mind is racing now. He wants to walk into the Hotel Adlon and be greeted by the manager, like in the good old days. '*Guten Abend Herr Baron*, it's good to see you again. Just like old times.'

First find the collateral.

He took out the pack of re-directed post picked up that morning from the box number he kept in London, dropped it onto the table and called for another slivovitz. The invitation to visit Seething Wells was lying on top of a pile of junk mail and he almost tore it up. It was the novelty of a handwritten envelope that caught his attention. He couldn't recall meeting an Adele Vincent, but she clearly remembered him and was suggesting he visit Water Lane, 'with a view to discussing an arrangement that could be of mutual benefit.'

Was it about sex? He attempted to focus his blurred imaginings on a young woman who may have crossed his path, a woman with a proposition. But all that popped into his mind was the nubile Polish assistant with the high small breasts who had given him a look of incomprehension when he'd attempted to engage her earlier about the origin of the smoked sprats.

* * * * *

Kitty was at her work table when she noticed the taxi's headlights momentarily illuminate the front of the house as it backed into the drive and then turned. It was not uncommon for cars to use the space in front of the garage to reverse once they discovered that Water Lane led to the river. Elsie had never bothered with gates. The end of the property was marked by a series of variegated shrubs that Rosario attempted to control with the shears but after the rain the laurel was shooting up and the Syringa was sending straggly new growth onto the road.

Kitty had been preparing a mould from rubber latex emulsion to fashion a new leg for Freddy when the light had startled her from the table and sent her into the kitchen. She was right about the car, a taxi from the sound of its ticking engine, but she wasn't prepared for the sight of the passenger stumbling onto her lawn and, after several false starts, weaving his way towards her door.

She was not expecting anyone at this time of night and ruled out the possibility that her visitor was a distraught collector clutching a broken piece of rare china. It had happened once but that was when she was younger and at the height of her restoration skills.

There was some kind of argument going on with the

taxi driver who had followed the man into the porch. Kitty heard him say, 'I'm not leaving here until you pay what's on the meter. You'd better be right about this.'

The bell rang and Kitty slipped on the safety catch and poked her face through the crack in the door.

'Ah, Mrs Vincent, Adele?'

'Adele doesn't live here.'

'It's Armin. Armin von Hassendorf. You wrote me, remember, inviting me to come and see you?'

Kitty thought she recognised the voice but it was too dim for her to make out the man's features.

'I wrote to you?'

'Your little dog, woof... woof.' Armin lurched forward and fell against the door, making Kitty jump.

The taxi driver was reaching into his pocket for his mobile. 'He owes me thirty quid and if I don't get it I'm calling the police.'

Armin was groping in his jacket pocket. 'I seem to have mislaid my wallet. I was wondering? Could you let me have a small loan until tomorrow? I am about to inherit a beautiful house, china, paintings worth millions. There's no problem about reimbursing you in full if you could help me out of this difficulty.'

The taxi driver had put his phone to his ear and it was Kitty's reluctance to have a police car turn up and wake the neighbours rather than Mr von Hassendorf's precarious situation that made her reach for the money she kept in the tea caddy.

As she paid off the cabby, Armin fell across the threshold and Kitty had no alternative but to let him in.

Chapter Five

It was the squirrels in the roof that woke him. They were running across the beams in the loft, chattering and screeching; a bust up in the community that continued outside on the mossy tiles where they scampered before taking flying leaps at the laburnum leaning into the guttering. Armin had no idea where he was or how he had got here. He was in a bedroom that smelled of mildew and outside the world was a gibbering mass of waving branches and flying objects.

Earlier, in that hazy half world of the hangover, where every turn of his head had sent a searing pain into his temples, he had heard geese honking and raising himself gingerly to the window above the bed had peered into the dawn to see a pinprick of light moving between earth and sky. A UFO he thought at first until reason told him that he was close to a river and the moving object was the bow light of an early morning sculler.

But how he had got here was a blank. He was still wearing his clothes, only his shoes had been taken off and placed by the side of the bed. It was too damned chilly for Florida.

He thought he heard voices downstairs but the house was full of echoes and he couldn't be sure where they were coming from. It was like being trapped inside a giant shell.

'He's here?'

Adele was incredulous as she followed Kitty into the front room where the cockatoo was perched on the table, its beak now intact.

For a moment Armin was forgotten as Adele stopped to appreciate Kitty's handiwork. 'You are so clever Kitty, no one would believe it was ever broken.'

'But I do,' Kitty replied, leading the way into the porch where she had already placed the teacups and saucers, each one different and all fine examples of her artistic flare and dexterity in the repairing and restoration of china. As if the parrot were not testament enough. She was up half the night finishing it off.

'Well how could I sleep with a stranger in my bed,' she argued, ignoring Adele's arched eyebrow.

'How indeed,' Adele murmured.

'This is serious, Adele. You invited this man to my house. He showed me your letter. What on earth were you thinking of, sending him here without consulting me first!'

'Because you'd never have agreed to it otherwise,' Adele replied.

'But he was drunk. He tumbled out of a taxi, which I ended up paying for and then he tumbled into my house. Without my leave. It was terrifying.'

'And now he's upstairs?'

'In my old bedroom, sleeping off his hangover.'

There was a thud from above and a crack forked across the ceiling, dislodging the plaster and sending it sprinkling to the floor like icing sugar.

A door slammed. 'The bathroom,' Kitty whispered, clutching the beads at her throat. They followed the progress of the crack as it travelled the breadth of the front room. It was like a river in spate and now with the heavy creak of the floorboards it was being encouraged to form tributaries east and west and north and south as Armin clunked across the upstairs hallway. There was the clink of china. 'The jardinière on the landing,' Kitty winced. The thumping footfalls were on the stairs now, and it would not be long before the swirling motes and miasma of damp announced the arrival of a dishevelled and apologetic Mr von Hassendorf into their midst.

'Ladies,' Armin announced in his sonorous voice and bowing slightly at the two elderly women watching him over the teacups, 'You have an infestation of squirrels in the roof.'

In Florida it was termites. In Palm Beach, he told them over a pot of strong coffee, they would eat their way to the foundations and the house would have to be vacated for months while joists were replaced and the whole building sprayed. It didn't stop them coming back. 'Like cockroaches, termites have developed an immunity to most chemicals devised by man.'

Armin's eyes had followed the expanse of water from the window where the glitter shot red hot pins behind his bloodshot eyes. '*Die Natur*, Nature,' he said, 'sooner or later she reclaims what is rightfully hers.'

'But we can postpone it,' Adele replied, hands folded in her lap to conceal their tremor. It had come on after Kitty's phone call summoning her to Seething Wells this morning. It was rare to hear Kitty angry but there'd been no mistaking the indignation in her voice. 'You invited a stranger to come here without asking me first? What were you thinking of Adele? How could you!'

What indeed but to offer a solution to Kitty's current financial difficulties by taking Mr von Hassendorf as her lodger.

Her hands continued to dance in her lap like butterflies wanting to be free to flutter over the bushes of elderberry and blackthorn now bursting into flower. Adele wished that her hands could take her there too and that with one huge beat they could lift her over the river to a quieter backwater beyond Kingston. She did not want to be here, on the receiving end of Kitty's displeasure and Herr von Hassendorf's bemusement. It was an ill-conceived idea to think that this wealthy if slightly crumpled aristocrat might choose to stay at Seething Wells when business brought him to London.

Armin had excused himself to take a call on his mobile in the garden. It consisted of long pauses and the occasional interjection of *ja* and *nein*. A voluble business partner at the other end, Adele guessed, unaware that it was Armin's cousin Karl who was irritable at having to waste expensive satellite time discussing the sleeping arrangements.

He was telling Armin that there was room for him in Trudy's house on the third floor. It had been cleared and was in the process of being turned into offices. It had a bathroom and a small kitchen and Crystal was going to arrange a camp bed.

Armin said, ‘Offices?’

Half the house belongs to me, he thought to himself. Why wasn't he consulted? No one had seen the Will and it was a little presumptuous of Karl to take matters into his own hands without discussing it first with him. An architect had already been hired.

Armin said that he had made no other plans. ‘If that's all there is then I'll have to take it,’ he said.

Karl was impatient to finish the conversation. He was expecting an important call from Brussels.

‘Where will you be sleeping?’ Armin managed to ask, wondering how Crystal would cope with the spartan arrangements.

‘We'll be downstairs,’ Karl said, ‘on the second floor.’

‘You've got camp beds down there too?’

‘No, Armin. The camp beds were bought for the restorers from Katowitz when they were working on the ceilings. That's finished now. Look, we've got plenty of time to discuss all this when you get here.’

And there was Armin thinking that the house hadn't been touched for over four decades.

'Painted ceilings?' Adele gently kneaded her knuckles when Armin mentioned it. 'It must be very grand. Like the villas on Lake Como. I went there with my late husband in the early seventies. It was late March and we drove through Munich in a blizzard and arrived at our hotel to find the peach trees in blossom and the meadows full of flowers. The Alps form a barrier against the harsh northern winds and spring comes early there. We had breakfast on our veranda overlooking the lake and watched the fishermen in their bright boats and I thought of all that ice and snow that we'd left behind in Munich.'

'Germany isn't always cold,' Armin said, raking back a slick of silver hair and smoothing his temples. 'We have heat waves too. Berlin is influenced by the climate of the central European weather system. It's similar to Warsaw and Moscow.'

'And Berlin is your home,' Adele concluded, taking the opportunity while Armin's attention was diverted by the jangle of his phone to reach for a slice of Battenberg. By lowering her head which had the habit of nodding involuntarily as though on a spring when she was stressed, she managed to negotiate the piece of cake from table to mouth. The sponge oozed over her teeth and she beamed triumphantly, savouring the sickly sweetness as Armin said, 'Sure Patty, I know. But I'll call you soon as I get there, hon.'

Adele wandered into the kitchen. 'Kitty darling,' she said to her friend who was gazing out the window at the squirrels. She had tossed crumbs onto the path and the squirrels were always first.

The stove had been left on and Adele watched in mute fascination as a tiny flame began to eat through the frolicking Yorkies on Kitty's tea towel that had fallen onto the hotplate. Without a word Adele seized the end of the smouldering cloth and dropped it into the washing up basin.

'I really think you should consider my idea,' she said forcibly as she switched off the gas. 'Not only would the money come in handy but you'd have someone to keep an eye on things.'

'I can manage perfectly well on my own. He'd only be in the way,' Kitty replied.

And now Mr von Hassendorf was on the landing, his tall frame blocking the light from the window, saying what a pleasure it had been but now he had to go to the airport. 'To Berlin. To my house,' he said with a thrust of his chest.

'And may it be good news all the way,' Adele said. 'Bring us some photographs of your lovely home, would you? I'm sure the china class would love to see it.'

'I will,' Armin said, stepping into the porch where he had collapsed last night.

He showed no sign of embarrassment. It was as if he had decided to forget his conduct on the lawn of Seething Wells when Kitty had given the taxi driver an extra five pounds to haul him up the stairs last night.

What must the driver have thought, Kitty had wondered when she'd found Armin lying fully clothed on the bed just as the driver had left him. He was wearing shoes made from the softest leather. They were dark brown and had neat little tassels on the front. She had pulled them off and a tiny sprinkling of white sand had spilled onto the floor and glittered in the moonlight. His feet were small for such a tall man, the nails expertly clipped and buffed and the toes curled like giant grubs. Deformed feet that came from wearing shoes too tight for him, Kitty thought, as she'd dropped them by the side of the bed. Mr von Hassendorf had not always enjoyed the luxury of well fitted moccasins.

'Ladies,' Armin said, opening his leather briefcase and taking out a jar which he placed on the hall table like an exhibit.

'A small thank you for your trouble. These are

gherkins from the Spreewald. The best in the world.'

Sprigs of dill and whole peppercorns floated in the vinegary liquid like detritus in a rock pool.

'Once I am settled in my new house and the renovations have been completed I invite you as my guests to Berlin.'

'And you must come back and visit us again,' Adele said enthusiastically.

Armin nodded but his eyes were invisible behind his aviator glasses and as he stepped onto the path Kitty could tell that his thoughts were already focused on a plane's vapour trail dissipating eastward towards Berlin.

* * * * *

After Adele had gone home, Kitty went to her table to finish off Bosco's cockatoo. She had decided to airbrush the area around the beak to give it a professional finish and was glad to have the house to herself to get on with her work.

Adele was disappointed with her for not having, 'pinned Mr von Hassendorf down.' He had told her when they were in the porch that he was between homes and Adele had looked pointedly at Kitty that here was her chance to jump in and offer Seething Wells as his base whenever business brought him to London.

Kitty had been about to say something when his mobile had gone off and he'd wandered into the garden to take the call from Karl.

When he'd come back he'd seemed like a different person. Sort of disconnected from the present, Adele had thought, as though speaking in his own language had summoned a different set of associations that were making him introspective and forgetful of his coffee going cold in the creamware cup.

Chapter Six

After the funeral Armin remained for a while by the graveside. Trudy had outlived most of her contemporaries but one of the nurses from the home had brought a frail old man in a wheelchair and Crystal and Karl had stopped to talk to them. Armin could see it was the kind of conversation that did not invite participation from outsiders so he had gone off under the trees and waited for them to make their way over to him.

He had arrived late, partly because he'd been bewildered by the new shops and restored buildings that bore no resemblance to the grim and crumbling area he remembered from his visit during the DDR years. And then for some inexplicable reason he had gone into Tchibo and ordered a cappuccino and it was only after he'd finished that he'd bothered to check whether he was on the right street or not.

The pastor was already reading the eulogy when he arrived but he'd managed to catch the tail end and then his thoughts had turned to the Koenigsberger Klopse, the small meatballs served in a sweet sour sauce that had been his and Trudy's favourite dish. In spring there had been asparagus from the allotment she'd kept near *Oma* and *Opa* on the outskirts of Berlin, the allotment where as a small child he had helped pull the purple tipped stalks from the sandy earth like so many needles in a pin cushion. And always potatoes. Potatoes the colour of the yellow soil, firm and buttery, never crumbly or knotted. He had not tasted such potatoes in England or America. Maybe he should export them?

He had slipped into a seat at the back well away from his cousin and his family. Karl was a little more stooped, a little greyer but Crystal looked very much the same, her black outfit contrasting with her immaculate brown coiffeur and buffed orange skin that reminded him of a Miami matron with no one to please but herself. He thought fleetingly of Patty's toned body and of the abundant secretions of youth, the pithy smell of seaweed between briny thighs that was a distant memory now. Patty's lotions bought over the internet were no substitute. She would flinch sometimes when he entered her. Well, money was his lubricant now and until he acquired the scent of it again his memory of the Polish sprat girl, golden as a Baltic summer, would remain just that.

Karl in his cashmere coat, had turned at the sound of his footsteps and acknowledged him with a sombre nod. He exuded an air of self-satisfaction, of someone who had seized his chance and made good his father-in-law's promise to underwrite his first venture into property if he could prove he was serious. Karl now owned three apartment blocks in Frankfurt and had his fingers in several projects including an out of town shopping complex near Munich.

The young woman seated next to him with the full fat creamy look of a daddy's girl had puzzled Armin for a moment until he realised he was looking at their daughter Julia. She was now a woman in her mid-thirties and still unmarried for he could see no sign of a partner in the front row.

It would be a daunting prospect for any man to assert himself between the shoulder to shoulder expectations of Karl and Crystal.

His own record would not bear closer scrutiny either but then Armin had always been an optimist and the future was his territory, the anticipation of better times ahead making him draw himself up to his full height as Karl gathered the glossy folds of his coat and came down the gravel path towards him. Armin was a good five centimetres taller than his cousin.

He was suggesting they drive into the country, to a small lakeside town about thirty kilometres away where they could have lunch. The first asparagus of the season. There was also carp from the lake. *Rote Gruetze* with vanilla sauce for dessert.

'I have to watch my cholesterol,' Karl said as he guided his Mercedes onto the road. He patted the centimetre layer of fat above his belt and the conversation remained with health matters, the advice of doctors, the benefits of vitamins and the latest diet fad, as the car glided down avenues of budding limes behind which fields of beet and barley were littered here and there with the dilapidated concrete silos and sheds of abandoned communes.

Crystal and Julia would not be joining them but they would meet later at the house for coffee and cake in the garden. His cousin taking the initiative as usual and when Armin murmured an objection, surely a lunch together to celebrate Trudy's life would have been more appropriate, Karl had turned on him and asked sharply if he was prepared to pay for it.

Armin had retorted, 'So you are inviting me?'

And when Karl said, 'You are my guest,' Armin had felt the first ripple of unease that not even a confident resume of his year in Miami, 'great potential, everything in place, just waiting for my go ahead,' could quite dispel. Karl had nodded encouragingly, 'Palm Beach must cost you a packet. And your new woman's called Patty, you say? Does that mean you've finally got over Angela?'

'We're still friends,' Armin said.

Her solicitor had recently sent him a letter requesting

a financial breakdown of his affairs, Angela being convinced he had secret bank accounts. She couldn't believe that the house, the business, everything had been taken by their creditors to cover the losses.

He had written back that they were free to investigate but he was confident they would find nothing. He understood his ex-wife's concerns and he was not trying to avoid his responsibilities. He recognised her support over the years and he was making every endeavour to build a viable business in the States where he believed there were ample opportunities for him to reclaim the position of trust and prosperity he had once enjoyed. It would take time however and although he regretted Angela's reduced circumstances (she was renting a leaky houseboat near Eel Pie Island and working part time at M&S as a shelf stacker) there was little that he could do to improve the situation at present. However, he was confident that this would change. A new and exciting proposal was currently being considered by a leading American finance company and he had great hopes that this would bring about a change in his fortunes.

Otto had helped him write the letter. 'No antagonism,' he had advised. If he came out on the defensive, Angela would smell a rat and know he had something to hide. The fact that Armin had no money was neither here nor there. 'It's the assumption people make about you,' Otto had said, his crinkly neck rearing out of his shirt like a tortoise emerging from its shell, 'that here's a guy with something big in his pants.'

Armin's hand had involuntarily reached for his fly zipper.

'Well look at the facts,' Otto had continued, ticking off the list on his fingers, 'You have an address in Palm Beach and the support of a loving and wealthy woman...'

'I pay my own way,' Armin had growled. 'We have

separate phone bills. I don't take advantage of Patty.'

'But anyone seeing you driving that big car, dining out at fine restaurants, sun tanning on the private beach. See what I mean about assumptions? Nobody mistakes you for the head waiter or the valet service. You look the man.'

Armin hadn't known whether to be flattered or peeved. His dealings had always been above board and yet here was Otto insinuating that he went about deceiving people. Okay, so sometimes he may have inflated the figures a little, but that was how businessmen talked when they were idling their time on the exhibition stand or meeting up for breakfast at the diner, it was all about show me yours and I'll show you mine. No one was going to admit to having a weenie.

Karl had brought the Mercedes to a halt in the car park of the hotel and was turning to him now with a conspiratorial smile on his lips.

'They do a very good massage here. A Hungarian girl, Esther, the most amazing fingers, not that there is anything improper.'

The massage was a weekly indulgence every Friday afternoon between three and four in the spa located in a sparkling new wing under a canopy of lofty firs. Karl had never been sexually adventurous. He had met Crystal at university and married her after graduation before setting out on his journey of speculation and accumulation.

They chose asparagus with a hollandaise sauce and Black Forest ham and Armin asked for an extra portion of potatoes on the side. His cousin did not drink but he ordered Armin a Riesling from a small vineyard he owned on the Mosel that specialised in the dry flinty white wines of the region. Karl kept a limited stock in the hotel's cellar for when he entertained clients. 'They are very accommodating here. I helped the owner with his planning applications and he obliges with these little requests of mine.'

Armin had purposely kept at a distance from Karl's sphere of influence. It had always seemed to him so cloyingly provincial in its ambitions. But he noticed that the waiters were attentive and twice during the meal they were to be interrupted by the warm greetings of friends, tanned men in golfing slacks and polo shirts with their blonde, spa toned women. They were bankers and investors, Karl told him, the second generation of post war children to inherit the fruits of hard working parents many of whom had died prematurely of cancers and heart disease in pursuit of *das Wirtschaftswunder.*

He and Karl had had no such benefactors. Only Trudy had sat tight and during the pre-war years begun her collections, her taste refined by frequent visits to Berlin's auction houses.

Yes, Karl had seen the catalogue. 'A fair amount of Meissen, most of it quite special. Kaendler from the mid eighteen century.' The series from the *Commedia dell'arte* were favourites of his. Then, 'Some cups with the Japanese brocade pattern, very early about 1720.' Karl mentioned a few names, Heroldt, Gottlieb. The insurance was immense. 'Ah yes, Boetger's red stoneware, also quite rare, and then the Delft from the Greek 'A' factory which was made around 1675. There is quite an art collection, not all of it to my taste, and furniture, some jewellery but too much for me to go into detail now.'

Over the *Rote Gruetze* with vanilla sauce they talked about family. Karl could see a time when he would hand more of the business over to Julia who had recently finished a course in business management. As a young woman she had studied music and had had hopes of joining an opera company if stage fright hadn't thwarted her ambitions. Soon she would be responsible for the day to day running of the property portfolio while Karl focused on projects that were still on the drawing board. He was still buying houses in old

East Berlin where it was cheap and advised Armin to check out the superb art nouveau villas that could still be had for relatively little in places near the lake, 'Where the *Bonzen* kept their villas.' Most of them required extensive renovation, nothing having been done during the DDR years, and there was sometimes a problem with sitting tenants or the original owners' attempts to reclaim their property. But he'd had a fair amount of success. 'Some of the balconies were so unsafe you couldn't go on them. Last winter one crashed onto the pavement and killed a pedestrian. The ice melted in the cracks and loosened the last of the grouting. These people can't afford the repairs and they eventually see sense. But you have to be quick. Demand is beginning to exceed supply.'

Armin listened impassively, sinking into the familiar role that had been forced upon him in childhood when his slow brain had been no match for Karl's sharp tongue and cynical put downs. He knew how quickly his cousin reacted to provocation and how as a boy he would lash out in frustration, his fists pummelling the bed they had shared after the war when their families had occupied two rooms in a Bremen tenement. Their mothers had been close then, brought together through adversity as they waited for their husbands to be repatriated from American POW camps.

Karl had called for the bill and still nothing had been mentioned about the house. Much had been said about family and responsibility, most of it from Karl's complacent perspective. He had stopped briefly to comment on Armin's divorce and how Crystal especially had been saddened to hear about it although it was no secret that she had not liked Angela with her arrogant English ways. And Alex still not married at thirty seven and settled in San Francisco?

Armin had been living abroad for most of his life and had always considered his world view superior to that of his cousin's narrow focus on the parochial. But arriving in Berlin to trees budding along Unter den Linden and a skyline dominated by cranes and the restless movement of the S-Bahn and Intercity expresses, he had felt something more than just the comfort of familiarity.

He remembered lounging by the pool one morning watching Patty count out her food supplements and suddenly panicking at the thought of dying here and his ashes being scattered over an alien ocean.

The breeze from the lake carried a miasma of water swollen by ice melt and detritus from the forest. During the journey he had heard birdsong so vibrant that he had wondered if his ears were becoming suddenly over sensitive as a precursor to going deaf. Thoughts of death and decay had nagged at him as though the underlying message in Karl's words had been to question his relevance, the eldest who had not lived up to expectations. The survivor of the flying coffin who had bombed as soon as he'd stepped out of the cockpit.

Now Armin leaned towards his cousin, his arms resting on the damask tablecloth where the sauce hollandaise had left small stains.

'Let's get down to business.'

Karl brushed at an invisible crumb by his saucer and then smoothed the cloth with his hand. 'By that I suppose you mean Trudy's Will? Well there isn't one.'

Armin took a deep breath and leaned back in his seat. 'You mean Trudy died intestate?'

'There was no Will. Instead we had an agreement.'

Was Armin part of that agreement? He could not remember signing anything. There had been no summons to a solicitor.

'You weren't here,' Karl said evenly.

'You had my address. I could always be contacted.'

'I can assure you....' Karl's hand fluttered. 'Can't we talk about this back at the house?'

'My inheritance. How much do I get?'

'To be blunt. Nothing.'

'Nothing? I don't understand. I was her favourite. She loved me. How can she have left me nothing?'

Karl shrugged. 'The circumstances did not give themselves to dividing up the estate. If you listen I will explain.'

'Explain nothing,' Armin said.

The blood was rushing in his ears and he got up abruptly and went off blindly in the direction of a track that rose steeply through a wood of beech and oak. Again he heard a burst of birdsong that was so strident and deafening in its energy he thought his head was going to burst. Karl had come after him and Armin stopped, waiting for his cousin to get closer and then when he was almost level, taking off and leaving him behind. It was a game he used to play when they were young; Armin mocking his cousin's lack of physical prowess. He had always been the stronger one.

'Go ahead, run away and leave others to clean up the mess. That's what you're good at, isn't it?' Karl gasped from below. 'Where were you when your mother died? Who had to pay for the funeral and maintain the grave? And I don't remember your visiting Trudy in the nursing home. There was nothing to stop you. Nothing! But you never came.'

Armin's feet slithered in the mud and he grabbed at a branch to steady himself.

Karl was pleading with him to go back. Crystal would be worried. There was no reason to get excited. Everything would be explained and Armin would soon see the benefits. No one had been sidelined or cheated out of anything. 'I understand your concern but really it's not what you think. There's a lot to celebrate.'

But it changed nothing. The house was Karl's now, irrespective of his assurances that it was not his home. Crystal was happy in Bremen with her tennis and ladies golf team. They had no intention of uprooting to the brutalism and concrete of modern Berlin with its graffiti, its anarchy. On a previous visit Crystal had been accosted by a young woman with a beetroot coloured quiff who had attempted to spray paint on her fur jacket. Crystal had elbowed her against a wall and called the police on her mobile.

* * * * *

'Berlin is not for us,' she was to purr later over *Kaffee und Kuchen*.

Afterwards he had walked from room to room, not saying a word, his mind a blank, while Crystal had pointed out the work they had commissioned. She had insisted that everything remain true to the original with the result that they had exceeded their budget by two hundred thousand euros. 'And still counting,' she had sighed, her blue lids flickering at the ceiling in the main salon with its cavorting cupids and wreaths of entwined vines and roses. Armin had glanced at the porcelain displayed in the vitrines, at the bejewelled snuff boxes, one of which Crystal informed him had belonged to *der Alte Fritz*. 'Trudy knew what she liked and she could be quite ruthless if she wanted it. She was not always the gentle soul she led others to believe.'

Armin had dismissed Trudy from his mind. Why should he care when she had obviously forgotten about him?

'It's attributed to Caspar Friedrich.'

He had stopped before a painting of a moonlit frozen landscape and had felt the coldness eating into his bone.

'It will be a living museum, a place for the family to come and spend some time. It's what Trudy wanted.' Karl had told him.

He had come into the room carrying something swaddled in white muslin and Crystal had fluttered her fingers as Karl went to put it on the secretaire, 'No, no Karl not there, here on the cloth where you won't scratch the wood.'

He had unveiled a plate decorated with a riot of flowers in shades of blue. 'I found this in the attic. It's Delft tin-glaze from the Greek 'A' factory, about 1690. It's worth fifty thousand euros.'

Armin went to touch but his cousin warned him off. He had been eating plum cake and his hands might be sticky.

'We thought of hanging it on this wall, what do you think, Armin?'

Crystal had stood against the green damask wallpaper and watched him with eyes that did not show contempt although it was in her heart.

'The diffused light from the window is perfect to bring out the colour, don't you think?'

She put her head to one side inviting a response as though she valued Armin's opinion about where best to display these artefacts. For they are his inheritance too, her smile implied, even though there was nothing to that effect written in the documents that Karl had shown him earlier.

'Let's get down to the facts,' Armin had said after coffee in the garden.

And he had followed Karl to the office he had created for himself next to his bedroom, installed with an oak desk and walnut bookcases upon which the busts of Goethe and Beethoven gazed with marble eyes at Julia in the garden talking earnestly into her mobile.

Karl had taken a thick file from the locked cupboard and flicked through the pages, removing papers from their plastic sleeves; signatures, agreements. Trudy's frail scrawl matched to Karl's vigorous moniker in blue ink. Karl told Armin that he had been the only member of the family with the resources to renovate and maintain the house.

'And Trudy understood this. She wanted to preserve it for generations. Remember, the contents had been catalogued in the DDR years and after her death the museums would have taken what they wanted and the house divided up into flats. Most of the detail, the stucco and stained glass on the landing, would have been damaged or destroyed. No sensitive renovation is possible when there is no money and the DDR was bankrupt as an economic force and as a political system. It was our luck that history was on our side.'

'And Trudy bequeathed it to you,' Armin had said at last, the words sticking in his throat, but they had to be said, the truth must come out.

'Bequeathed it to us on behalf of the family' Karl had corrected. 'Crystal and I are the caretakers. We have spent nearly a million euros, a million of our own money but once we had committed ourselves it was important for both of us that the work be carried out properly. We hired only the best craftsmen, bought only the best materials. Everything was matched for authenticity. In the kitchen we had the missing Dutch tiles replaced. Crystal went to Holland and miraculously the factory was still there. She has put all her energies into this restoration.'

Armin needed some air. The house was closing in on him, the windows bolted and the curtains drawn in the rooms where the afternoon sunlight would fade the furnishings. He left his cousin making a phone call and went down the stairs and across the flagged yard and then through the massive doors into the garden. He had forgotten that Julia was there.

'*Na,* Armin?'

He acknowledged her but would have gone on walking until he became invisible behind the fruit trees if she hadn't offered him a drink from the bottle of white wine on the table.

'I was twelve the last time I saw you. I was thinking about it. I was just about to start at the Gymnasium.'

He pretended to look startled. 'Surely not?' But then

Angela had never liked visiting his cousin's house.

'I hardly know you.'

He poured himself a glass of wine and dropped the empty bottle into the grass.

'I hope you'll come and stay. The house needs life.'

She had a light, melodic voice and he thought how attractive she looked in her lilac crepe jacket, her dark blonde hair spiking out from a cleverly constructed chignon. For a moment he forgot his anger. It wasn't Julia's fault.

'My companies keep me busy,' he said.

'Then you will have to make time Armin,' she said, reaching under the verbena bush and brandishing another bottle. She poured them both a fresh glass. 'Mum and Dad ought to relax more. Dad still thinks he's living in one room in Frankfurt Oder and any minute the Russians are going to burst through the door.'

She looked serious for a moment and he noticed that in repose the sides of her mouth drooped in an expression whether of disappointment, or disenchantment, he could not tell but he realised that she was not happy. Maybe it was too much wine. Or there was no man in her life. Nobody special. He seemed to remember Karl mentioning someone who had turned out to be unsuitable.

'They work so hard. They've been involved with this project for two years and it's still not finished.'

Armin had always believed that Trudy had continued to live in the house until her first stroke a year ago. He hadn't realised that she had been in the nursing home so long.

'She was becoming absent minded. She left the tap running and flooded the basement a few times. Dad went to see her and told her it couldn't go on. Frau Hubschmidt from the tenement opposite was bringing her coal for the stove and Mum found her in the front room one day, just standing there with her dirty shoes on the Persian rug and staring at all the priceless objects. Fortunately nothing was taken but you can see where it was leading. Something had to be done.'

She was looking at him now with grey eyes that had a challenging glint, as though she had not really convinced herself and with a little encouragement her true opinion would come spilling out. But Armin was too depressed to notice. It had finally sunk in that he had inherited nothing. No investment for his company, no fresh start in Berlin or anywhere. He was as broke now as he was ten days ago when he'd left Miami bursting with optimism about his future. All he had to show for it was a glorified timeshare where he would have to book his dates in advance and sign for the keys with Frau Hubschmidt.

He told Julia he was going out and would be back later.

'Mum's ordered dinner from Kaefers so don't be late.'

'It's business,' he said.

He went to the river and took a path through the woods to the lake. The house was still visible behind the trees but he could not bring himself to look at it. He found a small bar and was drinking steadily when Patty rang. Wasn't the funeral today? And the Will, what about the Will?

'Everything's just great.' he said, 'I was about to call you. Everything's fantastic.'

'I can hear you're having quite a party there. So tell me, how much, *schatzelein*, how much did your dear old auntie leave you?'

Armin tossed the whisky down his throat and indicated to the barman to pour him another.

'About two million.'

Patty said, 'Is that just the house? And are we talking dollars or euros here?'

'Dollars. It's what the house is worth, roughly, I haven't had time to get a proper assessment.'

'And that's not including the contents?'

‘Not including the antiques.’

‘You must be over the moon! Dear old auntie Trudy. She never forgot you, Armin. But then you always said you were her favourite. I feel like catching the next plane and joining in the celebrations.’

He groaned appreciatively. ‘Nothing I’d like more Patty, but I have a lot of loose ends to tie up. Meetings with attorneys and so on. I'm thinking of turning the house into some kind of museum for the family.’

‘That's very altruistic of you to give everyone a share in your good fortune. Have you spoken to Karl about it?’

‘That's what I'm planning for tomorrow. No point in your coming over until I've sorted things out.’

‘Listen, take my advice and make sure you keep the antiques for yourself. Don't leave them in the house. Have a list drawn up by an expert. From what I hear, your cousin’s no push over. Don't let him take any of the good stuff as compensation for losing out. When money's at stake it makes people do things they wouldn't normally do.’

It was late when he left the bar. He heard the pneumatic whine of the last tram as it snaked off towards the depot and went up the road looking for a taxi. The street was deserted and he had no alternative but to walk. The party was still in full swing when he rang the bell.

‘I'm Karl's cousin,’ he explained above the noise to a man in a yellow linen jacket. He was asked to wait while Karl was found among a group of friends.

‘You've missed a great evening,’ Karl said evenly, ‘but that's your loss. There may be some food left.’ He indicated the marquee where the caterers were busily packing away their equipment.

Armin's belly was hollow but he had no appetite.

‘Was there any money?’ he asked, ‘I mean, did she have any savings? All those years with nothing to spend her marks on. Bonn agreed to parity after reunification so what happened to it all?'

They were in the yard between the street and the garden where through the open great door Armin could make out guests grouped under lanterns strung in the trees. A woman raised a bare arm from under her heavy stole and he saw the flash of diamonds on her neck and wrist.

'I don't want to discuss such matters now.'

'So there were savings?'

'I told you, now is not the place. We can talk about it tomorrow.'

'I'm going to London tomorrow. What happened to Trudy's savings?'

'Keep your voice down, you're drunk.'

Karl closed the door to the garden but continued to keep a grip on the handle. He balled one fist and dug it deep into the pocket of his jacket, a jacket Armin noticed that had satin reveres. His cousin dressed for the opera and Crystal appearing now against the stained glass window in a shot silk cocktail gown, her arm encircled by gold bracelets.

'Oh, it's you?' she murmured when she saw him.

'Who did you think it was, a thief come to steal your precious museum?'

'He's been drinking,' Karl said with a shrug.

'Those things you're wearing were hers too,' he said indicating the bracelets. And I suppose Julia hasn't gone empty handed. Amazing!' Armin raised his face to the ceiling and glimpsed the faint outline of mountains at sunset painted above the lintel. A mural that had somehow missed Crystal's gimlet eye. The plaster was flaking and he almost rejoiced at it.

'And you? What would you have done? Sold up and spent the lot. You never could hold on to your money. Don't you think Trudy knew this and that's why she made sure you wouldn't get your hands on it?' The artery in Karl's neck bulged against his spotless collar.

Crystal had stepped between them with her arms raised like a hostage. ‘Don't say things you will regret. We have something for you, Armin. A keepsake from the collection. Come, follow me and I'll show you.’

‘He doesn't deserve anything,’ Karl snapped after them. ‘He can't just turn up here and make claims. It doesn't work like that. You have to earn the right. You have to work hard and pay your dues. You can go to hell!’

Crystal was calling him from the landing, her skirt rustling as she mounted the stairs to the living quarters and he stumbled up after her as Karl slammed the door behind them. He wanted nothing from them. Nothing at all. He gripped onto the door, swaying gently as Crystal went into her bedroom and came out with a leather box.

Most of Armin's memories of Trudy were from childhood and the trinkets that Crystal drew from the dark velvet had no meaning for him. He could tell that they were of little material worth; an art nouveau bracelet that smelled of tin, a lump of amber with the density of custard, some earrings of a uniform dullness. Everything had been sifted through many times and the tiniest glints of gold removed, leaving behind only their intrinsic value. He had loved Trudy and he had thought she loved him. He looked at the objects between Crystal’s manicured fingers, for he could not bring himself to touch them, to feel the links in a chain of finely wrought pewter when it was proffered. To him it would have meant colluding with everything Crystal stood for.

She was studying him with earnest blue eyes. He had never realised she wore tinted contact lenses until she'd lost one and he'd come across her frantically searching for it on the floor. All the years he'd known her, believing that the intensity of her irises was a gift of Mother Nature. It was like the dark hair, no woman of Crystal's age could maintain such a depth of colour unless it was out of a bottle. He moved his knee against her skirt and felt her leg withdraw to the safety of the table. Once she would have flirted with him. When his stock was high. The ex-Starfighter pilot who in more ambitious times had flown cronies of Franz Joseph Strauss on shopping sprees to New York and had stories to tell.

Karl was calling up the stairwell. Guests were wanting to say goodnight. Voices echoed in the courtyard. ‘Fantastic house. Wonderful piece of work.’

Crystal got up. ‘Take your time, I'll be back in a minute.’

He heard her girlish laughter accepting the flattery of her friends. It had taken both imagination and courage to restore this house. ‘And millions of euros,’ someone added.

On the ceiling of powder blue the nymphs eyed him mischievously as they romped among the exuberant swathes of roses and vines. Armin pushed the box to one side and got up. He had no investment here. In the morning he would leave early before they were awake.

He padded across the carpet and stopped before one of the vitrines, his attention caught by a pair of yellow birds perched upon a stump of sprouting pink blossom. On the shelf above was the figurine of a young man reaching for a maiden's hand, her wide skirt looped up in anticipation of his proposal. What was he suggesting?

The key was in the lock and he turned it and ran a finger now over her bosom and tightly corseted waist and down the folds of her skirt. How much was it worth? Weighing the figurine in his hand, gram for gram he guessed he was looking at tens of thousands of euros.

He felt something snap and fall onto the floor. At first he did not realise what had happened but on closer inspection he realised that the man's hand was missing. He got down unsteadily on all fours and began to search for it under the table, gently sweeping the carpet and wooden parquet with his palms and cursing under his breath when he found nothing. And then something hard digging into his right knee and an almost imperceptible crunch. Gingerly moving to one side, he saw tiny specks of porcelain, delicate as crushed shell, clinging to his trouser leg.

There was movement below, the conversation that had bubbled up from the courtyard had deflated to a few whispers and conspiratorial laughter. 'How about Sylt next weekend?' one of the women piped. There was a chorus of affirmation. Obviously these were close friends, the exclusive circle that earlier had been given a tour of the house and in this very room, champagne flutes raised, had toasted the new proprietors of Trudy's treasures. Where was Armin? Oughtn't he to be here, too? 'He sends his apologies.' Julia had said, 'He had some pressing business to attend to.'

He brushed the shards onto the floor and swept them with his foot under the carpet. Then he pocketed the figurine and rearranged the vitrine to cover the gap. He turned off the light and went into the corridor where his muddy footprints were all over the Persian rug. He had walked through the woods and bits of leaves and twigs were still sticking to his heels. He made a half-hearted attempt to rub some of it off but a little dirt on the carpet was the least of his worries.

Chapter Seven

In all her years as a china restorer Kitty had rarely held a figurine so precious. 'JJ Kaendler, one of Meissen's undisputed masters,' she had confirmed to Armin.

And Armin impatient to be off now that he had delivered the damaged suitor engaged in delicate fingerplay with his senorita (except there was no hand, only a rosy stump) had said he had a meeting in Isleworth at two and would call in later to see how work was progressing.

'Oh, but I don't know if I can,' had been Kitty's immediate response on seeing the porcelain unravelled from the bundle of newspaper. First Armin had carefully removed the padding of a vest and towel before the pages of *Die Berliner Morgenpost* had exposed the red and yellow plumes of the young woman's bonnet. The colours were repeated in the roses at her bosom and the rosettes on the young man's doublet and yellow shoes, the heels red tipped. The Spanish Lovers. Meissen about 1741.

'You will repair it for me,' he had said. 'I saw how you made a new beak for the parrot. You can make a new hand? How long will it take?'

'I have repaired Worcester, Chelsea, Limoges but never Kaendler Meissen. It is something for a museum. I suggest you take it to the V&A and ask their advice. And this is part of your legacy, you say? Oh what a pity.'

Kitty traced a finger over the folds of the young woman's floral skirt. Her suitor was pressing her, his toe blocking her progress across the flower strewn path. She looked bemused, a little reticent, Kitty thought and her hand without the steadying influence of his seemed to waver and be on the point of withdrawal.

She still hadn't got over the shock of finding Armin here. He had been sitting in the front garden when she had returned from visiting Elsie at the hospital and at first glance she had thought it was Jason.

Even when she heard the trill of a mobile and a German voice drifting over the Peace roses she remained convinced it was Jason. He had discovered Freddy in the porch and now he was waiting to confront her. She would defend herself of course and claim that she'd been unable to find any alternative to deceiving him if she wanted to stay at Seething Wells. Her cheeks were hot and her breath came in little puffs. But she could not deny there was also an underlying sense of relief that the game was finally up.

No more pretend. No more having to rack her brain for increasingly ludicrous stories which suggested that subconsciously she was already preparing herself for the day when Elsie would question the veracity of her little mutt's adventures. And then, walking into the ward of eight old ladies, who in their faded beige had all looked identical. That had distressed Kitty as much as finding her friend lying so deathly still, the way personality and life experience were subsumed by this ageing assertiveness of sameness. Like babies fresh from the womb recognisable only to their mothers.

And that dreadful hospital smell that remained in the clothes and nostrils and was still with her when she had spotted Jason, wrongly as it turned out, waiting for her to explain herself. She could have hugged Armin when she realised her mistake. Instead she had invited him inside and, going into the kitchen to make tea, had had one of her dizzy spells. They lasted no more than a few seconds but it was as if she had suddenly experienced the true nature of the universe with its violent and restless energy. The earth's spin sending her staggering against the side of the stove, arms flailing. But it had righted itself soon enough. The illusion of terra firma still maintained so that after a minute or two she could return to the front room with the tray of tea things, a little unsteady mind, but Mr von Hassendorf had had eyes for nothing but his Spanish Lovers spilling from the cocoon of laundry and yesterday's newspaper.

She had wanted to tell him nothing was that important once you'd understood your perception of the world was dependant on the fragile mechanism of the inner ear. That is what her doctor had told her when writing out the prescription for Stugeron. Take one after or prior to an attack if you were sensitive enough to feel it coming on. Well, she'd been very stressed after seeing Elsie and ought to have guessed it would happen.

A fractured coccyx, Dr Koshi had said to Kitty at the hospital. She had looked no older than a schoolgirl and with wrists so slender Kitty had thought they might snap under the slightest pressure. Elsie had had a fall in her room at Fircroft and had managed to crawl to her panic button and raise the alarm.

Kitty had whispered to Elsie through the light fuzz of her hair and smelt the hastily removed smear of vomit. She had stroked her hand where the thin wedding band had been embedded in her swollen finger as though the skin were yielding it now like a seam of finest gold. She had thought of all the years they had been friends, in the days when Alfred was forty and Derrick a young man fighting the insurgents in Jahore State. No, she wouldn't go there. She had promised herself. But driving through the endless plantations of rubber and palm oil trees, for after Alfred passed away she had suddenly needed desperately to find the place where Derrick had been killed, the taxi had stopped at a bend in the road and she had seen the sidelong ripple of a large snake crossing their path on the spot where the convoy had been ambushed.

Dr Koshi had said they could do little but give Elsie painkillers and leave the fracture to knit in its own time. No swathing in plaster for so inaccessible a region. Kitty had looked at her friend and wished she could take her home and repair her broken bone with love and attention and an application of Two Tube Araldite.

It would take much more than a little bonding to do what Armin was asking of her. A new hand no less, to be fashioned from a composition of kaolin, Araldite AY 103 and titanium dioxide powder, the mixture to be rolled out like pastry and then pinned before being applied as far as the knuckles. Thin wire to be used for each of the fingers and then more composition added. But Kitty knew she was not up to the challenge. She had lost her freshness of vision. Fine detail eluded her even with the aid of a magnifying glass. And although her hands were remarkably steady for an eighty year old, they could not compete with the supple fingers of someone half her age.

She had contacts though. Restorers she would be happy to recommend. The responsibility for a Kaendler worth thousands of pounds was too daunting a prospect.

'I don't think I could do it justice,' she said.

Armin had looked at her quizzically. He understood the word but not in that context. His justice was bound up with the overwhelming resentment he felt for his cousin and the treachery that he saw permeating every object on every floor of the Berlin house. Even his camp bed with the duvet neatly smoothed, a towel for his ablutions folded on the pillow, had made a mockery of his expectations. He had come to claim his inheritance and here it is, Karl was saying.

He had hardly slept and nodding off at last towards dawn had been woken by the roar of the first tram, a noise so thunderous that his first thought had been that he was in the cockpit preparing for takeoff into the lilac and rose of a Colorado dawn. The dark mountains flattening out like the crushed spine of a mackerel, the earth a blur of light honey as the nose lifted.

And then the reality kicking in.

He had left the figurine, incautiously, on the chair by his bed and on a rare impulse had been about to lob it out the window when he'd heard Julia calling him up the stairwell. He’d tucked it under the duvet and opened the door. She had made coffee and bought fresh rolls from the baker. Did he want to join her for breakfast?

He'd washed and shaved in the guest bathroom on the landing and gone downstairs, his footsteps cushioned by the Persian rug where all traces of yesterday's transgression had been erased. It was common courtesy to leave dirty shoes outside, Julia would tell him later in a tone reminiscent of her mother until she had broken into a grin. ‘Breaking the rules, Armin, that's what you're about, eh?’ He had never seen himself as a rebel but was flattered that she should think so.

He'd found Julia alone in the kitchen, dressed for business in a grey pants suit and white blouse with a cascade of frills at the throat that rippled when she moved, a constant reminder of motion that he had found unnerving. He could be very still. Patty had remarked upon it. ‘You're like a big old ‘gator,’ she'd said to him once, intimidated perhaps by his ability to sit for hours at his desk or watch TV. Inactivity was one step closer to death, or perhaps she begrudged the exclusion.

The tiny kitchen table with a dazzling white starched cloth had been set for two. He saw dishes of glistening raspberry and apricot jam and whirls of pale yellow butter, a plate of cheese and *Wurst*, yoghurt and a basket of fresh rolls, sunflower, poppy seed, white and brown, a couple of pretzels splintered and encrusted with grains of salt. He hadn't eaten since yesterday lunchtime.

'Mum and Dad had to leave early this morning. They thought it better not to wake you but they wish you a safe journey.'

Armin said nothing.

There was a layer of fat on Julia's thighs, a gentle rolling of flesh which he found compelling. He found himself watching her as she went back and forth dipping into cupboards and then hurrying into the corridor to answer the telephone, her vitality expressed in the brashness of her laugh and the liveliness of her hands. She was like neither of her parents. Armin wondered where she had sprung from.

She had returned looking preoccupied and then burst out, 'I don't understand men. I can't get into their heads.'

'Your father...' he had begun but she had dismissed that idea with an angry shrug. 'No, I mean men in general. Their assumptions. Their expectations. What they expect of me.'

'So many men,' Armin had replied, bemused. He felt he could relax at least for a moment. Karl and Crystal out of the way and no mention of a disappearing figurine.

Julia was dribbling honey onto her roll. 'If I tell you, you promise to keep it to yourself?'

'Who would I tell?' he said. Uncomfortable with secrets. The machinations of family. It was one of the reasons why he had left.

'Dad doesn't like my friends. Mum just hates them.'

'Well, that's at least unanimous,' he said. 'No conflict of interest, just plain disapproval. You can deal with it.'

He had gone into the front room while Julia was clearing the table, his eyes settling immediately on the vitrine of opalescent Meissen. It was not immediately obvious that the Spanish Lovers was missing. He had filled the gap with another study in gallantry; a young man in frock coat, tipping his tricorn hat at a flounce of petticoats.

Julia suddenly had been in haste to be gone and he had closed the door softly behind him, assuring her that all was safe and secure in there. She was on the landing, her overnight bag strung over her shoulder, activating the security system.

'If I want to spend some time here, how do I get in?' he asked and she told him about Frau Hubschmidt opposite who kept a set of keys and whose job it was to clean up after they had left. She offered her cheek to him, tilting her nose as if he were a bad smell and then clamping both arms about him in a bear hug. He felt the thrust of her breasts and her soft excitable skin against his cheek and he slid his hand against the dimpled hollows of her back and held her. A moment too long perhaps, but she didn't resist. When he released her she said, 'Don't wait another twenty years.'

He went back upstairs and packed his few belongings and then took the tram to the main station and made enquiries in a few antique shops on the Friedrichstrasse about the restoration of Meissen. But no one could offer him the quick fix he was hoping for. His mention of the Spanish Lovers awakened curiosity about provenance. It was unusual for such a rare piece to come onto the market. Most Kaendler was in museums or in private collections. Was it genuine and if so how had he come by it? Aware that he was arousing suspicion he had made a hasty retreat before anyone got the idea of contacting the police.

* * * * *

Kitty sat at her table. The oilcloth was her CV, besmirched as it was with dried kaolin, paint, the bleached spots of spilled peroxide, the rust of old razor blades and the crumbs from one of Millie's cookies that Armin had spilled over his plate before taking his leave.

His last words to Kitty had been, ‘Just put the hand back on. It doesn't have to be perfect.’

Chapter Eight

VJ was waiting for Armin when he walked into the Kerala Garden. He was at a table with two other Indians, Tamil like himself with neat features and smooth gelled hair that left a dribble of curls at the nape. Brothers Neel and Sam. VJ's nephews. Dabblers in whatever turned a profit. They owned a mini-mart in Shepherds Bush and besides the usual array of dry goods, offered a photocopying and fax facility, cheap phone cards for overseas calls, a shipping business for the subcontinent (no packages too big or too small), internet banking and a twenty-four hour cab service. A large fluorescent sign over the counter indicated that no cash was kept overnight on the premises but this was to be no deterrent to the crackhead or daytime opportunist. Three months ago Neel had been held at gun point while two youths had straddled the counter to rifle the till. Vodka was grabbed from the shelves, bottles smashed and chocolate bars sent skittering across the floor. Now he was terrified they would come back.

Business doesn't have to be at the sharp end of retail. VJ's words over the dhal and onion bhajis, the vegetable curry with its gluttonous ladies fingers, coconut milk and coriander. There were safer ways, more lucrative too.

At this Armin felt a familiar stirring in his blood and a resurgence of interest in prospects that at first sight had looked as bleak as the hemp walls and maroon tablecloths of the Kerala Garden.

‘What do you have for me?’

VJ reached into a plastic bag and pulled out a smoky glass bottle with an old fashioned spring stopper. On the label was a picture of a castle resembling Neuschwanstein and above its crenulated battlements written in gothic script on a sky blue ground was the word 'Klug.'

Armin had never heard of it.

'It's new to the market,' VJ said. 'Neel and Sam here are sole agents for the UK. How about some mango and breadfruit sorbet?'

'German beers are over represented in the UK,' Armin said.

'But Klug isn't German,' Sam said, breaking into a grin. 'And it's half the price too. I defy you to tell the difference; Löwenbräu, Pschorr, Becks, Thurn und Taxis, Weihenstephaner, Klug. They all sound German but one of them is brewed right here, not a mile from this restaurant, in Hounslow.'

'They're good, eh?' VJ chortled. 'I told them about your business in America, World Trade Emporium... my big shot friend who went to Florida and started an empire.'

'World Trade Agency,' Armin corrected.

'If people see a German beer that's half the price of its competitors they'll buy it,' Neel said.

'But it isn't German,' Armin insisted.

'And the Taj Mahal isn't Indian, strictly speaking, it's Mogul,' Neel said, calling for fresh glasses. 'And anyway in America, they have no idea where Germany is, right? But they understand that it means quality, efficiency, reliability like BMW and Porsche.'

It was easy to be beguiled by these glossy skinned young men, their lips hovering with eager smiles, scented and so smart, button down shirts and Levis. Hands nimble as spiders. They caressed the dumpy bottle, proffered it for inspection, drained one and then another and smacked their lips at the salty sweetness. Beer bubbles burst into a head of froth and lathered their upper lips. 'I might know a few people,' Armin said.

The CEO of World Trade Agency offering a helping hand for him and VJ went way back to the golden years of Liebfraumilch when England couldn't get enough of it and the vineyards had imported grapes from Greece, Spain anywhere to keep up with demand. Until the shipment from Austria had been impounded amid rumours of tampering with glycol. Anti-freeze added to evoke the honey fermented sweetness of *Spaetlese.* It had almost ruined him.

The thought added more rancour to his heart, the past and present stirred now to a thick dark stew of thwarted ambition, the underhand actions of people he had thought were friends. Were cousins. He looked at these brilliant itchy nephews with their business degrees and was reminded of a tailor shop in Hong Kong, years ago, where bolts of cloth had lined the walls, iridescent satins and Chinese silks, Irish linen and Harris tweed, Swiss cotton, French voile, and the shameless hustling of the young men unravelling the billowing materials across the counter, no trouble spared, 'a coke sir, a whisky soda?' And the tailor on hand with his tape ready to snap for collar size even before he had ventured through the door.

Armin always experienced elation at the mention of business, the jangle of mobiles a reminder of his world of deals and talking up, of tips in smoke filled clubs and members only washrooms; the golf course where a hole in one had released from its triumphant executor insider knowledge about the real state of a rock solid company. 'It's on the skids, believe me.' And yet Armin had not acted, this man of trade, on the ephemeral, the rumour that could be put to good use and with the right tweaking be turned into a windfall. Angela had hated him for it. They could have lined their pockets many times over, others did. In her eyes everyone was at it from the rich with their offshore tax havens, to supermarkets, speed cameras, parking meters, public transport, shopping malls, restaurants, the government. You were being ripped off everywhere. What made Armin von Hassendorf so fucking special?

‘Because I'd get no pleasure from it,’ he had said disingenuously and releasing a torrent of abuse from Angela who had tossed a blizzard of unpaid bills at him and slammed the door.

Why was the truth sometimes so unpalatable? The simulated cockpit of a fighter jet could never compete with the fear and elation of flying the real thing. He needed to touch what he traded, to hold and taste it and judge its potential not bring it up on screen and project its future from a barrage of statistics. He had wondered if those commodities really existed. Did someone eat the rice and drink the coffee of the future or were they all part of that virtual world, trapped in space like a quasar or supernova?

Klug. The correct pronunciation was Kloog. But the nephews liked its onomatopoeic suggestion of beer emptying into a glass. In German, Armin told them, Klug means clever, wise. ‘Yeh?’ they beamed. Then it was double karma. A beer that tasted great and sounded smart.

Later he would fan out the beer mats across the scratched mahogany counter of the deli in Ealing, splaying them like a winning hand in poker before the young assistant. Sonja. He had coaxed the name from her as he'd thumbed up the swing stopper, releasing a wisp of vapour and a prickle of froth that had dampened the counter and the knuckle of her hand, her hair, darkly streaked with unnatural red and polished hard like lacquer. ‘Sonja?’ he had repeated, pouring the beer into an empty jar, for she could not find a glass, and he was offering that to her now. ‘A fresh, full bodied taste. New to the market.’ She had raised the beer to her lips, wrinkling her nose at the effervescence, her eyes that were the folk memory of Baltic summers, the band playing at Bansin, the stucco villas with their germanic names, Elfrieda, Irmgard, Gerda, rising above the dunes, their balconies festooned with towels flavoured by the tarry aromas of the fish smokeries. 'Where was she from?' 'Cracow,' she told him. He had not been there. But his family had been traders in Danzig. A slip of the tongue. He meant Gdansk. Sonja tipped her head and studied the Disneyland label on the bottle. Perhaps she had not heard him.

The Russians into Poland, the Poles into Germany, a side step shuffle, the crab seizing with his pincers the small fish, the unwary. Karl of course had gone back to size up the other ancestral home on the banks of the Motlawa, a tall Dutch gabled house renovated by Stalin. They had no claim. But in the church there was a von Hassendorf plaque, a piece of stained glass that had remained unshattered by enemy bombs.

In the cusp of her breasts hung a thin gold cross. He would take her on a journey, his arm encircling her narrow waist where the flounce of her smock skirted the pleat of her crotch, his stride matching hers for she had long legs. Then he would lift the filigree chain with the tip of a finger and draw her to him.

It was not for her to make decisions, Maciej the proprietor was away but she would bring the beer to his attention. It was good. Cheap. The small teeth in wide pink gums had the milky enamel of late adolescence. How old was she? 'Twenty two,' she said, wagging a finger at him like a keep off sign. A man didn't ask a woman's age.

'So young!' he said, and realised too late that he had given himself away.

She had protested, 'No! You are not old, you are still fit, still working. It is good!' In the patronising way that a daughter would address a sprightly grandfather.

He left her two bottles quietly fizzing, brown on gold like a harvest and a clutch of beer mats and ballpoints, the nephews' promo material also stretching to a five day stay in a maharaja's palace for repeat orders exceeding 50K.

The river drew him, first to Richmond where he met up with an old customer, a German from Magdeburg who had opened a bakery and was doing well, rising at four to bake the batches of rye and *vollkorn,* the sour dough wheels embedded with sunflower seeds, walnut bread, the long brown caraway loaves. He was scornful of English bread. *Pappe,* he called it. No substance, nothing to chew on. No wonder English teeth were bad. Armin unzapped a beer. On the counter were trays of cheesecake embellished with slivers of lime, translucent glazes of blueberry, raspberry, strawberry, apple cake with a crumble topping, *Schweinsohren, Hoernchen* stuffed with cream, custard slices in filo pastry and topped with cherry jam. The baker held up his glass and said, 'Klug. It's not a brewery I'm familiar with.'

Armin left with a trial order for three cases and followed the river's curve through the water meadow where the cows grazed and then along the towpath pitted from the tidal flow that sucked the gravel and deposited the funfair colours of detritus along its edges. Only after Teddington Lock was the river limpid as a pond, tideless between banks of sycamore and alder.

He found Kitty in her front garden, a tiny crouched figure tugging at a shrub of yellow stars. Adele was reclining in a deckchair, her pale face tilted at a watery sun that made her whirl of hair almost transparent. 'Ah, Mr von Hassendorf. I have seen the Spanish Lovers - what a tragedy!'

She was beckoning Armin to join her. 'I don't think Kitty is up to it the poor darling. It is a tremendous responsibility to restore a Kaendler. I think you should forget about it, dear. She has enough worries already what with Elsie about to snuff it. Oh, no disrespect but she ought to have been more careful when so many people are depending on her. Jason will have Kitty out on the street while Elsie's ashes are still smouldering. My father used to play at funerals God rest his soul. Work was very hard to come by in the thirties. He was a saxophonist. A very good one, too. He used to practise in the lavatory for the acoustics. All six of us in two rooms and no bathroom. We went to the local baths for our weekly soak. Oh dear, me rambling on. My father had a friend, a violinist called Rosenberg. He was from Germany but he left when he heard there was going to be trouble, rumours starting about the persecutions, so he packed his bags and came to England. A young man, very talented. He'd played in an orchestra in Munich and my darling mother, such a soft hearted soul, put him up for a bit, gave him a rug and some floor space. That's how it was in those days.'

Adele's lament drifted past Freddy standing peg-legged on permanent alert at the window and on into the front room where it was drowned by the sudden throb of the airbrush as Sylvia stood poised to blush the cheek of her porcelain doll with rose madder genuine. Startled by Armin's long shadow, she let the stilo drop and watched in dismay as a spray of paint speckled the carpet.

The Spanish Lovers had been put for safekeeping on the topmost shelf of Kitty's bookcase, wrapped in muslin and then boxed and padded with bubble wrap. 'I'm sorry,' Kitty said, as Bosco reached up to retrieve it, 'but you'll understand Mr von Hassendorf that I couldn't do it justice.'

That word again, fermenting in Armin's breast and making him reply brusquely, 'Once something is in a museum who questions its authenticity? The Spanish Lovers in my vitrine has a hand missing, that's the only difference. Replace it and no one will be any the wiser.'

'But you will know,' Sylvia said, grabbing the side of the table and hauling herself up from the carpet where she had been dabbing at the stain with kitchen roll. 'And each time you look at it you'll see it's a botched job and you'll regret it bitterly.'

'Let me be the judge of that,' Armin said.

'A Meissen figurine worth thousands of pounds and you just don't care? We should be so lucky. Very few of us have that luxury.'

Doreen had come in from the kitchen where she had been washing up the afternoon cups. Behind her Milly and Molly flapped their tea towels in mild acquiescence. It wasn't a good idea to get on the wrong side of Doreen.

'But Mr von Hassendorf does care, otherwise he wouldn't have brought it all the way from Berlin.' Kitty said, 'It's only that he's come to the wrong person.'

'How much do you want?' Armin said.

'It's not about the money. It's about professional pride and expertise,' Kitty began.

'Five hundred pounds,' Adele said. 'Kitty needs the money. The roof leaks each time the rain comes from the south. Heaven knows, Elsie hasn't been able to write any cheques since her stroke and once that dreadful Jason finds out and applies for power of attorney, well, we're sunk. You might as well release the floodgates and sell us up the river.'

'But it would be taking money under false pretences, and I won't do it,' Kitty protested.

'You could have it restored for me by this time tomorrow?'

Armin was at the window, gazing out at the shimmering water that seemed to reflect the emotion in the room behind him, the ripples of excitement tugged by uncertainty, the undercurrent of greed, for few people were immune to its pull and he suspected that even Kitty under her mild exterior was already calculating what she could do with five hundred pounds. He had no problem with that. He was a businessman, after all.

'It's worth a try.' Bosco's voice boomed like a bittern. In his dark suit and white open necked shirt, a gold medallion suggested otherwise but he was a mummy's boy, his large jowls pock marked from a smallpox epidemic carried on a junk to Canton where Bosco's uncle had been in trade. His widowed mother kept house in their flat in Teddington, sallow skinned and white haired but in her dark eyes still a flicker of the beauty she had once been. Each Sunday she accompanied her son to Mass, her fingers clinging to his arm like the tendril of a flower.

Kitty was rifling through the boxes of china chips, the cup handles, the amputated limbs and heads of figurines that she could never bring herself to throw away. Perhaps in here somewhere there already was a hand that with the application of Araldite and kaolin could be made to resemble the original. If it didn't matter. If Mr von Hassendorf was absolutely sure that all he wanted was a cosmetic job, an illusion of whole, for his fabulous collection?

Chapter Nine

'An advance?' Patty sounded cautious. 'How much do you want Armin?'

'Ten thousand should do it. You know how it is Patty. On paper I'm a millionaire, but I'm walking round London with two dimes in my pocket.'

'What about your credit cards?'

'I've hit the limit. Okay, so I've had a lot of expenses these last few months. I can approach some of my old investors if you don't feel happy about helping me out.'

'You can't blame me for asking questions.'

'I appreciate that, Patty.'

'And you know how I feel about autonomy.'

'Sure, sure, so let's forget I ever asked, okay? I'm sorry.'

'Now you're making me sound like a mean bitch.'

'Patty, I respect you, okay? It's fine. I'm in Berlin tomorrow, I'll talk to my bank.'

'But I want to help you, sweetie, s*chatzelein*. My bed's so cold without you. Are we talking dollars or euros?'

'Dollars will be fine.'

In the garden a squirrel jerked its tail aggressively before taking a flying leap onto the mimosa. Armin went to the shadow of the lilac and tilted his credit card to catch the light. The digits danced before his eyes, spilling across the plastic as he read them out for Patty. Money like water through his fingers.

'You'll get it all back, with interest,' he promised, voice breaking with emotion.

He'll take Patty on a trip through the limpid backwaters of the Spree where the wooden houses with their slavic symbols squat on tiny islands; a fecund hydroculture of cucumbers on the vine swelling like cocks. He got her to repeat the numbers so there could be no mistake.

'I won't forget this,' he said and walked across the lawn and onto the road where the river curved like a scimitar, silver chased.

Patty was still there, pressed to his ear. 'Tell me some more about those salty *Spreewalder...*'

The sun hovered between the firs that stood on either side of the gate and sidled through their needles to gild the Spanish Lovers on Kitty's table. Bosco, matching dry powder pigments on a tile, noted the illusory quivering of two feathers on her bonnet. A trick of the light. He experienced the dull weight of loss but did not know why. Scarlet and gold. Blood and heat. The dazzle of the fort and the long curve of the Avenida Almeida where the fishing nets were suspended on bamboo poles and the sweat was still fresh on the young man's upper lip. Bosco tasted the velvet of his mouth and dipped his brush vigorously into cerulean blue, alizarin crimson, aureolin yellow, mixing and re-mixing with titanium white to erase the memory already darkening as the sun dipped behind the ait.

Kitty had bonded the pin under the ruffle of the young man's cuff and was now rolling out her composition of kaolin, Araldite AY 103 and titanium dioxide powder to wind around it. There it will be allowed to dry before the next layer is added. Electric wire for the fingers had been inserted into this soft dough and shaped to resemble the hand in the photograph. It was Sylvia on a chair leaning into the dusty top shelf who had plucked the volume from the squash of books on spiritualism, herbaceous borders, British flora and fauna and the King James Bible and waved it triumphantly in the air. 'Here it is!'

Kitty proving that some things remain indelible once put to memory for she had recalled seeing a full colour plate of the Spanish Lovers in Nathaniel Harris's *Porcelain Figurines*. Bosco had twinkled over, nimble for a heavyweight, and helped Sylvia from the chair and they had spread the book on the table and compared every detail, remarking on the balance of tilt and angle, or as Bosco called it, the yin and yang. Kitty would not have dreamed of attempting a restoration without a reference. Armin's blithe remark that she, 'do the best you can under the circumstances,' had been an insult to her professionalism. 'Did he expect that I would make it up?' she had asked after he had gone.

It struck them as profoundly odd that he didn't seem to care. Second or third best, it was all the same to Armin von Hassendorf. A Meissen of this quality when restored was still worth a lot of money. It was a rare piece.

'But once you know it's been repaired, it can never be the same,' Sylvia had said, 'and therefore to Mr von Hassendorf it will always be damaged goods.'

The team had to be satisfied with that.

Sylvia and Bosco had volunteered to stay behind and help Kitty after the sisters and Doreen had set off for Godalming in the coupé. Sun roof down and Dame Myra Hess on Radio Three. Doreen had played Wigmore Hall in the fifties, at a charity concert for Archibald McIndoe. She was hostile towards Germans and didn't want to help. It reminded Milly and Molly of their older brother Malcolm who had refused to buy anything Japanese. He had died in a freak accident in 1969 when he had tripped over his Belling fire and smashed his head against the mantle. A few years later when Hitachi and Sony were dominating the market, Molly was heard to say thank heaven it hadn't been one of their products that had brought about Malcolm's untimely death. 'People have short memories and the young have no memory at all.'

Kitty had said, 'We can't go on bearing grudges. There comes a time when we have to forgive, if not forget.'

'And it's that kind of wishy washy liberalism which makes me see red,' Doreen had cried, vigorously sanding the plaster filler on her ceramic cup. 'Sometimes I ask myself why am I bothering to hold the bits together? We're trying to mend the past and make out nothing's broken. Sometimes I think it would be better to leave it, just leave it there on the shelf as a reminder that some things can't and ought not to be fixed.'

Perhaps it was different for Armin. Perhaps the past for him was not repairable. But it still struck Kitty as odd that he should be so careless of what was, after all, a beautiful family heirloom.

Armin had looked exhausted that afternoon. More than exhausted, strung out, as though he had a lot on his mind and the last thing he wanted was to be reminded of recent events. Kitty was disappointed. A little muted joy would have been acceptable under the circumstances. She had even considered cracking open the bottle of Cava she was keeping in her refrigerator for just such an occasion. She would have been over the moon. No money worries for the rest of her life. And a wonderful house to call her own. She should be so lucky.

Kitty doesn't want to be reminded of Elsie. It agitates her and then she can't concentrate.

Bosco took the colour plate and held it under the fluorescent light. He squinted at the glossy page. Were the lovers' hands touching or not? Kitty's eyes were tired and she left Sylvia to add another layer of composition to the bonded pin. Sylvia attempted to spread it evenly but some of the mixture dripped onto the man's green jerkin. She hastily wiped it off.

'Are they touching or not?' Sylvia repeated crossly. Bosco was still deliberating. Composition clogged the pin, a lumpy pastry that resembled a closed fist. It was impossible to prevent the mixture from crumbling onto the young woman's outstretched hand.

'Not touching,' Bosco said.

But by then it was too late. The hands were joined. Sylvia had sealed the lovers' fate with Araldite AY 103, titanium dioxide powder and kaolin on 30G electrical wire. She removed her glasses and gave them a rub with a sheet of kitchen towel. Perspiration meandered down her cheeks and forged tiny tributaries through her tinted foundation. She took the scalpel and carefully etched the fingers, her lips pursed in concentration.

It was past midnight before they had sanded down the final layer, polished with Solvol Autosol and added the paint. Bosco had mixed and re-mixed his colours until he had achieved the faint bluish tint he thought came closest to the original. By then Sylvia was dipping her nose into the corky tang of her fourth sherry. Kitty heated up three Wiltshire Farm cottage pies in the microwave and served them with frozen carrots. For dessert there was chocolate mousse five days past its sell by date but Bosco insisted that manufacturers always erred on the side of caution. 'It means we can't sue if we get food poisoning,' he said, dipping his spoon into the dark sticky mix.

Kitty insisted on driving them home, it was the least she could, she said, unlocking the Micra and backing out of the garage, her headlights bringing up the yellow eyes of the fox slinking across the lawn to eat the leftovers put out for it in the porch. On the ait the Canada geese were squabbling over territory and in the sky the planes seemed to be heading for a collision with Mars and Jupiter.

Bosco asked to get out before Teddington, easing his bulk off the back seat and standing for a moment on the empty street, sniffing its potential like a rogue bear in an Alaskan ghost town. In his hand were two plastic bags with his mother's shopping. He had phoned to tell her he'd be late. Then he ambled off in the opposite direction to home, animated by a sexual restlessness that went undetected by Kitty. But Sylvia knew what it was.

In the morning Armin turned up as promised, rousing Kitty from her doze for she was a light sleeper and waiting in the kitchen while she pulled on her dressing gown. A reminder that it was very early. ‘Five o'clock,’ he said, checking his watch. ‘I am sorry for waking you.’ And Kitty accepting his apology with a wave of her hand as if it were nothing. Adele's last words to her had been, ‘Make sure you get your money!’

Did he have time for a coffee?

He smelled of the air, did Mr von Hassendorf, as though he had been sleeping in earth and grass under trees. His coat was expensive but crumpled, grey like a blanket but with the recognisable sheen of cashmere. The red lining was silk if Kitty wasn't mistaken but still it looked second hand on him, his shoulders not quite fitting and the sleeves a little too long. A family heirloom Kitty decided, and was not far from the truth, for the coat was a gift from Patty and had been bought for her late husband on one of their autumn trips to New York.

Would he be coming back to England? Kitty wanted to know as she heated milk on the stove. She had gone with her father to Brittany in the summer of 1939 and would always remember the jug of warm frothy milk that was served with their pot of coffee. And big creamy cups like bowls. The hum of insects in the garden and the sea foaming like the milk blur on her upper lip. That September war was declared and she never went to Brittany again.

'I have some business interests here.'

Should she mention the question of payment now? Kitty had always been too polite when it came to money, marking down her china at bring and buy sales. Fifty pence, a pound? Still counting in the old money when fifty pence was ten shillings. Adele had told her sharply to think big. Five hundred for an evening's work on the Kaendler. Armin slurped his coffee appreciatively but Kitty knew that he had only one thought in his head.

They went into the front room and she raised the blinds. The Spanish Lovers was on the table covered by a piece of muslin like a prize jelly at a birthday party. Kitty removed the cloth with a little flourish. 'I'm afraid it will never even come close to the original...'

Armin peered at it. 'You can't see the join. It's very good. Excellent.'

'Oh, I wouldn't say that.'

'But it is. No one would guess it was broken.'

'An expert would notice at once.'

Armin glanced at Kitty and she saw an expression of uncertainty cloud his face, 'Really? Well let's hope it won't be put to the test.'

He was wrapping the figurine that Kitty had already covered in bubble wrap into the soft fold of a towel. He fitted the bundle into his holdall and then reached inside his coat and drew out his wallet. He counted out the fifty pound notes and dropped them on the table.

'I am obliged to you, Kitty, for your assistance. And now I have a plane to catch.'

Chapter Ten

He called Julia from Schoenfeld, stepping into a raw Berlin morning with the air tasting of ice and his coat tails flapping in a wind that came straight from Siberia. He had forgotten how cold Berlin could be in April, his blood thinned by the heat of Florida's eternal summer, his tan puckered and yellow.

Julia's mobile was switched off which was annoying. He hadn't thought to check whether the house would be empty, and it had suddenly struck him that Karl and Crystal might have cut short their stay in Frankfurt to throw another party to celebrate their latest coup. And, knowing Karl, he would have noticed by now that his precious Spanish Lovers was missing. Julia would have been able to tell Armin if anything was wrong. It brought a darkening to his mood. But not for long.

In the departure lounge at Heathrow he had made a quick call to VJ to discuss the future of Klug. He was thinking of placing a trial order subject to his credit being extended to sixty days. 'Some of my bigger customers don't like to be pushed. They will pay but in their own time.'

'Personally I don't see a problem,' VJ had said raising his voice above the background chatter. He lived with his parents and calls to the house were invariably disrupted by a lively domestic debate. His daughter Marie Christine had answered the phone and spoken to Armin in French before covering the mouthpiece with her hand and yelling for VJ as though the extension to his home in Wembley was the size of a football pitch.

VJ had sounded breathless. 'Too many stairs, man,' he'd wheezed.

His office was at the top of the house and he was considering installing a lift. 'One of those old people things. My mother's got bad hips and knees.'

'I've been talking to my associates in Miami,' Armin said, 'We think Klug's got potential in the niche market. Better than the *Katzenpiss* they have over there.'

'If anyone knows the market, it's got to be you,' VJ replied.

'World Trade Agency will be huge when we go global. I invite you all to Florida, to Palm Beach for our next board meeting.'

Encouraged by VJ, he had phoned Otto in Miami and caught him at the end of a poker game. 'I'm doing pretty well. I'm up five grand,' Otto had said from outside the Yum Yum restaurant where he'd been playing in a back room since seven that evening. He'd been about to light a celebratory cheroot when Armin had interrupted him.

Armin told him about Klug. 'I'm organising samples to be sent to your office. Can you get the sales team together? Mini marts, gas stations to start. I'll be meeting with the big players once I'm back. I'll calculate prices and send them over.'

Otto said, 'You really think we need another beer?'

'I have the sole agency for the States, it's got to be good.'

He could feel Otto deliberating. 'I wouldn't do this for anyone else.'

'I know.' Armin said trying to sound humble.

He took a taxi and asked to be dropped off before they reached the house. He didn't want to come face to face with anyone he knew and have to explain why he had come back so soon after the funeral. He got out and followed the configuration of the streets that had been reshaped by the path of bomb clusters, the craters transformed into open spaces with park benches, flower beds and saplings where once houses had stood. Some of the buildings were still pock marked from shell spray and the crumbling masonry looked downright dangerous. The question of ownership had not been an issue. The State had been the sole landlord, omnipresent and bankrupt.

He called Julia again as he sipped a cappuccino in one of the cafés overlooking the Spree but there was no answer. Between the trees he had a good view of the house with its white and primrose facade and the great wooden doors coated in thick green paint.

Frau Hubschmidt lived in one of the tenements opposite, *ein Familienhaus* that had gone the way of most of the others on the street, the large rooms partitioned and much of the embellishment removed as they'd crumbled beyond repair. Armin had waited in the narrow hall, its linoleum winding like warm toffee through the small apartment while she went off to fetch the keys. A middle aged, wide hipped women, she had eyed him suspiciously from a crack in the door when he had rung the bell. She had not been warned about a visitor. 'I can phone my cousin if you want identification,' Armin had said giving her his card. She had weighed him up for a few seconds and then they had crossed the road and she had unlocked the door. He was aware of her hostility, the several degrees of permafrost under the icing of her smile. Karl had mentioned that many of the older generation still hankered for the days of Honecker.

On the landing Frau Hubschmidt had tapped in the numbers to disable the security alarm. She showed him how to re-set it and asked him to drop the keys into her mail box when he left.

'*Alles klar Frau Hubschmidt*, *vielen Dank*,' he murmured. She lingered on the landing, 'Herr von Hassendorf has done such marvels to this house, so much money invested. Hundreds of thousands of euros I hear? Of course, your aunt had good friends. How else to explain so many treasures left undisturbed?'

He closed the door and leaned against it. Frau Hubschmidt had said that she did not expect Karl until next week.

He had all the time in the world but now that he was free to explore he found his curiosity diminished. He had no interest in examining the furniture and paintings and went instead to the kitchen, spooning coffee into the filter and then laying the table with the designer jams and deliberating over the Tupperware boxes of muesli and other breakfast cereals.

Clearly this was going to be a living museum as far as Karl and Crystal were concerned, the dusty image dispelled by parties and the bubbling percolator. This was their home. It belonged to them. Their food was in the refrigerator, (unsalted butter, free range eggs, organic ham and in the freezer tiger prawns, a French chicken). He had thought he didn't care, the urge to smash the china and scrawl graffiti across the walls, childish things that nonetheless would have been hugely satisfying, suppressed by an innate sense of his superiority. He was older than Karl and things should have come to him first.

But he had to satisfy himself that it was as he suspected, and their clothes were already hanging in the wardrobes: Karl's suits and casual wear and Crystal's costumes and those peacock dresses that were always scoop necked and nipped in at the waist in a fifties metamorphosis. Crystal had never changed her look. Consistency. Yes. That is what had paid off in the end. The fact that his cousin had always been there. And as for family, family was to be exploited and to be cosied up to in anticipation of returns. It was the smell of profit that had kept Karl close.

Soft footing it over the Persian rugs, he had gone into the first of the bedrooms and flung open the door, only to be stopped short by the movement of someone under the duvet. He had thought the house was empty.

'Armin?' Julia's voice was dreamy with disbelief.

She was looking at him through a nest of dark blond hair. 'What the hell are you doing here?'

She had lunged at him, full breasts between strong brown shoulders and he saw the shock darkness of her pubes and then a long white arm shot out from the duvet and pulled her back. The other woman began to giggle.

Julia groaned and buried her face in the pillow, her buttocks raised above the damask sheet to display the bikini line in her faded tan, the subtle strength of limbs outstretched, feet yellow soled and tipped with varnish. The tangle of their bodies. They exchanged glances that he could not interpret, a secret code of understanding that kept him pinned against the wardrobe with its silvered mirror reflecting the woman, Sabine was her name, bemused and defiant.

He burst out laughing.

'*So was.*'

Sabine followed him into the kitchen, pulling about her body a thin silk gown that emphasised her nakedness and drew his attention to her full breasts and the long line of her hip bone, her flat belly and the haphazard protuberance of her pubes in that carelessly gathered morning gown. And Sabine, aware of her affect on him; men loved a challenge, loved the idea that they could be converted by a bout of rough lovemaking, the arrogance of men, how she hated them, had taken a seat by the window and crossing her arms under those luscious breasts had demanded to know what Armin was going to do about it.

'What do you want me to do?' he asked.

Sabine had looked at him evenly, ‘They put you up to this, *Julchen's* parents, didn't they?’

Julia was standing in the doorway, a frotteé cream housecoat pulled up to her chin. She was nibbling nervously at her fingernails.

Why was he here if he hadn't been sent to spy on them?

Armin was indignant. ‘You think I work for Karl, that I do his dirty business?’

‘You haven't answered the question. Why have you come back? What do you want here?’

‘It's my home too,’ he'd replied unconvincingly.

There was no bread. He had set the table and realised only now that the most important ingredient was missing. He had imagined a pleasant hour by the window eating his breakfast. He hadn't planned to barge in. It wasn't a put up job. Nor was sex a mystery to him. It wasn't all consuming as it had been once. The other person in the room, a constant itching presence. He was just a little surprised at Julia, for he had not thought her, what? Butch enough?

Was it serious, he'd thought briefly waiting in line at the bakery for the assistant to tilt her chin at him, paper bag at the ready to be filled with seed rolls, pretzels, three custard slices and half a sunflower loaf. Chocolate ladybirds and maybugs encased in silver paper stood on a glass display shelf and he bought half a dozen. He would put them on the white cloth as a peace offering, as proof of his neutrality.

They were waiting for him when he returned, Julia in jeans and a Lacoste shirt, Sabine in chinos and a chequered blouse, her auburn curls wound hastily about a comb that sagged under their weight. A tall, handsome pair, he thought and suppressed the urge to add, ‘such a waste.’

He was of an age when his opinion did not matter. Only his presence, his intrusion into their secret life had roused feelings of indignation and betrayal.

'I came to see the treasures,' he explained, 'to look round the museum at my leisure.'

Sabine glanced at her watch. She had to get back to her studio. She was an artist, a sculptor and offered to show him her work one day. Perhaps she was beginning to accept that he had not been sent to spy on them.

He returned the Spanish Lovers to the vitrine while Sabina and Julia were downstairs saying goodbye. The room had a smell he associated with a laboratory, all imperfection cleansed from it. He found to his disgust that he was tiptoeing over the carpet. He unzipped the holdall and unravelled the Meissen from the folds of a towel and Kitty's bubble wrap. She had done an excellent job. Nobody would suspect it had been restored. He put it back on the shelf and experienced the slight dip that came with the completion of a journey. He saw Julia in the corridor and closed the door behind him.

'Everything okay?' he asked.

She didn't answer and disappeared into her bedroom.

He decided to make full use of his day in Berlin and visit some minimarts and beer and soft drinks wholesalers to get an idea of what was already on offer. He also wanted to inspect the refurbished KDW on the Kurfuerstendamm with its food hall that was said to rival Harrods. A dozen rock oysters at the new zinc bar. With Patty's money already in his account, he could afford a little indulgence. A glass of Bollinger or two.

She would get it back with interest, he'd insisted on that, even though ten thousand meant nothing to Patty. It was the cost of a new fur coat, a cruise across the Pacific. She had gone to Bora Bora, Fiji, Tahiti and then to Indonesia, after Irwin's death and told Armin that she had been disappointed to find the ship full of widows like herself. Only a few men aboard and those accompanied by wives who had gone to extraordinary lengths to keep all single women at a distance.

'And Irwin only a few months taken from me,' Patty had wept.

Julia was in the courtyard when he came downstairs. She had yanked her hair into one of those consciously untidy bunches that reminded him of a palm tree lashed by a hurricane and was hugging herself in a thick navy jersey.

'Are you very busy? I'd like to take you on a little trip.'

She was looking at him with serious grey eyes and he said, 'I have a lot to pack in today. Meetings with associates and so on.'

'My guess is that a Palm Beach millionaire has no experience of the real world. Let's have a ride in the Trabi.'

'You're still driving one of those things? They can burst into flames without warning.' He had read of such a case in the Berlin paper.

'Not if you brake carefully,' she said.

He followed her across the cobbles and waited while she unlocked the stable door. A marble bust of a Roman emperor stood on the shelf, Caligula possibly. The Trabi was covered in a blanket and she pulled it off dramatically as if she were unveiling a plaque.

'Great grandfather used to keep a goat and trap here. There's a picture of Trudy as a little girl in a white dress and button boots holding the reins, a whip in one hand and looking very much in control.'

Crouched in his seat with his knees almost to his chin, he clutched onto the dashboard as Julia careered around corners. Each time they went over a pothole his head hit the roof. By the end of the journey Julia's face would be speckled with oil that had worked its way through a hole in the dashboard. Another design fault that didn't seem to bother her.

'There was a ten year wait for a Trabi in the DDR days but Trudy got preferential treatment because of her job. She was an agent for the state insurance company and had to visit all the farms around here and check that they were covered against fire and flood.'

They were in countryside now and bowling down a long straight avenue bordered by limes. Later, Julia would turn onto a sandy track and he would see the first burst of cherry blossom in the knotted trees that defined the undulating rise to the village.

He recognised the church spire and was suddenly moved, 'I've not been back since,' he murmured in Julia's watchful silence. 'Not since I came here when I was eight. We stayed for seven months in 1945 but mother wanted to move on. It was better for us to be with the Americans. Ah, yes...'

They had passed the yard where a woman had kept hens. His mother had bartered one of her rings for eggs. 'We didn't starve like some. But I often went to bed hungry.'

'What is hunger like?' she asked. 'Sometimes I get shaky if I forget to eat.'

'It went beyond that,' he said.

Houses hugged the road, stooped and watchful. Most of them were one storey barricades, all life turned inward to the *Hof*.

On a bench three old men in blue overalls were chatting to a woman in a floral pinafore, her bare splotched arms hooked under a bowl. Julia waved at them as they passed. 'That's Frau Auerbach.'

'You come here often?'

Noting the surprise in his voice she said, 'Why, what's wrong with that?'

They passed grey blocks of flats where washing flapped in the *Hof*. There were satellite dishes on some of the balconies and he thought moodily how all these places reverted to type wherever they were, graffiti scrawled and youths in baseball caps hanging about, the uniform of stunted, incurious lives. At their age he had taken his bike and cycled from Kassel to Hamburg and slept rough under hedges and in barns. But he had been used to discomfort. Foraging the fields for food.

His grandparents' house was in a clearing at the end of the village. Identical to its neighbours in khaki coloured plaster, it stood as camouflage against the suspicion of difference. Julia had got out, her face pinched by the wind and he had caught a glimpse of her mother in the imperious shake of her head as though she could toss off the elements at will.

He told her how they had piled logs across the road when they heard the Russian artillery in the forest. The women, old men and children thinking they could stop the Red Army's advance with a few trees. 'Quite useless, of course. They simply went round.'

He'd had to raise his voice against the wind, and couldn't be sure she'd heard him. All about him the sweet smell of resin from the cut logs, that is what had reminded him. Why had she brought him here? Strangers lived in the house now and he was sure they were watching from behind the nets.

'They made us assemble in front of the houses and because I was the tallest of the boys they gave me the flag and we had to march through the village.'

'Did nothing terrible happen to you, Armin?' Julia seemed disappointed. A German who had escaped the war unscathed. It was not allowed.

'What do you want me to tell you?' he replied with a flash of irritation.

But she had left the house behind and was striding now towards an unruly patch of ground. He waited by the car, weary of his journey into a past that Julia clearly found disappointing and thinking of the oysters served on a platter with thick wedges of lemon and a dash of Tabasco. The chilled glass of champagne.

Then it dawned on him that this was where he had picked the vegetables.

'Red and green peppers, shallots, tomatoes, butter and haricot beans, peas and of course potatoes, yellow as butter with skins you could scrape off with your fingers. Trudy's potato salad was the best.'

The land belonged to the church but during the DDR years the buildings had been neglected, (he had gone to Wittenberg once and seen pigeons nesting above the altar in the All Saints Church where Luther had nailed his 95 theses to the huge wooden door, the windows smashed) and Trudy had taken it over and begun an allotment. But now the church had reclaimed it. He noticed the labels on the roses and the fresh compost worked into their roots.

'When I heard they were going to grass it over we came and harvested what was left. There were potatoes and the asparagus had re-seeded itself. We had quite a feast. Sabine and I are vegetarians.'

He thought he detected a challenge in her voice. 'We went digging that day and found something. Over by that tree where she grew her runner beans. Sabine's spade hit a box. Inside was a tankard with a Chinese scene painted on it. It had a silver lid. I took it to Dad and he showed it to some people and they said it was very rare. Apparently there's a similar one in the Smithsonian in Washington. It caused quite a stir.'

She was shivering inside her big pullover, the sleeves pulled over her knuckles, the white tips of her long fingers fiddling with the chain at her neck.

He didn't want to hear about the tankard. Another good luck story from a cousin who had a surfeit of them. No thanks. But Julia wouldn't let it rest and so he shut off, his eyes drifting over pasture flattened by the last snowfall where patches of it were still visible in the ditches and under the trees, thinking about business and suddenly Angela popping up to add to his discomfort. When he thought he'd put that particular business behind him for good. But he'd brought

Angela to visit Trudy in East Berlin before driving south and that was why she had come to mind. He had forgotten all about that until now.

There were graves in the village square with epithets in cyrillic script. 'The whole area's a graveyard,' he grunted. 'Dig a garden and you turn up bones.'

She wouldn't let him go and when they reached the Berlin suburbs she insisted on having lunch in the *Ratskeller.* He agreed reluctantly. The gothic cellar with its stained glass and jazz posters would have to sub for KDW's oyster bar for the time being at least.

He ordered the *Koenigsberger Klopse* and Julia had *gnocchi*. In Florida he explained, he lived on Patty's salads and take out Italian. Julia was incurious about his life, she wasn't fond of Americans was all she said and he replied that it was impossible to generalise and he had made some very good friends in the US. He found it odd that she should be so sniffy about what she called his extravagant lifestyle when as far as he could tell she was still being supported by Karl and flitting from course to course with no clear idea of what she wanted to do.

The dumplings were a poor imitation of the dish he remembered as a boy when their cook Martha had brought a chair up to the stove and let him drop the floury balls into the broth. The flavour wasn't there. It had become depleted by acid rain and intensive farming and an old man's desensitised taste buds.

He asked for a chaser with his second beer and savoured the caraway burn at the back of his throat. In the corner three couples were enjoying lunch, the men dressed like a rash in floral shirts and chinos, their womenfolk coarse featured and with mannish haircuts. It made him ponder briefly on the effects of hormones built up over a lifetime that blurred the edges between the sexes, or perhaps it had always been like that only he hadn't noticed.

He knew that Julia had something to say to him. All through the meal he had felt the anticipation of thoughts waiting to be aired.

'You didn't know Trudy well?'

The question took him by surprise. 'I knew her when I was a small boy. She was kind to me. She used to take me to the cafés on the Friedrichstrasse. She liked to treat me. She was a little subversive, I guess. And then I moved west and she stayed here to look after *Oma* and *Opa.* I don't know if it mattered to her. She made a life for herself, but whether it was the one she wanted I can't say.'

He had no intention of giving the impression that he was bitter about what had happened.

'I've been thinking about Trudy's collection and where she got it from.'

'She went to a lot of auctions,' Armin said.

'But what about the DDR years? Trudy was in a privileged position going into people's homes. Some of the farmers around here were rich and they hung on because they were hoping one day to get their land back. They believed communism was just a passing phase.'

'As it has proved,' Armin said,

'Yes, but what did they do with their family heirlooms when they realised they belonged to the State? The State confiscated everything. There was no private wealth. What did they do with the porcelain, the works of art?'

'The rich will always find a way,' he said.

'Not all of them, Armin, not the naive and the trusting ones. You don't believe in God?'

'What has God got to do with Trudy's bits and pieces?'

'In God's grace,' Julia persisted.

'I don't think about it,' he said.

At her age she ought to be focusing on her career or finding a husband, having children. He was tempted to ask if it was just a phase, this business with Sabine. Her parents might tolerate it for a bit but they would be devastated if Julia failed to produce a grandchild. He wondered if she realised this?

The dumplings sat like small lead weights in his stomach and he shifted uncomfortably in his seat. He needed to walk for his digestion and breathe in a fresh lungful of Spree air.

Julia said, ‘We're trying to find out about the tankard. Sabine's been looking at archives. We're hoping it will be listed somewhere, such a valuable piece is sure to have provenance.’

‘Good luck,’ he said. He didn't care one way or the other and called for the bill.

‘Either it was hidden before the estate was ransacked by the Russians or it came into Trudy's possession in the DDR years.’

Armin said, ‘Why bother your head about it, what does it matter? Let me tell you a story. Patty has some Jewish friends in Palm Beach. They were from Berlin. When it was time for them to leave they buried the family silver in the forest near their house and came to England. After the war they could not bring themselves to go back, they had lost family there, but their son wanted the heirlooms, the family history so he travelled to Berlin and he found the spot where the silver was buried and dug it up. He took it back to London and displayed it in his home and then a few weeks later he was burgled.’

Chapter Eleven

The old adage about casting your bread upon the waters had been uppermost in Kitty's mind as she'd waited for the fireman to pump out the lake that had formed under the railway bridge. She had got caught in a cloudburst on her way back from the hospital and while she had been sitting in her car watching the road turn into a torrent it had occurred to her that she had just said goodbye to Elsie for the last time and that, for all Kitty's good intentions, she had turned out to be a deceitful friend. Once Elsie departed this life she would look into Kitty's heart from her new position of omnipotence and find it a very dark place indeed.

Kitty had been preparing herself for the worst for a long time but it had still come as a shock to peer into Elsie's wizened face cupped in an oxygen mask, eyes tight shut and such sparse eyelashes like the legs of the spiders that dangled from the windows in late summer, and see the change in her. But Kitty had been determined to remain cheerful and had maintained a monologue of neighbourhood transgressions; the request for planning permission to build a second house in the garden of the Pantiles, the rumours of wild parties in the grounds of number sixty-six and Trish causing a rumpus by blocking opposite's drive with her Ferrari. Elsie's laboured breathing had brought Kitty into a panic. So much left unsaid and so little time to say it.

And so she had moved the wisp of hair covering Elsie's left ear, the lobe disfigured by the weight of a pearl drop, and whispered, 'I'm so sorry Elsie but I have lied to you. Freddy's been dead for over a year.'

And realised even as she spoke that in that ear Elsie was stone deaf.

Dismayed and yet relieved that her confession had gone unheard she had taken the photographs and pressed them close to Elsie's face.

'And here he is at Ham pond getting into all kinds of scrapes with the muscovy ducks...'

Startled into wakefulness by Freddy's derring do, Elsie had opened her eyes wide.

Kitty had sat squeezing Elsie's hand unaware of the stirring of the atmosphere, the deepening of shadow as Jason had come towards them. He had been there for ten minutes talking platitudes to a shrivelled lookalike at the top of the ward until Kitty's animated curls had alerted him to his mistake.

He had given her a curt nod and then thrown off his jacket and loosened his tie with a thrust of his chin that exposed a scribble of fiery chest hair. Like an encroaching forest fire, Kitty had thought uncomfortably. She had leaned over Elsie and whispered in her ear, 'Darling, Jason's here.'

But Elsie's breathing did not falter and after a while Jason had got bored and gone to the window to gaze on the grim cigarillo of the incinerator chimney. Kitty remembered a mother telling her fractious child that they put the naughty babies in there. Oh, the ignorance of people and the anxiety they engendered.

Dark clouds massed behind Jason's large pink torso. In his youth he had been a promising rugby player until injury had forced him to give it up. Elsie had told Kitty that every so often he had to go into traction to stretch his damaged back and this could explain his tetchiness.

Kitty experienced a little burst of it now.

'Do you have a contingency plan ready?'

Kitty did not understand.

'For when you leave Seething Wells,' Jason said a little too loudly. 'The Council is legally obliged to rehouse you and contrary to what you think Marion and I do care about your welfare. You have been a good friend to Aunt Elsie.'

'We go back sixty years. I knew her grandmother. She had a big house with an orchard near Cobham and Elsie and I would lie under the trees and eat the green apples. They gave us terrible stomach ache. Our mothers were best friends, you see. They were members of the Guildford Philharmonic and sang for the wounded soldiers in the local infirmary during the Great War.'

'You do know that my aunt has made a Will?'

'But of course!' Kitty replied scornfully. 'And you are the sole heir. You don't have to remind me, Jason. I am well aware of my situation and I am not interested in your aunt's money if that is what you are thinking. It is enough that Elsie gave me a home after Alfred passed away.'

Elsie's breathing had suddenly become more laboured, her complexion more bloodless now that her nephew's shadow had fallen across the bedside.

* * * * *

Kitty took Jason's call as her china class was assembling. They could tell from Kitty's voice that it was serious. They went into freeze frame; Milly and Molly poised with their patches of sandpaper over the Mason teapot bought at a car boot for twenty pence, Doreen with the frothing cafetiere, Bosco turning from patching the Parian cupid with its arch smile to shifting his gaze to Sylvia balanced on a chair by the bookshelf.

Only Adele was outside the enchanted circle as she

made her way up the garden path, catching sight now of Lee crouched on the roof like a leprechaun where he had gone to replace Kitty's missing tiles. The lawn shimmered with light and water, the trees diamond drops, the wooden porch and window sills steaming. From her basket Adele took one of the iced buns that she had brought for their elevenses and handed it up to Lee who reached down with an inky mermaid writhing the length of his muscular forearm. A fish tail the colour of burnished copper wisped the knuckles where FUCK was on fistful special. He beamed and Adele could see the attraction for Trish and any number of women, age being no barrier to desire. If I was only sixty years younger she mused, picturing herself with Lee's naked body arched above hers in all its sinewy strength, a script as yet unwritten as she rings the bell.

'Elsie's passed away,' Sylvia said, opening the door.

* * * * *

Kitty told Lee to go ahead with the roof. What had been started had to be finished in spite of the opposition of her friends.

'Why make it easy for Jason? Let the house fall to bits, let it rot.'

But Kitty hated the timpani of raindrops hitting the pots and pans and of having to get up in the middle of the night to empty the tin bath and basins when the rain came thundering in. It was she who had to feel the carpet tiles squelching between her toes and suffer the frantic coupling of the squirrels above her head. Birds too. Magpies strutting their stuff and starlings nesting in the guttering. It was all right for the china class to be indignant on her behalf. They went back in their cars to watertight cream carpeted cottages in the Surrey hills and could afford the luxury of vindictiveness. The roof needed fixing whether Kitty was to be there for one month or two. And she owed it to Elsie. This was still her home and it was her legacy. How could she live with herself if she allowed the house to go from rack to ruin?

Elsie was kept chilled in the morgue and bundled out of sight until the day of the funeral when her insect fragility was encased in polished wood and carried into the chapel by Jason and three bearers from the funeral home. Kitty wept through the hymns. *Oh God our help in ages past. All things bright and beautiful*. The reedy voices of her friends were drowned by the vibrant thrust of Jason's baritone and Marion's soprano. A few unknown faces swelled the mourners, curious onlookers Kitty supposed, and glimpsing Maria from Fircroft, red eyed, for the young took death seriously, had given her an encouraging smile. 'A life to celebrate not to mourn,' the pastor had said. But there was too much of the past among the chipped angels and epithets and Kitty had left the gathering to seek out the memorial rose garden where Elsie's standard hybrid was to be planted. Elsie had hated roses. Something to do with childhood trauma after losing her younger brother to scarlet fever. But Jason would not have known about that.

There were refreshments in the hall at St John's. Jason had ordered a spread from Marks and Spencer and occupied himself with the vicar and anyone else he thought worthy of his attention. Marion in an ankle length black skirt and loose fitting jacket clung onto her shoulder bag and like a minor royal leaned forward to speak to two ladies in wheelchairs.

'Lord and Lady Muck,' Sylvia muttered, adding hot water from the urn to her tepid coffee. And then Bosco had uttered what was on all their minds, 'Why didn't Elsie leave the house to you Kitty? You did more for her than Jason ever did!' Offering her a plate piled high with what she mistook for giant liquorice allsorts.

'Sushi,' he corrected.

On the grassy verge, Doreen was puffing at a cigarette with the relish of an abstainer. Later, Marion would join her and they would strike a match behind cupped hands and discover a shared passion for Brahms. 'One of my favourites, too,' Doreen was heard to say as she siphoned smoke towards the steel and concrete steeple. 'And I don't find him at all brown.'

Sushi, red bean wraps and free trade coffee. That wasn't Elsie.

When she got home, Kitty realised how few reminders there were of Elsie in the cluttered house. Her furniture groaned under the weight of bric-a-brac and chinoiserie, of mismatched dinner services, tea and coffee sets and countless ornaments bought at car boots and bring and buy. There was not a surface that did not bear witness to Kitty's occupancy. Crammed in the corners of the sofa with its William Morris print were reference books, invoices, magazines and scraps of paper with the telephone numbers of clients some of whom were still waiting one or two years on, for the restored plate or vase to be returned to them. Kitty would repair them all eventually but by then the owners had often moved or lost their enthusiasm for a piece that could never again be called quite perfect. Kitty tried to talk them out of thinking that way. 'It's what it means to you that is important,' she would say, 'not whether it has a crack in it.'

So where was Elsie? Kitty had walked restlessly through the house playing hide and seek with her thoughts. Where indeed? Elsie had left Seething Wells long ago and Freddy standing sentinel at the porch window looked increasingly like the false representation of a friendship that had meant more to them both than the antics of a mounted pooch.

Elsie would forgive her. She probably already had, up there on her astral plain. Kitty smiled and then gathering

Freddy in her arms carried him outside and left him by the hedge while she went to the shed to fetch the garden fork.

'Just playing for a little time Elsie, I meant no harm,' she murmured, levering the fork from behind the hosepipe.

Soon she would not be needing Rosario to coax the old mower into action and turn the lawn into the variegated stripes of a football pitch. Kitty would miss him plodding back and forth in his gum boots, just as she would miss the scent of jasmine and her first sight of the pipistrelle against April's lemon sky.

Freddy lay on his side, his beady eye lit by Jupiter's glimmer as he waited for Kitty to prepare his final resting place next to the mouldering embodiment of himself.

Dark clouds billowed above the ait and in the half-light Kitty did not recognise the figure walking up her garden path until he came to a halt under the pebbled glass of her porch lamp. Contrary thoughts ran through her mind. Was this a friendly visit or had the Spanish Lovers proved unconvincing and Mr von Hassendorf was here to demand his money back? She slipped Freddy under the bushes and went off to find out.

* * * * *

'A favour?' Kitty repeated.

'Yes,' Armin said, 'A small favour. I would like to use your shed to store some goods for a few days. My warehouse is full and I don't have time to relocate. I would pay you of course.'

Armin had taken the Victorian chair by the fireplace but it was much too narrow and he was perched on its edge, his shoulders hunched and his long arms almost touching the carpet like a supplicant.

Kitty said, 'Elsie died last Monday. Her funeral was

today and I am going to have to move.'

'I am sorry to hear it.' Armin said.

'This has been my home for over ten years. But it's all about to change. The house will be demolished, including the shed, the trees, the lilac bushes that Elsie loved and all the little creatures that have made their home here....'

Kitty's lips quivered and she couldn't stop herself. Tears of anger and regret clogged her nose and throat until she was squeezed dry like an old mop. She must look a sight, her cheeks inflamed and her curls sticking to her brow. Eyes reduced to tiny slits and her lids so heavy she could hardly keep them open. The indignity of tears. The self-indulgence of crying out loud. Sorrow was a private matter to be stifled in the pillow at night or in a quiet corner. She was ashamed that she had made such an exhibition of herself. And in front of a stranger, too.

Armin had put his hand on her shoulder that in its leadenness had kept her grounded in this room, in this house until it's heaviness had become unbearable and she had removed it with shaking fingers.

'Whisky,' he said. 'I find whisky very good in such circumstances.'

She had directed him to the single malt kept by the serving hatch with the tumblers and box of Ritz crackers and gone into the bathroom only to be sent lurching against the side of the bath as the giddiness had come over her. The spin of the universe that had sent the talc and loofah flying. She had reached for the shelf to steady herself, the mechanism controlling her equilibrium humming in her ears until it had stopped as suddenly as it had started, the ground settling at her feet, the walls again acquiring the semblance of solidness. She'd picked up the tooth mug and her tubes of face cream, the Anne French cleansing milk that had crashed into the bath. 'It's all right,' she had called shrilly, 'Everything's under control.'

These turns were thankfully brief and yet in their

violence a reminder that she was no more substantial than a speck of dust.

And then nipping her whisky she had said, ‘I must warn you Mr von Hassendorf that the shed has mice and there's an old rat who comes out sometimes to gobble up the bird seed that the squirrels tip from the feeder. But if you don't mind all that, then you can store your goods in there for as long as I am still at Seething Wells.’

Chapter Twelve

When Patty rang Armin she sounded wistful. She was missing him. She had never thought she would be happy again but their meeting in the Sunshine Fruit Basket had changed everything. She didn't like dried fruit and yet something had drawn her to the store that afternoon and guided her footsteps past the mountains of pecan, cashew and shocking pink pistachios to where Armin had been sampling the figs and apricots on special.

She had said to him, 'Be sure they're sun dried, too much sulphur is bad for you.' And Armin had given her one of his dark blue stares and Patty had been smitten.

That same afternoon she had left him sipping his mojito and popped into the drugstore and bought a vaginal lubricant and Armin had gone back to the Villa Carmina with her and a day later he had brought his few belongings over from Jupiter and moved in. Patty had had no misgivings. It had been her idea that she put her gowns and shoes into storage so Armin could use her dressing room as an office. Temporarily of course until his suite in the new state of the art business park over at West Palm Beach was ready.

Patty couldn't believe her luck and it made her nervous. She had met her late husband Irwin in a lift at the Waldorf and was aware of the temptations that lurked in airport lounges and five star hotel lobbies. She had seen how hungry those young East Europeans were with their long legs and strawberry mouths. They had a voracious appetite for rich older men and no amount of vitamin popping, exfoliation and lubrication was going to hold Armin true to the *idea* of Patty once his dick became engaged instead of his brain.

Patty had begun to notice that Armin was being evasive when she rang, as though she had interrupted something important, something intimate that had nothing to do with their life together in Palm Beach and everything to do with his life in Europe *sans* responsibility and *sans* Patty.

And Patty hated sharing. The rumours still circulate about how she had banished the portrait of Irwin's first wife from the dining room once she and Irwin were married. Then she had drawn up visiting rights for his two children, citing health grounds for why they should not make unannounced stopovers with their spoilt brats in tow. Boundaries had to be drawn in the interest of Irwin's heart condition and blood pressure.

Armin was in the Ealing deli when Patty rang. He had just learned from the slack jawed, sandy substitute of a young man behind the counter that Sonja was at her English class; the grit in Armin's oyster arousing in him such irritation, that he had snapped at Patty and asked what she was doing phoning him when it was, he had checked his watch and done a quick sum, 'three o'clock in the goddamn morning your time.'

'I want to see your house in Berlin.'

'You're phoning me in the middle of the night to tell me this?'

'We're drifting apart Armin.'

'How did you figure that one out, Patty?'

And then she had come in and stirred the motes and brought hopelessness and joy to Armin's heart. Sonja in low slung jeans with a studded belt and some kind of fur substitute knotted about her neck which she had tugged off and tossed behind the counter as if it were a poor defenceless animal. She said something sulky in Polish as she stomped off into the back.

'Berlin isn't ready for you,' he said.

The heels of her boots were worn. Her clothes cheap. She ignored him when she returned, an old man on the phone attempting to placate some silly woman. She'd clocked his interest though.

'Look Patty, it's much better if you stay put for now. Berlin's not ready for you. In another month it'll be warm and we can sit outside and have coffee on Unter den Linden. We can go to the opera. You should see the cakes in the opera café. *Fantastisch*.'

What does a young girl want of an old man but his money and the influence it can buy her?

She stretched to reach the topmost shelf and flicked a jam pot into place, exposing the bottom rung of a creamy ribcage and a mole dark as cinnamon in the hollow of an unshaven armpit.

Armin turned to the window where the streets were thronged with people in all shades of spice from ginger to clove, and heard Patty announce that she was on her way. 'I'm booked on the morning flight from Miami. I arrive at Schoenfeld Saturday morning around ten o'clock your time so be sure and meet me.'

'The hell you did,' Armin growled and ended the conversation.

He bought more sprats. The girl served him but he was preoccupied, speed dialling VJ to confirm the first trial order for Klug, fifty cases to be delivered to his temporary warehouse, 'at Water Lane number 105. I'll warn Kitty about the arrangement.'

'Kitty? You never told me you had a little kitten tucked away!' VJ gurgles down the phone, and Armin replies, 'Kitty's the housekeeper.' Unaware that for a few seconds he had Sonja's attention as she plucked the fish by their tails with maroon tipped fingers and smacked them onto the sheet of greaseproof paper; a dozen coppery, fat bellied sprats that exuded the sharp smell of tar tacked roof tops and salt smoke drifting towards a sea that glittered like the scales on a mermaid's belt.

* * * * *

'Fifty cases?' Kitty exclaimed as Neel opened the doors of the van. Crates up to the ceiling and jiggling merrily as he and Sam began to unload them onto the drive. She'd had no time to clear the shed, hadn't dreamed that when Armin had asked her about it yesterday afternoon that he'd planned delivery so soon. And Kitty still in her dressing gown and wearing the hairnet which she fingered like a cat's cradle to release the flattened curls, sculpted by Dawn at the Waves Ahead salon every Friday week.

The shed was full of boxes and old suitcases, rolled up carpets, bits of furniture, a broken pair of venetian blinds; some of it Elsie's stuff, most of it Kitty's. She had forgotten she had so much stored away; jars of kaolin, titanium dioxide, pollyfilla, marble powder, barytes powder, bottles of peroxide, meths, turps, cyanoacrylate, acetone. On the shelf were two large pots of cup handles, in another the body parts of dismembered porcelain figurines, the fingers and toes of shepherdesses, the cloven hoofs of animals, horns, talons, beaks, kaleidoscope into an Hieronymus Bosch nightmare. And on the wall a fly specked picture of the Pieta and a tea towel depicting the castles of the Highlands.

'You've got no space in here,' Neel had said to her and the floor had tilted with his weight and sent the china chattering as if they were at a séance. Crates were piled high in the driveway, their red labels imprinted with Klug in gold script.

They were waiting for her answer. Where to store this precious cargo? Not in the shed or the garage where the Nissan Micra took up all the space.

'You'll have to take it back,' she said crossly. 'I've got nowhere to put it.'

'We can't do that,' they said. 'No way, man. It ain't ours to take back.'

'Well telephone Mr von Hassendorf and tell him to take it back.'

They grinned at her confusion. Tall, black eyed, their sights went over her head to settle on the twitch tailed squirrel gnawing at the pear florets.

'Can't leave it here. It'll get nicked.'

'Then it will have to go upstairs,' Kitty said. 'And you can tell Mr von Hassendorf that I am not at all happy and he is to make other arrangements as soon as he gets back.'

They cursed in French as they heaved the crates into her old bedroom. The ceiling shook with their thuds, loosening more plaster that swirled in the air like talc and created an ominous swelling over the door leading to the back porch.

* * * * *

It would be Bosco who after some deliberation got up from the Casa Pupo leopard and beckoned Kitty to come and look. He positioned her to the left of the bulge so that she could appreciate it in profile like a bruise on the forehead. 'Did it come on all of a sudden Kitty?' he asked in a dark voice that Kitty always associated with bosky.

Bosco took an affectionate interest in Kitty. She was the one who had encouraged him in his china mending after he had nursed his mother Vida through a particularly bad bout of depression. Kitty had met Vida years ago when she had been looking for someone to translate the provenance notes on a Chinese vase. Vida could speak five languages including Mandarin and Cantonese. Kitty used to stop and chat to her when she saw her walking down the towpath; a vigorous woman who was now too anxious to leave the house.

'She starts shaking and talking gibberish!' Bosco had confessed to Kitty one day. 'She worries about getting the washing and ironing done when she's got all week and now she's roaming the house at night and keeping me awake.'

Vida was taken for assessment and prescribed antidepressants but by then Bosco had grown used to popping in to talk to Kitty and having the table to himself. Soon the Monday sessions had become three times a week. He preferred working on his own, he told her, especially when it was a particularly demanding task, like the piece of T'ang pottery that he'd found under Vida's bed. She had dug it out of her wardrobe one day and had been using it as a chamber pot.

Bosco was an excellent restorer but erratic. Sometimes he would leave a plate in the base of roma plasticine or abandon a vase halfway through the process only to disappear and pick it up weeks later as though nothing had happened. Doreen murmured darkly about boys, one of whom had been seen loitering on the towpath outside their window before heading off in the direction of the Ham Lands. The Ham Lands was a notorious cruising ground. Kitty turned her mind from such gossip. There were many things she would rather not know about, and people's sex lives was one of them.

Kitty and Bosco were still contemplating the bulge in the ceiling when Jason came and told her about Elsie's Will. Elsie had left her twenty thousand pounds and first refusal on the house.

Bosco went into the kitchen to make coffee and Jason puffed up like a robin, jiggled the change in his pockets and took up his position by the window.

‘No dog?’

No frenzied yapping at his heels and piss glistening on every chair leg?

‘Freddy's gone out,’ Bosco said, bringing with him from the kitchen the aromatic scent of a Turkish cigarette and coffee which had induced a bout of homesickness for the Praya Grande and the fishermen's nets strung like vast spider webs across the bay.

‘Funny,’ Jason frowned, ‘I could have sworn...’ and then looked sly.

The coffee was thick and black and undrinkable except to Bosco who slurped it from his chair by the work table where Kitty had suggested he remain while Jason explained this first refusal business.

‘It means,’ Jason said, ‘that the house will be valued by an independent chartered surveyor who does not represent the interests of an estate agent and you will be given first refusal on the price.’

‘And what if Kitty can't afford it?’ Bosco asked.

‘Then the property reverts to the trustee who can offer it for sale on the open market. Elsie's solicitor will be writing to you and you have three months to make your decision. If you decide to take up the option then you have a further three months to complete. According to the instructions of the Will the house has to be sold within six months of Elsie's death. I'm telling you this in plain English as I know the legalities can be confusing to someone of your age. I take my responsibilities seriously and I suggest you find a solicitor to advise you.’

The coffee being undrinkable, Jason had taken a moment to survey the room in all its dusty clutter and Kitty had seen its shabbiness through his eyes; the mess that momentarily made him falter in his estimation of the house's worth until his glance drifted to the open window and the glorious stretch of river with its aits and towpath winding through budding apple trees self-propagated from the old Dysart estate at Ham. The site was undoubtedly worth a small fortune. Even in her wildest dreams, Kitty could never have afforded to buy it.

She went to say something of that nature to Jason but he was already out the door and crossing the lawn where he stooped to pick up what looked like bits of rubbish scattered near the verbena bushes. The fox was her first thought. They were destructive animals and would tear a plastic bag to shreds if there was anything edible inside.

But there was something about Jason's demeanour that disturbed Kitty and as he came towards her brandishing the stick it suddenly dawned.

'And what's this?' he demanded.

What indeed, when it was obvious to anyone with even the most elementary knowledge of anatomy what Jason was holding in his great fat paw.

Or as Kitty bravely put it, 'That is Freddy's second leg modelled from Araldite and kaolin after the first one got gnawed away by mice.'

'And where's the real one?'

'The real one?'

Kitty clutched at the brooch at her neck. Did he mean the original leg as opposed to the peg leg?

Jason was brandishing the shovel. The original as fashioned by God was interred with the other Yorkies in Elsie's pet cemetery near the verbena hedge.

Which is where Kitty had intended to bury her White Lie if Mr von Hassendorf hadn't surprised her in the porch last night and made her forget all about it.

Chapter Thirteen

Frau Hubschmidt levered the key from the hook and handed it to Armin with a thin smile. Her husband, a wizened man with a complexion yellowed by tobacco, passed down the narrow hall behind her and Armin heard him cough and smelt the sour odour of pickled cabbage as he disappeared into the back room.

He would be staying for two nights, Armin confirmed, and there was no need for her to bother coming over now that he knew the security arrangements. The housekeeper told him that she had already spoken to Frau von Hassendorf and for a moment Armin had stared at her, thinking she meant Crystal until it dawned on him that she was talking about Julia. He had gone away wondering when she had stopped being the nubile *das Fräulein* and become the matronly *die Frau*.

He had phoned Julia last night about the possibility of spending the weekend in the house and she had told him that her parents were in Sylt until Monday and so the house was his. '*Viel Spass, Armin*,' she had said and then before ringing off had added, 'Oh, and we're getting somewhere with the tankard. I'll tell you about it when I see you.'

'Next time okay? I'm tied up with meetings all weekend.'

He unpacked his clothes and hung them in Karl's wardrobe. He and Crystal kept separate bedrooms and Patty would have to share the single with him if she didn't want to sleep alone. Years ago Karl had confided that it kept their sex life fresh when in truth it was Karl's use of the bathroom during the night that had made Crystal insist on the arrangement. It didn't seem to have done the marriage much harm, although Armin guessed that it was the topic of money rather than love making that preoccupied them now.

Crystal's room was further down the corridor and he had gone to inspect it, his memory stirred by its previous two occupants whom he had surprised tightly wound under the duvet. It brought his mind back to sex and the promise of the little blue pills that would give a satisfactory boost to his weekend, although they tended to leave him with a thumping headache.

He bundled Crystal's clothes into bin liners and took them upstairs, any misgivings he might have had about appropriating the house for the weekend dispelled by the sight of the camp bed in the office. It was a reminder, if he needed one, that he was here on sufferance only.

He returned to the first floor and, pouring himself a generous Red Grouse, propped his feet on the mahogany table and waited for Patty's call.

After a couple of glasses he felt relaxed enough to take a closer look at the objects in the vitrine. The Spanish Lovers hadn't been touched as far as he could tell and they smiled out at him with what he interpreted as a conspiring air. They seemed to dominate the rows of crinoline maids and foppish young swain engaged in a courtly dance on their flower strewn paths.

He hadn't understood at first what all the fuss was about until unravelling the Meissen under the glitter of river light he had seen it through Kitty's eyes. The exquisite moulding, vibrant colours and the deceptive softness of the girl's cheek had encouraged him to believe it would yield to his touch. He had felt but a brief pang of guilt at having damaged something so precious. The lovers had survived three centuries of upheaval only to fall foul of a clumsy pair of hands. Well, what was done was done. He had gone to a lot of trouble and expense to make amends and with luck no one would ever know. And if they did, then it would go to prove the old adage that nothing was forever.

He went for a pee before leaving for the airport and found to his horror that Crystal's cosmetics littered the bathroom shelves and her robe courtesy of the Four Seasons in Marrakech was still hanging on the hook by the door. He scooped the fragrances and lotions into the housecoat and dumped everything upstairs with the rest of her stuff.

His plan was to hire a Volkswagen Polo at the airport knowing that Patty would insist on an upgrade and pay for it with her credit card. He had never been one for status symbols but Patty liked a limousine and he was dangerously low on funds again until orders for Klug began coming in. The first consignment was already at Water Lane although Kitty hadn't sounded very pleased about it when he'd phoned her from the airport bus.

'It can't stay here Mr von Hassendorf, not in my bedroom it can't. It's buckling the floor. No, I won't have it. You must come and remove it as soon as possible.'

'I'm at my house for a couple of days. But I promise I will see to it on my return.'

'I'm having to clear everything out. Everything. Seething Wells has to be sold within six months.'

'Don't worry about it Kitty. I give you my word as a businessman. You will have your house back by the end of next week, latest.'

'But it isn't my house to give back, Mr von Hassendorf.'

'Leave it with me,' he'd said absently.

Patty's plane was taxiing down the runway and he'd rung off.

Patty had required a little warming up on that brisk Berlin day of high cloud and low temperature, a twenty degree drop from poolside Palm Beach to the arrival lounge where not even a mink jacket could protect her from the *frisson* of seeing Armin again. She had told her best friend that she would know in an instant if Armin had been unfaithful but as soon as she had seen him by the barrier in his grey coat and blue scarf, his silver hair reminding her of a mature Giovanni Agnelli, she had made up her mind to hold onto her man, no matter what.

Questions would come later, after the public embrace and the appraisals.

'You're looking great!'

'You're not so bad yourself. New outfit?'

'Love the scarf, it matches your eyes, who helped you pick it out?'

'A very helpful young woman behind the counter at KDW,' he'd reassured her.

Patty had nuzzled up to his shoulder and smoothed his nape with her long fingers as he'd turned the upgraded Mercedes in the direction of the autobahn.

'I can't wait to see the house. I've been dreaming about it since you told me.'

'I hope you won't be disappointed,' he said, 'You can get the whole of it into Googie Wallenstein's shoe closet.'

He'd turned to her and caught the crepe apricot of her cheek cruelly highlighted by the cold Berlin light as she'd rummaged in her big designer handbag.

'I'm going to adore it whatever,' she'd said, and he had pulled up at the crossing and watched a girl with long legs, her hair a startling orange above a chalk white face, stride past them. 'Why do they go out of their way to look so damned ugly?' he said.

They made love on Crystal's bed, a little hurriedly but he managed to perform to Patty's satisfaction after weeks of celibacy. But if it was Sonja who yielded instead of Patty in his mind's eye, cast upon the dune maiden that made him thrust into Patty with the potency of memory, then what did it matter? Patty gave her wittering cry and her body slackened under him, her lace bra strap dangling from a freckled arm, its cup still warm from a breast that had grown briefly taut with fondling.

Afterwards they slept and when they awoke it was early evening. Patty had pulled her satin housecoat about her shoulders and asked Armin to show her his museum.

'Are you sure you're up to it?' he'd said, insinuating that their lovemaking had been more wearing than was true.

He could tell by the tightening grip of her hand as he'd led her from room to room that she was impressed. She would stop before an object and murmur that it brought to mind the eighteenth century marquetry table at Sans Souci (near the glorious grotto constructed from seashells and mother of pearl) or the Meissen at King Ludwig's castle, Schloss Linderhof. Everything delighted Patty and she congratulated him on his aunt's good taste and her foresight in making Armin her sole beneficiary. 'I guess Karl must be green with envy.'

'It will stay in the family,' Armin said. 'It's here for all of us to enjoy.'

He was nervous about spending long periods in the house and suggested dinner at a small restaurant he had discovered in Mitte where a wall to wall display of pre-war posters would compensate for the rumblings of the S-Bahn on the bridge above them. He thought Patty might appreciate the raw often provocative art of an era that she was familiar with although she would of course deny it.

But Patty wasn't keen to go out. She had taken her serotonin tablets but was still finding it difficult to keep awake and so he had gone to the local Turkish and bought two kebabs, his with extra pickle, and a double portion of green salad, stuffed olives and a selection of halva dripping in syrup and encrusted with sesame and pistachio and they had eaten them in front of the TV in the sitting room after taking the precaution of covering the table with newspaper.

'I hope we can come here often,' Patty murmured, 'and use it as our base when we're in Europe.'

'I don't see why not,' he said.

The next morning he broke it to her over breakfast that he would have to cut their visit short. An unforeseen hitch in a deal back in London needed his attention. 'I'm sorry Patty, I just got the call. VJ needs me there. Negotiations are at a sensitive stage and he wants my advice'

'When?'

'Monday afternoon at the latest.'

He watched as her disappointment turned to petulance. Didn't he have people to sort these kind of things out for him? She hadn't flown half way round the world to spend just forty eight hours with him in his house.

'You can stay here and do some sightseeing,' he suggested, 'but I can't guarantee how long I'll be gone. These things blow up in your face and it can be weeks before the pieces are put together again.'

'Weeks? What am I going to do here on my own for weeks?'

'Visit the Museuminsel, and Schloss Charlottenburg, see the Nefertiti over at the Neues Museum, take a trip to Spandau. There are plenty of galleries and shopping malls. Or is there some place you can go until I get back? Maybe a trip to Baden Baden to see your sister?'

'I came here expressly to be with you, Armin!'

'I know and I feel as bad about this as you do,' he said earnestly.

She went away and sulked for a while and then he heard her on the phone talking to Gilda.

When she returned she was still annoyed with him

and he decided not to push it and continued to take down details of the wholesalers he was planning to visit. Once he saw a return on his investment he would hire a sales team to cover the rest of Germany and then move into eastern Europe. The challenge of succeeding in countries with a proud brewing tradition gave him an adrenalin rush. It was the fusion of exhilaration and fear that got him every time. His flights in the Starfighter to meet the horizon and the unknown, the unaccounted for, like the UFO he'd seen skimming the top of the Arizona desert like a Frisbee in a dust devil.

He'd felt something of the old twitchiness when Patty had come into the room and started to examine the cabinets, acutely aware all of a sudden that they were the aliens here and that none of what Patty was scrutinising was his. The Grecian urn, 'around 100BC I guess,' the eighteenth century secretaire with its illuminated portal (he heard the creak of the leaf as she'd tugged it open), and of course the figurines in the vitrine.

'I'm going to stay with Gilda in Baden Baden,' she announced. 'The Kneipp baths are good there and my circulation could do with gingering up. They have an excellent pool, something I'm already starting to miss. City life is fine but it lacks the amenities I'm used to having on my doorstep.'

'It's all my fault and I'm sorry.'

He reached for her hand and she let him hold it limply.

'Have the whole package on me,' he said.

'I don't need your money, Armin.'

'I'll make it up to you Patty, I promise.'

'I guess,' she said and moved away from him.

'In a year or two...'

'At our age we count in days, weeks...'

'We've got another twenty years! Look at Ronald Reagan; he wasn't president until he got to be seventy.'

'You work too hard,' she said and alerted by the distraction in her voice he looked up in time to see her opening the vitrine. After a moment's hesitation she plucked a harlequin from the shelf.

'Isn't this just great?'

Armin didn't think so. The masked harlequin had the predatory litheness of Spiderman and looked as if it was about to hit someone with the tankard gripped in its hand.

'But it's so alive, so vital,' Patty enthused, reaching for its neighbour on the shelf. Armin found it equally unattractive. There was something coarse and malign about the figure, another harlequin grimacing at them through his fingers.

'They're old Meissen,' Patty said, turning them over to study the crossed swords mark. The first figurine with its small head and diamond patterned dazzle reminded Armin of a poisonous reptile. He grimaced.

'I just adore this.'

'Then it's yours,' he said.

'You can't be serious?'

'Sure, I am. Here, take them both. I've got plenty more harlequins. And you deserve them seeing how I've spoiled your trip.'

* * * * *

Patty decided to cut short her visit and drive to Baden Baden that same afternoon. Armin wanted her to stay until the next morning. Why the hurry? He proposed lunch at the Hotel Adlon and then a stroll through the old town. They could visit the Bundestag and walk the spiral path under the great plexidome and watch democracy at work on the floors below. But Patty shivered in her Miami skin at the prospect of long hours outdoors and Armin guessed that she was still angry with him and making her own plans was her way of getting even in spite of the two harlequins bubble wrapped in her suitcase.

A telephone call earlier that morning had left him feeling a little edgy and maybe it wasn't a bad thing if Patty left before an unwelcome visitor turned up at the door. She had intercepted a call for Karl and he'd had to fob off the caller by telling him he had a wrong number before switching to voicemail.

But it didn't stop him pushing his luck and suggesting that Patty invite Gilda to come and stay with her rather than make the tiring journey south. He was sure that two beautiful women could find plenty to keep them amused in Berlin. And then he'd gone to the window, his breath coming in little bursts and his pulse quickening with suspense as Patty had pondered the idea.

But as he'd silently prayed, she had decided against it.

He would miss her though. Patty's glamour and the pheromones of money that upped his game and renewed his confidence. It wasn't over yet, he told himself, reciprocating her wave as the Mercedes carried her over the Spree and the widening lake with its flat northern light.

Age was no hindrance to success. He still had the energy of a man half his age. He was still hungry. Always hungry.

There was wild salmon in the refrigerator and a half ounce of caviar that Patty had bought at duty free with the idea of a celebratory dinner in his new home. A bottle of Bollinger on ice. Patty had wanted to set the table with the Meissen plates and the crystal glasses she had discovered during her forage in the cupboards. Nothing had been barred to her, Armin had seen to that. Only the rooms upstairs were double locked. 'They're offices,' he'd told her. 'Nothing for you up there but spiders.'

Five hours later Patty was phoning him from Stuttgart

where she had decided to spend the night. She wasn't ready for the Black Forest. Too many trees gave her the creeps. The Russians had caught up with her mother on the edge of a forest near the Lithuanian border in 1944. 'They put a gun to her head but I was a feisty little thing, half-starved but still tugging at her skirt and screaming at them to let her go. We were lucky they didn't shoot us there and then.'

He could hear that she'd been drinking. 'We ended up in a labour camp but I promised myself, in that filthy place with my aunt dying of starvation on the floor next to me, that if I ever got out of there alive I'd make sure I never lived like that again. Not ever.'

'I know,' he said.

'And we've done well for ourselves, haven't we? Me, in Palm Beach with my own fortune and you my handsome millionaire.'

Armin tipped the last of the champagne into the flute.

'Go to sleep Patty, you've got a long journey ahead of you.'

'Along the Tittisee,' she said laughing. 'It was good, wasn't it? I mean we had a good time even if you decided to make it short and sweet. And I have the Meissen to remember you by.'

'Be sure and take good care of them,' he said and felt a momentary pang of remorse for splitting up the collection.

'Good night s*chatzelein*,' Patty said drowsily.

'Good night, Patty,' Armin said.

He placed a forefinger on the speck of caviar on his plate, a clump of egg that had the rich darkness of loam and left them to dissolve on his tongue before finishing the champagne.

Above him the ceiling shimmered with the blue of waters not traversed, the tendrils of vines trailing the ankles of maidens with flesh so luminous it made him ache.

Chapter Fourteen

Jason's exhumation of Freddy's remains had proved traumatic for Kitty and she had lain awake for most of the night going over events in her head. Towards dawn she had sunk exhausted into a deep slumber only to be woken by the slam of the car doors as the Rover parked in the drive.

Eleven o'clock and no oilcloth wiped clean, no work in progress taken from the shelf for the final rubbing down. What would they say when they found she had not yet colour matched the leopard's ear or prepared the soak for Doreen's jug in the de-ionized solution?

She had pulled on her paisley skirt, blouse and red cardigan and dabbing powder to hide the dark shadows under her eyes had gone to the door to greet her friends coming towards her down the path.

'It was the final nail in the coffin,' she was to tell them after she'd described how Jason had found faux Freddy's leg on the lawn and dug up the pet cemetery.

'You deceived and you lied to Aunt Elsie and to me,' Jason had shouted stabbing at the coffin with his shovel, 'and don't tell me that it was in her interest that you did this vile thing. I know where you're coming from. This is all about you.'

As Kitty said when they were seated at the table, what did it matter? In the grand scheme of things they were nothing more than a tiny spark quickly extinguished. Whatever happened to her was of no consequence to the parakeets gobbling the pear buds or the bees nuzzling the daisies on her lawn. And the frogs that lived in the overflowing drain each spring would continue their cycle of regeneration whether she continued to flush them out with her bathwater or not. The planet, Kitty had already decided, could well do without her and mankind in general.

'Oh dear, what is it all about?' Molly had sighed and Bosco, opening a carton of chocolate fingers, had said, 'Molly darling, that is best left to God.'

It had been a while before they could settle. Kitty had had to go over every detail and then when Adele arrived late as usual, she'd had to repeat it again with contributions from the class. Disgust and indignation had heightened the atmosphere and made it impossible to focus on the whisper of a paintbrush on a hand modelled petal or the delicate separation of a tin-glazed earthenware pot. Talk of revenge and retribution was high, flushing Milly's cheeks the colour of a Capodimonte cherub and generating a wealth of ideas, none of which was very helpful for Kitty was feeling her age that morning and everything required so much effort.

Adele suggested they form a syndicate and do the lottery but although Kitty agreed in principle she was too aware that luck favoured the Jasons of this world and she had lived too long on a wing and a prayer to change now.

They had just begun work in earnest when Adele came hurrying into the room to announce that Kitty had a visitor.

'It's Mr von Hassendorf and it was lucky for him that I was in the garden. He nearly fell into the trench.'

Armin had been making his way across the lawn when Adele had appeared from the shed and uttered a little squeal.

'Be careful! It's Freddy's grave,' she'd cried coming towards him with the jar of kaolin spilling over her skirt and leaving a powdery trail across the grass.

'Or it was until Jason dug it up. It's terrible what he's done, upsetting our Kitty like this.'

Doreen had greeted Armin with a frosty stare. She refused to fall for what Milly referred to as Armin's, 'old world charm.'

'There's something about that man I don't like,' she was to mutter when they went into the kitchen to make coffee.

'Just because he's German?' Sylvia had asked. 'I lost a brother in the war but you can't go on bearing a grudge forever.'

For all Doreen's hostility, there was no denying that Armin had brought some much needed light relief to the mood of the china class that day. Adele's mid-morning muffins had done nothing to dispel the pall that had descended on the house like a Thames fog. And even Bosco's new find from the treasure trove that was Tiffin Boys car boot, a badly cracked slipware bowl depicting a jaunty octopus that had all the markings of Bernard Leach, had been unable to arouse more than a glimmer of interest from the depressed Kitty.

And Armin was doing his best to be amenable, apologising for the interruption for he could see they were busy but he had a proposition he wanted to discuss with them.

Much to Doreen's irritation, for what could be more pressing than the piecing together of the Caughly jug she had promised for the arthritic society's annual bring and buy? They had eagerly begun to clear the table, Milly picking up the razor blades and toothpicks and Molly carrying the dish of liquorice allsorts to the shelf. The rest of them were quite happy to make space on the oilcloth for the German's James Bond briefcase. Armin had matched the code on the locks and they had sprung back with the force of two striking cobras.

First to come out was a copy of a tabloid with a topless model on its front page. Armin dropped that into Kitty's bin and then dug out several plastic files, neatly labelled and exuding the chill air of a Berlin spring. There was also a leather diary, a digital calculator and columns of figures on a scrap of paper, written in a surprisingly cramped hand for such a big man.

'My office,' Armin said, bemused by their curiosity.

He tapped his temple where a stray strand of silvery hair posed a question mark. 'All my business is up here.'

From one of the plastic sheaths he drew out several colour photographs.

'These are from the collection in Berlin,' he said. 'Harlequins from the *Commedia dell'arte.* Columbine, Scaramouche, Pantaloon, Harlequin and others. Meissen of course, with the distinctive crossed swords on underglaze blue.'

'The Italian Comedy figurines and all quite wonderful!' Kitty said, cheering up. 'These are some of the finest I have seen. Kaendler did you say Mr von Hassendorf? Kaendler was a master of porcelain sculpture, quite the best in my opinion.'

'What an incredible inheritance,' Adele murmured.

But Armin had not looked particularly grateful on that grey afternoon of low cloud where even the river's sluggish meander seemed to collude with the air of despondency at Seething Wells. The first pleasure boat of the new season had chundered past unremarked, its sole passenger on the top deck sheltering under an umbrella inverted by gusts from a rising westerly. The photographs by contrast were dazzling and yet somewhat sinister.

Kitty thought she misheard Armin when he asked if she could make copies of two in particular. The harlequin with monocle and the harlequin with tankard.

Copies? No, she didn't know of any copies but he could contact the Meissen factory and find out if they did limited editions.

'I need copies of these by Friday,' Armin explained, indicating the picture of the two harlequins that were now on the top of Gilda's bookcase in Baden Baden. 'Can you help me? The originals are on loan and I have visitors to the house this weekend.'

Sylvia was puzzled, 'But why should it matter? Just tell them that two are on display.'

'It is important to me that the whole series is represented. I do not want to compromise,' Armin said. 'They will not be allowed to inspect them, they are far too delicate for that, only to view them in the vitrine. The question of their authenticity will not be disputed. If they are told that the whole set is there they will believe it. It is a game of bluff and the suggestion of a strong hand is enough to convince a weak opponent. Can you make me some reproductions?'

'In just a week? I'd say it was out of the question,' Doreen said.

'Where would we start? Do you want them made from scratch?' Milly wondered.

Bosco had picked up the photographs and said he'd check them out on e-bay. Maybe there was something similar out there that would need just a little adjusting. A spot of the right coloured paint, a few extra flowers on the pedestal. Adele promised to talk to Gordon. There was always the chance that something might turn up on the bric-a-brac stall.

'Good,' Armin said in his deep voice. 'I will of course reimburse you for your trouble. Would five hundred pounds for each harlequin be satisfactory?'

It was the thought of money that drew Bosco to examine the harlequins more closely. Surely not a difficult job, he murmured. Not like the floral crinolines and bewigged young shepherds that required so much attention to detail. If they all worked together surely they could come up with a reasonable likeness? He could make a frame out of wire and pack it with playdoh. It would be the sculptural equivalent of

Seething Wells, he said, turning to Kitty with a grin, ‘a metal skeleton hung with cladding.’

‘But we are talking Meissen,’ Kitty exclaimed.

‘And what does that mean exactly?’ Bosco replied.

‘It means that you cannot replicate something that is the result of hundreds of years of mastery. It denigrates the artist and all his endeavours to think you can reproduce his work from a child's modelling kit.’

‘That may be true for an artist like yourself, Kitty. And I mean no disrespect to Mr von Hassendorf, but what's the point of all this stuff gathering dust on the shelves?’

Armin looked at him quizzically, ‘I can assure you, there is no dust.’

Bosco said, ‘I was speaking metaphorically. If these belonged to me I'd sell them and live on the proceeds.’

Armin closed his briefcase with the distracted look of a man with other things on his mind. His gaze drifted now to the horizon where the planes were stacking above Heathrow. The sun was a tremor on the water. He had a business appointment but he would return later to see if they had come up with any ideas.

He crossed the darkening lawn, avoiding the pot hole by the verbena bushes and travelled to VJ's favourite restaurant in Slough.

For part of his childhood VJ had lived in an ashram and was a strict vegetarian but Armin noticed, after they had made themselves comfortable in his private banquette which VJ cheerfully labelled his second office, that this had not prevented him from piling on the pounds.

When Armin commented that life was obviously treating him well, VJ looked dejected and confessed that he'd recently been diagnosed with Diabetes B and was being urged by his doctor to go on a diet.

‘No more chapattis, cooking with ghee, no more pain

au chocolat. No more life!' he'd grumbled, until the waiter arrived with the menus and he'd announced with a sudden burst of fervid determination, 'the new regime begins tomorrow.'

Over the onion bhaji and saffron rice, the spicy ladies fingers and dhal, Armin had talked about his plan to make Klug the number one selling foreign beer not only in Germany but throughout eastern Europe. 'I like a challenge and it'll be one in the eye for the big boys when Klug starts outstripping them. I don't see why we shouldn't plan for this year's Oktoberfest in Munich. It's high time those Bavarians opened up the tents to some healthy competition. Klug's cleverer on price and taste.'

'Not a bad sales pitch,' VJ had replied, glancing at the BlackBerry by his plate.

'What I'll be needing from you is more promotional material; beer mats, mugs, posters, key rings, anything you've got. You can send it to my address at Water Lane. I'm keeping storage space there while I look to establish an office.'

They both agreed it was unwise to grow too quickly. It had been the reason for Armin's last crash; his over optimism in a burgeoning market that had encouraged him to borrow heavily against his assets. It did not take much to make the banks nervous: rumours of a rise in interest rates, a glitch in the housing market or in Armin's case the hostility towards German and Austrian white wines after the glycol scandal. A ploy Armin guessed cynically that was intended to protect the wine growers of California. It had reduced his collateral to nothing and been the reason for his having to camp out in Otto's office until the serendipitous meeting with Patty had whisked him away to Palm Beach. 'You're one lucky sonofabitch, you know that?' Otto had said when Armin had come to collect his few belongings the day before he was to leave for Europe. Armin had examined hands manicured that morning by Ming, Patty's Vietnamese manicurist, and played with his signet ring that had the family crest engraved upon a lozenge of lapis lazuli.

VJ had known Armin from the days when he was still with Deli World and had come into his corner shop on the Portsmouth Road to regale him with his price list and brochures of air dried hams and sausages displayed on platters in the white wood kitchens of toothsome *Hausfrauen*. VJ had eyed the looped blonde plaits and full breasts bursting from the dirndls of these latter day Brunhildes and indulged himself in this most innocent of food porn; a voyeur in the flesh pink world of skinless and vacuum packed, the weenie and the ball breaking *Berliner Bouletten*. Later had come pickles, dumplings and herrings silver skinned or dunked in creamy sauce, chopped and marinated, sweet and sour. The burgeoning demand from the first wave of Poles had encouraged VJ to reorganise his shelves.

Ten years later and competition was fierce. Even the supermarkets had a section devoted to the salt and vinegary preserves favoured by those where winter froze the fields from November to March. But by then VJ had moved on, expanding into property and buying up corner shops that he planned to sell to the twenty four seven stores and Tesco and Sainsbury locals.

VJ respected Armin for his resilience. A year ago Armin had looked like a bum, unshaven and on his uppers but now his shirts were blue Egyptian cotton, his ties red and gold silk and his loafers polished to the high shine of a maharaja's waxed moustache.

‘I have a proposition to make to you,’ VJ had said over coffee. ‘It only came up yesterday.’

Armin said, 'I'm all ears, but could we discuss this over a drink? Flying always leaves me with a mouth like a camel.'

They had gone to a hotel VJ knew with a small

mahogany bar and there VJ had told him about his idea of buying the brewery.

'Is it for sale?' Armin asked, his interest roused.

'No. But it soon could be.' VJ twirled the ice cubes in his bitter lemon.

'I know the owner from way back. He's retiring and handing the reins to his son Edgar who isn't interested. He prefers flowers, plants, that sort of thing.'

'He's a florist?' Armin had asked curiously.

'A Kew thing. A botanist,' VJ had replied dismissively. 'I think we should make him an offer. If we produce our own beer it means no middle man. We go straight to the retailer. We can't lose. I know breweries in India who'd be delighted to deal with us. Kingfisher and Cobra are not the only animals in the zoo.' Here VJ had given a chuckle.

'How much is he asking?' Armin said.

'I thought a partnership. You put in as much as you can afford and I'll do the same and then we'll borrow the rest. One million, two, three, it's up to you how much you want to invest. But since you're a rich man with a fabulous house full of treasures, you shouldn't have any trouble finding collateral. I don't see how we can lose.'

Armin studied his friend over the rim of his glass. He'd known VJ for years. Known him and yet not known him. He'd never been invited to the house or met his wife. In the shop he'd been introduced to a succession of young assistants who judging from their bright smiles and darker complexions had not been in England long. From what he gathered they came in on tourist visas but how VJ managed his business affairs was of no concern to Armin. He had been a good friend, they had been through a lot together.

'One million, two or three. Whatever you can afford.' VJ's words resonated in Armin's head as he made his way back to Seething Wells later that night.

He had never had that kind of money, not even in his

best years. Angela had always spent as much as he earned, first on a bigger house and then on horse riding lessons, private education for Alexander, all the musts a move to Oxshott had demanded.

There was Karl but he had no intention of asking him. Patty had an investment portfolio but she had told him that money was the cause of too many fractured relationships and the topic was taboo. Money was boring and besides, neither of them had financial worries. Irwin had been generous in his provision for Patty's future and Armin had his businesses as well as a home in Berlin worth millions. They could count themselves very lucky.

Business and pleasure. Patty was for the latter and Armin was inclined to go along with it when she left him in peace to sip his breakfast smoothie by the pool.

One million. Armin would be lucky if he broke even after covering his expenses on this trip.

He began to feel queasy and by the time he reached Seething Wells he was sweating and wanting to vomit. He rang the bell and the smell of Araldite and damp hit his nostrils and sent him clutching the lintel for support. He felt his legs buckle and suddenly someone was helping him into the house.

He heard voices as though they were coming from the bottom of an aquarium and then he dropped to the floor.

Chapter Fifteen

When Armin collapsed in Kitty's front room, her first thought was that he had suffered a heart attack but Bosco who had trained as a nurse said it looked more like the result of a dodgy curry and they shouldn't call an ambulance. That was after Armin had thrown up and contributed yet another yellow stain to Kitty's carpet.

Men were such babies when it came to being sick, Sylvia had said, holding the glass of water to Armin's lips. It was years since she'd been this intimate with a man, her arm hooked under Armin's senatorial head with its prominent beaked nose and looking for all the world like Julius Caesar or so she imagined.

It had been a combined effort getting him to the spare room, each of them grabbing a limb and Bosco doing the heavy work by hauling Armin by the shoulders up the stairs. Adele had wondered how anyone managed to hide a body, it was such a dead weight. Once Armin was on the bed she had volunteered to sponge his face and then Bosco had taken over the more intimate task of dressing him in Alfred's pyjamas. Kitty had kept a pair all these years in the airing cupboard but when she'd shaken out the trousers she'd found a pubic hair snagged in a button. It had given her a jolt, this connection with her sexual past and she had tugged it free and spirited it out the window.

Adele insisted on staying with Kitty overnight and together they had made up the put-u-up and Adele had slept quite comfortably in the front room surrounded by china that over the years had become old friends. She had gazed at the statue of the nymph with her flawless Parian skin and then peeped under the sheet at her own body that was yellowed and barnacled like an old whale. When had that happened? When had she turned into this hag? She had been a beauty once. In her head she was still eighteen.

The next morning she was in the front room when the fissures in the ceiling suddenly exploded into puffs of plaster above her head.

'He's getting up. I'll put his clothes on the landing,' she called to Kitty.

Last night she had bundled his shirt and trousers in the wash and then ironed them and hung them to air in the porch. In the early hours she'd woken with a start to see the shirt trembling in the breeze from the open window. It had got her thinking about Mr von Hassendorf. He reminded her of Dad when he used to come home from playing with one of the Big Bands and all the air was sucked out of him. Not difficult for a trumpet player. Dad in his black jacket with the satin reveres and tuxedo looking like a toff and all this frustration and anxiety building up inside him.

Adele thought she had caught a glimpse of that potent mix in the German's eyes after Kitty had told him that she couldn't possibly attempt to copy a Kaendler harlequin.

'It would be sacrilege, Mr von Hassendorf. I am really not up to it.'

But Adele did not agree and she had taken the Parian nymph off the top of the cupboard and shown Armin just how good Kitty was at restoration, 'Look, part of the back was missing and Kitty rebuilt it. It's a wonderful piece of work.'

'But that took me several weeks,' Kitty protested. 'And I can see the joins even if you can't.'

* * * * *

Armin put both feet on the floor and sent the Klug bottles chinking in their crates. Someone had attempted to put him into pyjamas but given up after the jacket proved too tight. They had left him to sleep in his boxer shorts. He looked for his shirt and trousers but they had disappeared.

He heard the women below and then the distinctive smell which was part clay and glue, part weedy river dank, came to him now up the staircase as the door to the front room opened. He felt a wave of nausea but there was nothing in his stomach and he eased himself up from the bed, placing one foot cautiously before the other.

'Mr von Hassendorf, are you awake, are you decent?' Adele was on the landing, a bobbing shape of violet and turquoise. A large paste brooch flashed at him like the evil eye.

'You'll be wanting these.' She placed his clothes on the top step as if he were a leper.

'Are you feeling all right? Bosco thinks it was something you ate last night. He's a nurse and knows about these things. Dry bread and a little gruel that's what my mother used to give us when we had stomach troubles. Doesn't excite the juices, you see?'

She threw him a casual wave and disappeared. As he dressed he heard them talking in the kitchen in their thin piping voices.

He went into the bathroom and stuck his head under the cold water tap and ran a damp hand through his hair. He had thought of taking a quick shower but the bath was stacked with books and a menagerie of china animals. There had been a rumbling sound when he'd tried the hot water tap and then the pipes had begun to vibrate alarmingly before giving off several loud blasts like a fog horn. He guessed it was trapped air.

Kitty and Adele were waiting for him in the front room. 'Ladies,' he said, 'I owe you an apology.'

Kitty said, 'You couldn't help being taken ill.'

'.... for your kindness and consideration,' Armin continued, following them through to the porch. He gazed ruefully at the table where his photographs of the harlequins were still on display.

'You would not reconsider?' he said to Kitty. 'I am not asking you to imitate Kaendler, I know that would be impossible. Just a reasonable copy is all I want. I will pay you for your trouble. A thousand pounds for each?'

'This isn't about money,' Kitty began but Armin stopped her with a warning hand.

'Kitty, in this life, it is always about money.'

She agreed to think about it and busied herself pouring the coffee and asking Adele to find the doughnuts that Bosco had brought yesterday. They might be a little dry but they were still perfectly edible.

The coffee made Armin feel better and he was soon making preparations to leave. He had business to attend to.

'Always so many appointments,' Adele said admiringly.

'And you will give some serious thought about the harlequins?' he said at the door. 'It doesn't have to be special, just a representation will do. Just something to suggest to my friends what the originals are like?'

He took the tube to South Kensington with the idea of visiting the V&A and inspecting the Kaendler on display there. He was still hoping Kitty would change her mind. One figurine would be enough. All he needed was to fill the gap in the vitrine.

He was idly examining a harlequin holding a cherry when a call came through from Julia.

'Julia? What can I do for you?'

'You're coming on Sunday? Mum's got loads of eggs she'll be hiding in the garden. It's having no grandchildren and her way of making a point. I can't face it unless you come.'

Armin didn't understand.

'It's Easter, remember?'

'Easter?'

'This Sunday. Don't tell me you've forgotten Armin? What are you thinking about? We always have an egg hunt on Easter Sunday. It's tradition.'

'No, no,' he protested,

'So you're coming?'

'Florida has messed up the seasons for me,' he said, 'I've made other plans.'

'Well break them. This is important. Please... please.'

He paused and then said, 'I'll think about it, ok?'

He phoned Patty while he waited in the café for his double espresso and left a message that he would call again in the evening.

In his House of Chocolate days Easter would have been impossible to ignore. The catalogues arrived six months in advance, their glossy pages spilling with the fecundity of eggs of all sizes, dark, white and milk chocolate, hollow and filled. Pipe cleaner chicks the yellow of yolk and fondant hares rampant under marzipan toadstools. Eggs as tiny as rabbit droppings sheathed in multi coloured foil or ostrich sized and ribbed with icing, adorned with satin bows as flamboyant as a little girl's party dress. Boxed in the pastels of spring flowers, he had taken delivery of samples at his warehouse in Chessington and distributed them to his customers. The patisserie that spent ten thousand pounds for its six outlets, the independent shops that although decreasing in number still commanded his special attention. He'd order extra cellophane and sprigs of silken blossom.

The invitation, though not welcome for he had no appetite for Karl and Crystal's preening, did have the effect of making him focus on his priorities. A closer look in the vitrine and it would be clear to anyone that some were missing. Karl and Crystal might not examine the Meissen every day, but they were aware of the volume of figurines in their possession if not the nuances of each piece. They were not connoisseurs, he had already gathered that.

But he had expected to have more time to get the copies made. He had not envisaged that it would have to be this weekend. 'Damn Easter,' he muttered.

He spent the rest of the day scouring markets and the china departments of the big stores but could find nothing suitable and the adrenalin rush that had kept him on a high now began to dissipate into frustration. Too many frosted fairies and franchised bat mobiles and limited editions of unbearably cute birds and gold chased turtles. Armin looked in vain for harlequins that would deceive the eye but the only figurine that came close was a Lladro rascal that he examined thoughtfully but did not buy.

He'd read in one of Karl's files that extravagant table displays had been a sign of wealth and power in the days of August the Strong, Elector of Saxony; the mermaids, tritons, swans and rushes sculpted by a creative wit that had made Kaendler much sought after by Europe's nobility. Frederick the Great and Catherine the Great, Madame de Stael, Louis XV and his Queen. Harlequins from the *Commedia dell'arte?* No one he asked had heard of them.

He returned to Seething Wells later that evening, oblivious to the activity inside the house although the neon light casting a flickering blue glow over the Peace roses ought to have prepared him. Bosco had let him in and Armin had smelt the familiar mixture of damp clay and Araldite washed by river water, more penetrating than usual he thought as he'd followed Bosco into the front room.

The three women were at the table; Kitty and Sylvia

with Adele flitting about on the periphery and giving what she trilled, 'moral support to the little elves.'

It had been a stroke of luck that Bosco had happened to walk past a junk shop in Surbiton that morning and found a harlequin.

'Bought for a fiver,' Bosco said with a laugh.

And now Kitty had remodelled the arm into the out flung position as seen on the photograph and Sylvia had made the tankard from a latex mould.

'It hasn't been without its dramas,' Adele added darkly. It was touch and go for a time when Kitty's eyesight had suddenly gone wonky and Bosco had had to deal with the Chintex glaze.

'And then Adele heated the oven to 94C and got muddled with the time and instead of leaving the figurine to cool off she brought it out too early and the arm was covered in air bubbles. It almost ruined it.' Sylvia was weary and grumpy.

'But all's well that ends well,' Adele reminded her.

'Only after we'd woken poor Kitty and got her to dribble glaze medium into the holes with a brush,' Sylvia shot back.

Armin had sat on the sofa with his long arms touching the carpet and said, 'So it will be ready for me to take to Berlin this weekend?'

One piece was better than none and with a little nudging of the Meissen he was sure no one would notice the difference.

He had eaten nothing all day and now suddenly he was very hungry.

'Potatoes,' he said, 'do you have some Kitty? I will make us a special meal to celebrate. *Bratkartoffeln mit Speck*. Fried potatoes with bacon if you have it. Onions. You have onions? A simple dish but the secret is to boil the potatoes in their skins and then slice them into hot fat. I will make us dinner. And Bosco will bring down a few beers and we will drink a toast to a successful day's work.'

Chapter Sixteen

The scillas in the garden were almost over, their intense blue faded to the insipid grey of Berlin's sky that Sunday morning. The sudden but not unexpected cold snap had frozen the buds on the damson trees and brought Crystal out in her fox fur. On first sighting, Armin had been struck by the variety of so much auburn and orange, the hennaed highlights whisked from under the Cossack style hat, the buffed cheeks that under closer scrutiny had the porosity of a clementine (she had pressed one against his in a display of affection he did not trust) and then the coat falling to the ankles in thick skeins of dark apricot that ruffled in the wind to reveal the pale almond beneath. A magnificent apparition he had first thought on seeing her poised amid the fading scillas, and she aware of her effect had allowed him to plod the thirty metres down the path before stepping forward to greet him.

It was the first time he'd been able to relax since arriving at the house, the impossibility of getting a flight over the holiday having forced him to wait until now for a cancellation. He had left Kitty's at five this morning and when he landed at Tegel he'd phoned Julia who had picked him up in the Trabi. With her lack of makeup and dark blond hair straggling to the shoulders of her crumpled sweater, she'd looked like any one of the hippy daughters rich parents seemed to generate, either in rejection of their values or in Julia's case a way of avoiding male attention. It did little to detract from her beauty. In fact Armin thought her scruffiness only made him look harder at the flawless skin and clear eyes that for all their youthful sparkle were guarded and slightly mocking.

'Mum and Dad are on the autobahn and should be with us in about an hour,' she had announced brightly over the phone. 'They were supposed to have come yesterday but someone jumped from the roof of one of the flats and Dad's been dealing with the police.'

'I know. I've spoken to him. Some people have wretched lives,' he'd murmured.

Julia had invited him back to her flat for breakfast. There was little point in going to the house until Karl and Crystal arrived and then they'd need time to arrange things. Everything had to be just so and there was no point in rushing. Julia guessed it would take at least another two hours.

'It will give us time to talk. And Sabine will show you what she's found out about the tankard. It's not very pleasant. I don't want to think the worse of Trudy but maybe living under the *Sozis* made her secretive.'

He wondered aloud whether they could make a brief stop at the house.

'My shaving kit,' he said rubbing his chin. 'I left it in the guest bathroom.'

Julia had driven him to the top of the road and then dropped a set of keys into his lap. 'Don't be long. Sabine's blinis have to be eaten warm.'

He unlocked the great doors and entered the yard and then climbed the spiral staircase to the first floor. He disabled the alarm and went in. The house had a dry chemical smell that he associated with formaldehyde and he grimaced at these rooms that had been buffed and polished of their vitality and were now quite dead. Then he caught a faint whiff of dankness from the river that reminded him of Seething Wells. Both houses were built too close to water.

It took him only a few seconds to unfasten his briefcase but he was surprised that his hands were trembling. He took out the figurine bandaged in folds of lint and bubble wrap and gently unwound it. His first impression on seeing it again was that it looked surprisingly authentic. It was only when he examined it more closely that he noticed the too heavy application of paint but he didn't think it lacked the vigour that Kitty had warned him about and which made this so obviously a copy. 'Kaendler was famous for making porcelain come alive.'

Armin padded over to the vitrine. He had only the one harlequin, but of the two, this was the most striking and therefore most likely to be missed. He rearranged the shelf and drew the figurines closer together, retrieving a plump little figure in yellow pantaloons from the back and putting him in the foreground to cover the one still with Kitty. In his black boots and red vest he looked like the prosperous owner of a brewery. Armin locked the vitrine and without thinking pocketed the key.

Over breakfast Sabine told him that her research into the tankard had so far been inconclusive but she had located two estates and a *Schloss* to the north of Berlin that might have kept an inventory. Many records had been destroyed during the war but something as valuable as the tankard she guessed would have been noted before it was hidden.

She had pointed to the two white chairs by the window and said that her mother had found them in a forest in 1945 after the Russians had ransacked the neighbouring houses. 'They must have dumped them when they couldn't fit them into the truck. They aren't worth much. The really priceless stuff was hidden away. Trudy dug her hole and buried the tankard in her allotment.'

Julia had said very little. She seemed uncomfortable

with the conversation and it occurred to Armin that she wasn't convinced of Trudy's complicity but preferred to keep her opinion to herself. Sabine was the dominant personality and Julia was too dazzled by her lover to openly oppose her. There were moments when a smile would pass between them as though a casual remark had reinforced a world of secrets that Armin would never be privy to.

When he returned to the house with Julia, Crystal had decorated branches of forsythia with coloured eggs and set them in a vase by the window. Miniature hand carved wooden rabbits and chickens were displayed in groups on cabinets and side tables. Some of them were pre-war, Crystal was to explain, and it was their duller shades and more elongated shapes that distinguished them from the modern brightly painted ones.

On a given signal they trooped down to the garden to start hunting for the chocolate eggs that Crystal had hidden. Wrapped in her furs she encouraged them by calling directions, 'closer, a little to your left, no Karl, *left*, I said.'

Armin found a clutch nestling in moss under the marble statue of Diana and others in the fork of the plum tree as though dropped there by an absent minded cuckoo. Julia whispered that the best cache was near the old stable and he had gone over and plucked the gold foil rabbit from under the raspberry bush. Julia came up and asked if he didn't find the whole thing a little ridiculous? It was for children, not grownups. But he was enjoying himself, peeling off the thin silver paper and relishing the flavours, some of them filled with liqueur that burst into his mouth.

Afterwards, Crystal went with Julia to the end of the garden to inspect the fruit trees. She didn't think the gardener had done a good job with the pruning and wanted a second opinion. Karl invited Armin upstairs for a drink. It was time for a little bonding.

How was business?

'Great. I'm toying with the idea of buying a brewery.'

'Here in Germany?'

'No, in England. But I plan to franchise my beer with one of the Bavarian brewers before moving into eastern Europe.'

'English beer has a poor reputation over here. Why would anyone want to buy it when we have our own excellent brands? If you have that much capital to play with why don't you invest it in real estate, something that will bring you a higher return? I've turned down three projects this week because I can't commit the time to them. Money isn't the problem. I only have to pick up the phone and the banks will give me whatever I ask for. But you can't buy time. I want to enjoy this house and appreciate what's here.'

While they were talking, the sun appeared over the roof tops and flooded into the room, spot lighting the harlequins in their vibrant yellow, black and red. Karl got up at once to adjust the blind but not before Armin said, 'Can I take a closer look? That fellow in there...' he nodded in the direction of the vitrine.

The urge to push his luck to the limit was irresistible.

Karl followed his gaze.

'The Scaramouch there, the harlequin.'

Karl went to turn the key but it was missing. Armin watched as Karl grew increasingly anxious. He could swear it had been there this morning. Armin peered under the table. Perhaps Julia or Crystal had taken it by mistake? Karl paced the room looking confused and checking his pockets. The key was kept in the lock, they all knew that. It was forbidden to remove it. Maybe Frau Hubschmidt? But she had no authority. No right.

'You should reconsider your security,' Armin said. 'A key in a vitrine full of Meissen is asking for trouble.'

'We are all family here,' Karl shot back angrily, 'this

is a house not a fortress.'

Later he would hear them rattling through drawers and examining bunches in their possession, the colour coded tags of coppery chubs and mortises giving access to treasures not only here but in the safe at Bremen. Armin had no idea what riches were stored there but he guessed that it must be some of the smaller more valuable pieces, the jewellery and snuff boxes that they'd smuggled out on their visits during the DDR years. Julia had told him with a mixture of pride and faint disgust that her mother had once smuggled a pair of diamond earrings over the border in her vagina.

'At least the Meissen's safely locked away,' Armin said when Karl came back.

His cousin turned on him, 'Everything's just a big joke to you. That's why leaving you in charge would have been a disaster!'

He went off to see Frau Hubschmidt and Armin sat contemplating the vitrine from the sofa, suppressing the urge to finger the missing key lying in his pocket. He didn't hear Crystal come in. She had taken off her boots and put on a pair of felt slippers which had the advantage of buffing the parquet while making her approach soundless. As silent as a cat ready to pounce, he'd thought.

She took Karl's seat and looked at him with her head to one side as though he were something she'd just found in the attic and was dubious about its provenance.

She smelled of flowers and warm chocolate, her beige cashmere roll neck defining a prominent chin in a face that looked distinctly Russian. The blue contact lenses added to the intensity of her gaze. How was life treating him? Was he going to be spending more time in Europe or did he prefer America? She had never liked Americans herself, too superficial. They were easy to get to know but did not make true friends. 'They seem to be acting out roles they have picked for themselves from their favourite movies.'

Patty though, must be different.

'She was born in Germany but she's a naturalised American,' Armin said.

Crystal had heard she was a widow. Probably Julia had told her.

'Her late husband was in manufacturing. He had a company in New Jersey making valves for the aircraft industry. His first wife died of cancer some years ago. There are a couple of kids, grown up now with families of their own but they and Patty aren't close.'

Crystal had stroked her hair and sighed. 'Children can be a problem. But Alexander's turned out just fine, yes? San Francisco's an attractive city, very liberal I hear, very accepting of all types of people.'

Armin nodded, 'Seems that way.'

'I hope Patty will come and visit us again soon.'

Armin was suddenly alert. He peered at Crystal through hooded lids. 'That can be arranged.'

'Preferably when we're here,' she added pointedly. 'Things go missing and cannot be accounted for and then the wrong people get blamed.'

Armin said nothing.

'The key's here somewhere. Karl's getting forgetful. He'll find it when he remembers. Perhaps though, you could have a word with Patty just in case?'

'Who told you Patty was here?'

'A little bird. Don't worry. Next time I'd prefer it if you cleared it with us first. It's not a problem.' She smiled at him but her eyes were hard.

Karl was calling from the garden and she went down. Armin watched from the window as they walked the path under the trees. The lost key had brought them closer for a moment but they had always pursued a common goal. The fruits of it were all around to see.

He waited a few seconds and then unlocked the vitrine. He felt like a kid in a candy store but knew it was not wise to indulge himself for too long. A young woman, simply dressed, caught his eye. She was in pleasant contrast to the row of baroque shepherdesses and fawning swains with their knowing coyness that took up most of the shelf. He wasn't prepared to be affected by her, she was only a lump of clay and water, but he found himself wondering about the letter she was holding and whether it was good news. Her expression was bemused, a touch cynical even.

He placed her carefully in his Easter basket and covered her with moss and the chocolate eggs he had collected. Then he rearranged the shelf and locked the door before dropping the key back into his pocket.

Crystal returned muttering about keeping a spare in the office. They had so many keys, some of them for cupboards here and others for furniture they were storing in the cellar in Bremen. She was going to prepare an inventory once she found the time.

They would not let the topic rest and spent the afternoon speculating on how the key could have got lost. When Julia came in to say goodbye, Crystal questioned her again. Could she have taken it home by mistake?

'Why would I?' Julia had snorted. 'It's probably on the floor or under the carpet.'

Armin followed Karl into his office. He had furnished the spare room with a desk and a couple of easy chairs. It had the usual antiques, a few choice paintings on the wall, one of which he told Armin was by a promising young Berlin artist that he had been advised to buy as an investment. Armin found its scribble deeply depressing. 'But do you like it?' he asked and Karl said, 'It's growing on me.' A Chinese vase painted with ebullient red peonies stood on an ebony stand and Armin concentrated on that instead. Karl sat behind his desk where he seemed to be more at ease and Armin settled for one of the yellow cushioned chairs opposite him.

There were several photographs in silver frames on display and one in particular caught Armin's eye. It was of Trudy as a young woman snapped on the decked promenade of a Baltic seaside resort. She was leaning languidly against the iron railings, her chin tilted towards the sun, her dark blond hair bleached and frizzed about her face. It was a small face and the skin was stretched tight across the cheekbones. He remembered that she tanned easily and that this accentuated the blueness of her eyes. His gaze drifted to the swastika held taut by a brisk wind on the flagpole behind her. It gave him a jolt of recognition and revulsion. In the corner written in Trudy's cramped hand was, 'Zoppot 1939.'

He would have been four years old then and when Trudy returned to Berlin they would have resumed their weekly assaults on the cake shops and cafés on the Friedrichstrasse. He experienced a moment of regret for things he could not change and indicating the photograph said, 'At least it's different for our kids.'

'Each generation brings its own challenges,' Karl replied briskly.

He studied Armin closely. 'I hear you've managed to angle yourself a fine fish?'

A marlin? A swordfish? They were to be had off the coast of Florida but Armin had never been one for big game sports. Hated to see the poor brute flailing at the bottom of a boat gasping for its life. What was the sport in killing things?

'I mean a woman,' Karl said.

'You're talking about Patty?'

'Crystal would like to invite her to stay. Get to know her a little if it's serious between the two of you. She lives in Florida?'

'In Palm Beach.'

'A smart address. So you have managed to angle

yourself a wealthy widow. Good. Something to secure your future is sound thinking.'

Karl had got up from the desk, preoccupied now with locking the house before they returned to Bremen. Audience over, Armin retreated to the landing while his cousin went from room to room double checking the window fastenings and the doors, his gaze assembling the artefacts in his mind, yet not seeing that in the vitrine the shelves were beginning to resemble a set of milk teeth, the gaps obvious to those who really saw.

In the hall the rugs that had the habit of slipping on the highly polished floor were straightened, the alarm about to be set when Crystal came hurrying up the stairs.

Was Armin really sure he didn't want some little memento of Trudy? She still had the box and he only had to ask. Armin could see that it would make her happy so he said, 'okay, let's have another look.' They sat at the table in the kitchen and he closed his mind to the heavy chains that smelled of metal, the glass beads and plastic earrings that she held up for his approval. He had no intention of accepting a peace offering. He did not want to make her feel better by accepting this junk. Then he noticed the lump of amber, dense and waxy as Dutch cheese. Crystal noticed his hesitation and thrust it upon him. 'Maybe Patty would like it as a small token of her homeland?'

He had overlooked the amber and now he saw it rolling under a lustred wave beneath a small child's toes, a connection with a scimitar of white sand that had been lost forever. 'Okay, I'll have it,' he said.

He was in the yard when Karl called him. Hadn't he forgotten something?

He was coming down the steps holding Armin's Easter basket of eggs and moss.

'You keep it,' Armin said.

‘You found them so they’re yours. Here!’
Karl thrust the basket firmly into Armin's hands.

Chapter Seventeen

Kitty had been restoring the paw of a King Charles spaniel when the letter arrived from the solicitor with the surveyor's report. She already knew from a review of the property pages that if she wanted to take up her option of first refusal on a house by the river it would cost her close to a million. She had decided therefore to leave the letter unopened on the draining board until another day.

The phone call from Mr Bellamy who had been waiting six months for the return of his King Charles spaniel had been another of those odd things that had happened to her recently. She had been searching high and low for the piece of Staffordshire creamware but hadn't been able to find it. Then a few minutes before his call she had gone into the porch to tidy up and there was the spaniel tucked behind a stack of Elsie's books and The Tablet magazines.

Adele had said that if anyone was responsible for this coincidence it must be Jason who had set the wheels in motion by telling Kitty the valuer would be coming round that afternoon to see what could go for auction. She wouldn't have tackled the porch otherwise.

'So why bother to make the place presentable?' Adele had argued, flicking the bangles up her skinny arms. Let Jason take care of it.

But accepting a sensible argument meant that Kitty would have to acknowledge the seriousness of her situation. And she couldn't go that far. Not yet. Secretly she was hoping that whoever or whatever was responsible for that one coincidence might pull another out of the hat that would allow her to stay at Seething Wells until she died.

Adele had run a damp cloth along the edges of the shelves and then she and Kitty had carried boxes of old china and materials into a garage already stacked high with Elsie's stuff. Adele had contemplated the suitcases franked with labels from the Italian and Swiss lakes, the tea chests of a hidden life soon to be exposed to the rifling hands of the house clearance and said it was always a good idea to have a regular clean out.

She had suggested they dump what remained in the roof but no one had been up there for as long as Kitty could remember and what with the squirrels and birds and the grime that had settled about the trapdoor, Kitty said she was not prepared to go into a part of the house that had already reverted to the wild.

The valuer had arrived and then Jason had turned up and together they had inspected the various items that would be sent to auction. The valuer had taken Polaroids of the French sideboard and the writing desk with its marquetry of flowers in slivers of plum and walnut wood, the water colour of the Highlands that Kitty had always admired and a few other pieces that Elsie had not been able to squeeze into her room at Fircroft. It was not much to show for a life, Adele had commented as the men had moved upstairs.

When Jason came down again he had demanded to know why the bedroom was stacked with beer crates.

'She's storing them for a friend. They'll be collected soon, no worries,' Adele had trilled as she and Kitty had retreated to the garden.

'You're too kind Kitty, that's your trouble. Always seeing the best in people when they're taking advantage. Ring that German now and tell him to move his beer. You don't want to give Jason reason for making it even harder for you.

If he accuses you of running an off licence on the premises, how are you going to prove otherwise?'

Kitty had phoned Armin as soon as Jason and the valuer were gone. Armin had his mobile on voice mail and she had left a message.

'Mr von Hassendorf, this is Kitty. The beer you have stored in my house must be moved immediately.'

'Otherwise we're emptying it into the river,' Adele had added over her shoulder before Kitty could ring off.

The next day Armin had turned up at the door. The young woman with him had Armin's caramel complexion and light blue eyes and the detached air of someone not quite belonging. A misalignment which was evident to a lesser extent in Armin too. Kitty wondered if she was Armin's daughter. They made an intriguing couple.

'This is Sonja. She works in the biggest deli in Ealing,' Armin said.

Sonja had given a crack of a smile and offered Kitty a limp hand.

'And I do apologise for the trouble. I would have come earlier but negotiations abroad took longer than expected.'

Kitty had fluttered her hands as though it had been the last thing on her mind, this business with the beer. She had far more important matters to attend to.

Armin stood by the window, blocking the light and casting a shadow, a bulk of a man in a smart blue blazer (a gift from Patty when they'd met up in Baden Baden over the weekend) and grey slacks, his shoes twinkling like Fred Astaire's. Those small feet again. And with this incredible capacity for calm which Kitty found both reassuring as well as slightly intimidating. Armin seemed to be able to dream while awake, conserving his energy yet remaining alert. And the girl? Kitty wondered about that.

'I am from Cracow,' Sonja said when Kitty asked after Armin had gone upstairs to look at his beer.

'So you are not related?' Kitty concluded, waving at the ceiling where heavy footsteps could be seen to judder the neon strip and send the china cups clinking on their hooks like an earth tremor.

'No, not related,' Sonja said, looking quizzically at Kitty from under a frond of dark hair.

'Have you been in England long?'

'Five months,' Sonja said, looking around her. 'So many cups and plates. So many vases and animals.'

She had seen Kitty's front room and was suddenly animated.

The King Charles spaniel was perched on the worktable, his paw waiting for the fizzy spurt of Kitty's airbrush. Sonja bent to stroke him and the amber pendant, dense as a lump of cheddar, suddenly swung free from the swell of her breasts and clinked gently against the creamware.

'I have dog at home. She is Labrador called Suzie from Everly Brothers song, you know? I am fan of American music. Fifties style.'

She reached inside her denim jacket for a pack of Marlboro Lite and offered Kitty a cigarette. They went into the garden and Sonja blew smoke between her lips and sent it drifting above their heads to mingle with the early blossom and the burst of exhaust from Trish's Ferrari as she roared past on her way to the shops.

Armin had come downstairs with a crate of Klug against his chest and swaggering like a sailor under its weight had carried it to the boot of his car. He handed Sonja the keys and asked her to wait. Later Kitty would hear music thumping from the car radio.

'Kitty, I have a little request.'

For the first time on that bright afternoon Kitty was aware not so much of the urgency in Armin's voice but of something else that jarred with the impression of a man of calm. Perhaps it was Sonja's doing, feet propped on the dashboard as she rifled through the CDs stashed in the glove compartment. She was to make little sense of the bangla and hip-hop left there by Neel and Sam on their recent trip to Leicester. Perhaps it was youth's impatience transmitted now by a sharp blast of the horn that had made Armin too hasty with the unravelling of another treasure.

‘Columbine, from the Italian Comedy,’ he had said as the narrow waisted figurine had unfurled from the bubble wrap. A young woman in red beribboned shoes. She displayed all the vivacity of Kaendler at his best.

‘You will be pleased to hear that Bosco has found something similar to the monocle harlequin on that e-bay thing. It will mean adjusting the leg, snapping off the original and remoulding. And making flowers for the base....’

‘Whatever it takes, Kitty,’ Armin said, ‘Can you make me a copy of this one too?’

‘But I'm not sure I will be here to finish it. I'm going to have to move shortly.’

Armin had patted her gently on the shoulder and then taken out his wallet and placed five twenty pound notes on the table.

‘A small deposit. I will pay you a thousand pounds for a Columbine. It does not have to be perfect, only a representation. The originals will be put in the safe, you understand? Try your best Kitty. This time I am not in such a hurry. I will be in touch.’

‘And the beer? Jason's been asking about it. I can't keep it up there for much longer.’

‘It's all in hand. I just need a little more time. Orders are coming in and soon it will all be sold. I appreciate your co-operation Kitty. It means a lot to me.’

He had given Kitty a cheery wave as he'd retreated

down the path to where Sonja was waiting in the car.

It had been his idea that she come with him. It was a beautiful spring day and the shop was quiet. A couple of hours would do no harm. The pimply youth could watch the place while they were away.

Sonja had reminded him that she was not the owner and it was not up to her whether they order the Klug. Maciej made all the decisions.

'But I am sure you can persuade him to take a case on sale or return,' Armin had said and, seeing the BMW outside, Sonja had considered Armin through a fringe of dark lashes and then pulled on a faded denim jacket with a grubby lambswool collar and accompanied him onto the street.

She hadn't had much to say for herself. When he asked her a question she mumbled yes or no but he did manage to discover that she wanted to go to the USA where she had a cousin. 'In Belmont, a small town near Milwaukee.' He had told her he didn't know Milwaukee but he had flown over the Arizona desert and seen a UFO once. He had waited for her to say something and when she did not respond he wondered if she knew what a UFO was. There was a peasant coarseness about her and he imagined that she came from a small village with no roads just muddy tracks and chickens running all over the place. Women in headscarves and thick shapeless coats. No big city girl then. Her background was ingrained like dirt under the fingernails. She was not the mermaid of his Baltic idling, the pearl encrusted creature that had entered his dreams the moment he had set eyes on her.

And yet he was enchanted by her and alert to her slightest gesture, the folding of her hands, the fingers flat tipped with one of the nails snagged.

Once or twice he had glanced at her tawny profile and thought her not beautiful at all and that her silences were the result of a lack of curiosity. He doubted she had a secret world where few were admitted.

On the way to Kingston he had taken a detour through Richmond Park to show her the deer. He had parked at Pembroke Lodge and they had gone onto the terrace, the yellow of the oaks glistening on the slope that fell away to more green, more trees lining the river bank and keeping it from view.

He had suggested coffee but she told him she had promised Pavel to be back in two hours.

On the path he had pulled the amber out by its chain and left it to dangle between his fingers, pretending to be mystified as to how it had got into his pocket. Did she know what it was? Sonja said, 'Of course.'

'Then it's yours,' he said, pressing it into her hand.

'I couldn't.'

'Sure you can.'

Her teeth were small and there was too much gum. He went ahead and waited for her in the car.

After they'd picked up the beer he'd driven her back to Ealing and then parked and gone to a café. He was so used to acting on his own with no consideration for others that it came as a shock to realise that he missed her. It was as if she had grasped the essence of life in a chunk of amber and spirited it away by sleight of hand.

Afterwards he made a few stops to see some old customers. One of them warned him that the new rep had heard he was hustling on his patch and was making a complaint to Deli World. Armin didn't work for them anymore. Furthermore his catalogue was out of date. 'Old habits,' Armin said. He couldn't resist the urge to trade and stack an empty shelf. When he had control of the brewery things would be different.

The brewery. He had spoken to Otto when he was in Baden Baden last weekend visiting Patty. He'd told him he was looking for backers. People with a couple of million to invest.

Otto had said, ‘Come on, Armin, you know I can't deal without having all the facts. I'll need accounts, a business plan, all the stuff you know they're going to ask for if you're serious about it. Are you serious, Armin?’

‘What do you mean?’ he'd demanded.

‘At your time of life I'd be thinking about taking it easy. You've inherited a house for chrissake. Enjoy it. Take Patty on one of those cruises she's always talking about.’

‘Patty hates cruises,’ Armin said.

‘A word of advice. Don't put your own money into this.’

‘I don't have any money,’ Armin said. ‘That's why I'm asking you.’

‘Come on, who are you kidding here? What about your big fat inheritance?’

‘There isn’t one. I lied. I inherited nothing,’ Armin said.

There had been a long pause at the other end. Long enough for Armin to consider the shrivelled state of his toes. He'd been on one of the spa loungers wrapped in a frotteé dressing gown, sunlight splintering the water into facets of blue and silver while in the exercise pool and well out of earshot Patty had been doing aqua aerobics with a young instructor in pink lycra.

‘Listen Otto, you're my oldest friend and that's why I'm telling you this. But not a word to anyone ok? If Patty gets to hear about it I’m finished.’

‘You mean you haven't told her yet?’

‘It's none of her business.’

‘But you're in the house, right?’

‘We're in Baden Baden at the spa. I've just done thirty lengths and now I'm relaxed and talking business. Patty has seen the house and has fallen in love with it. You see my problem?’

‘She loves you Armin. She’ll be okay with it. ’

'I appreciate your confidence, Otto. See what's out there for me, okay? I'll send you more details once I've spoken to VJ. I'll e-mail them or send a fax.'

Patty in a flowered bathing cap and emerald one piece had been waving to get his attention and he'd dropped the phone into his pocket and gone over.

'Who was that?' she'd asked, breasting the water and peering up at him now from the spangled mosaics of poolside.

'Someone reminding me I've got to give you my full attention,' he said and Patty had smiled and lowering her floral head had nibbled at his shrunken toe.

Armin thought about Patty as he made his way to the bistro where he was meeting VJ for a briefing. She had told him she was going to stay in Baden Baden for a full course of treatment. There was so much else to enjoy in the daily concerts, lectures and tea dances where men in the Heinz Ruehmann mould were only too eager to take her and Gilda for a spin across the parquet.

'You'd better watch those lounge lizards,' he'd growled.

'Nothing I can't handle,' Patty had replied lightly.

He'd seen the figurines in Gilda's apartment when he'd stopped by to pick her up. Gilda was out and they'd made love on the sofa and when he'd looked over Patty's shoulder he'd seen the snake head harlequin on the top shelf reflected in the baroque mirror. And his own face, his blood up and his hair a curtain of sweat over his brow. Patty had left him to go to the spa and after he'd rested and showered, he'd brewed some coffee and taken down the figurines from the shelf, wondering what all the fuss was about for he could find no beauty there.

* * * * *

VJ had some good news when they were seated at his favourite table in the bistro. The nephews had been busy and had managed to introduce Klug to a small but expanding chain of cash and carry. They would be doing a promotion next week and Armin should come along and see for himself how popular it was becoming.

'Developments are going well,' Armin had responded when VJ had asked about progress at his end. He'd had a limited amount of time on his last trip.

Baden Baden had been a no show. People there were more interested in strawberry and blueberry frappés and herbal concoctions than a new budget priced beer. The Berlin wholesalers he'd contacted on his way to the airport had been equally unimpressed. Why should they stock English beer with a German name? They didn't get the irony. He hated the idea that Karl could be right.

VJ had played with his tortellini. In a nod to fashion he'd had his head shaved and with the dark circles under his eyes looked like a disenchanted monk. A man with too many things on his mind and God no help at all. Last week he'd gone swimming and pissed blood. He was going in for tests at the end of the month.

Edgar was pressing him for an answer. There were several other contenders, a cartel from Mumbai and a brewery in the Midlands.

'Is that what Edgar's telling you?' Armin had asked, prodding at a particularly fleshless plaice. Fish were taken too young. Food was getting leaner and people fatter. The couple sitting behind VJ had thighs oozing over their chairs.

'We have to show him we're serious,' VJ said, jabbing a fork into his tomato salad. 'Keep him focused on us. We don't want him sniffing around.'

'No fear of that,' Armin said tetchily, pushing his plate away. He was still hungry. The plaice had been all bones.

It had been an unsatisfactory meal all round. VJ was worried about the tests, 'They're going to stick a tube up my dick,' and then, just as Armin had been digging into his tiramisu, he'd received a message from Karl on his pager asking him to call back. It occurred to Armin that his cousin might have noticed one of the harlequins was missing or some other irregularity in his precious vitrine. Armin would of course deny all knowledge.

Like a niggling pain, he had found his senses heightened by the uncertainty. The faded bistro had suddenly burst into life; the strings of red peppers draped about an old cartwheel, the straw donkeys and patterned plates feeding the owner's nostalgia for an artless charm that rarely existed in modern Tuscany. Even the staff had a stocky old fashioned look.

He phoned Karl while VJ was in the gents. Whatever was coming his way he could deal with it. He heard his cousin's clipped voice on the other end as he gave his name.

Armin said, 'What's up?

'Crystal wants to invite you and Patty for a long weekend.'

'Patty's taking the *Kur* at Baden Baden.'

'When is she free?'

'She'll be going back to Florida soon after.'

'But you'll talk to her?'

'What are your plans? When are you expected in Berlin again?'

'Not this weekend, I've got to see the architect about a new project. But we're having people over in a fortnight. Some dealer Crystal met at an antique's fair. It's a bore and I don't want to encourage this kind of thing. Word gets round that we have valuable objects at home and before you know it we're on someone's wish list. It will mean having to install a more sophisticated alarm system and that's not the idea. This is our home.'

'One of them,' Armin said under his breath. Then, 'I understand. I'll talk to Patty and let you know.'

Chapter Eighteen

'Seven hundred thousand pounds!'

In the kitchen Sylvia whistled through her teeth as she read the solicitors' letter. She was used to dealing with money but a sum of that magnitude wasn't brought to her attention every day.

There again, money didn't have the value it once had. In 1961 Sylvia had bought her house for three thousand pounds which had been a huge commitment for a young woman just starting out on own. She'd worked her way up from dusting the Pyrex in the basement of the store to becoming chief buyer for gift articles and sundries. Every week she'd put money aside to pay off the mortgage at four pounds sixpence a month.

The day she had redeemed it she had poured herself a Campari soda and gone into the garden. The cherry tree, planted the year she'd moved in, was in bloom and at the sight of it, the blossom always reminded her of tiny ballerinas in their pink tutus, she had burst into tears. She still couldn't understand why it had affected her so badly. Here was one of the great milestones in her life and yet her abiding memory of it was one of bewilderment and embarrassment. Her neighbour had heard her sobbing and asked if she was all right. Would she like to come round and talk about it? Sylvia had ignored her and dashed inside.

'So what does it say?' Kitty had called from her work table. 'Is it a million or more?'

Sylvia had come into the front room with the letter

and said, 'Actually it's almost as bad as that, Kitty. It's seven hundred thousand.'

Kitty had given the composition of Araldite AY 103 and titanium dioxide powder another roll on the glass plate and then she'd handed Bosco the spatula and said, 'I think I need some fresh air, would you take over for me please?'

When Kitty had gone up the towpath Sylvia told Bosco that in the hiatus following Elsie's death Kitty had started raising her hopes that Jason had changed his mind about selling. Nothing more had been heard from the valuer and even Sylvia had begun to wonder if Kitty may be right. As sole trustee Jason could challenge the Will and arrange to proceed at a later date once Kitty was settled somewhere else.

But seven hundred thousand pounds typed in bold and underlined was not something that could be dismissed lightly. It was what Kitty had been dreading. The solicitors' letter not only set out Jason's intentions but introduced a new reality. The reality of time passing.

'I've been doing some research,' Bosco said, easing his bulk out of the wicker chair and opening one of the plastic bags he always carried with him. He produced a laptop and jiggled it gently like a baby that needed to be turned right side up before being set down on the work table.

'Kaendler, am I right?'

Bosco tapped at his keyboard and pictures began to pop up. He scrolled down a series of Meissen figurines that Sylvia recognised as old friends from the reference books.

'Sold at auction, New York. Wait for it. Two hundred thousand dollars. That is for *one* figurine.'

'And here. Zurich. Four hundred thousand Swiss Francs. Rare Kaendler. Provenance: once part of a table centrepiece for Augustus the Strong, Elector of Saxony 1739. And there's more.'

Sylvia caught up with Kitty on a bench near the great black poplar. She hadn't got far.

'The mind's willing you know. In my head I'm already in Richmond. It's the body that's so pathetic. There's no joy in getting old. All that rubbish about a golden age,' Kitty exclaimed.

Sylvia had been having some trouble herself recently. On her way to Kingston she'd lost the feeling in one of her legs and for a few seconds had been unable to take her foot off the clutch.

'You can always come and live with me, Kitty.'

They could look out for each other. If she was suddenly confined to a wheelchair, Kitty would be there to help.

Kitty had gazed wistfully across the river at the ait where the chestnuts were already festooned with their white and pink candelabrae. It was the lushness of the landscape that so appealed. She would miss it terribly.

'Bosco's got something to show you,' Sylvia said getting up. 'It's about those figurines. He thinks you should get in touch with Mr von Hassendorf.'

* * * * *

Armin took Kitty's call while he was making an unannounced visit to the brewery. His first surprise had been Edgar himself. He was a Sri Lankan in his early forties, slightly built and with the demeanour of an academic and judging by the botanical prints on his office wall had interests that went beyond the humble hop. When Edgar caught Armin looking at them he told him that once the brewery was off his hands he planned an expedition to central Borneo to look for rare plants.

Armin had liked the feel of the brewery even though it was run down and would require a massive injection of cash. The bottling floor was so antiquated he'd seen a group of women fixing the old spring stoppers by hand. Edgar had explained he was still producing a local bitter but wouldn't go into full production of Klug until the orders were more substantial.

They were back in the office when Kitty phoned to tell Armin that his harlequin was ready for collection. 'I shall be out tomorrow, so would you mind picking it up this afternoon?'

There had been just enough nervousness in Kitty's voice to arouse his suspicion.

'Is something the matter Kitty?'

'No, Mr von Hassendorf. Everything is just fine. But space is tight and I wouldn't want anything to get broken. And I'd sooner you took Columbine home with you and left me to work from photographs. It's just too precious. I have no security. Sometimes I forget to lock the porch door and anyone could walk in off the towpath and help themselves. Usually I don't have anything of much value but with Columbine it's a totally different story.'

'I'll come as soon as I can,' Armin said.

An accident on Richmond Road delayed his arrival at Seething Wells. Kitty had been watching out for him at the kitchen window and she'd begun to worry that he had forgotten or an important business meeting had sent him abroad again. She was relieved when she saw his silvery head appear above the hedge.

'I was beginning to think you'd gone to Berlin!' she said.

'Not until the weekend Kitty,' Armin said. 'I shall be at my house on Saturday.'

He had followed her into the front room where Sylvia and Bosco were sitting at the table with the finished harlequin.

'It looks fantastic,' he said, thrusting out his chest and throwing up his arms.

'It's not all my doing,' Kitty said, fluttering her hands in a disclaimer as she disappeared into the kitchen to prepare supper. 'It's Bosco's work as well and Sylvia's been a great help too.'

'Kitty can be a little too trusting sometimes and I have to watch that people don't take advantage of her good nature,' Sylvia said pointedly.

Armin was peering closely at the figurine. It looked perfect to him but then he had no eye and did not see the beauty in a cold piece of clay.

'The harlequin is as good as we can make it given the time restraints,' Bosco said, suppressing a burp. He leaned back in the chair, arms folded across his chest in an effort to hold himself together. A half empty crate of Klug was tucked out of sight under the table.

Kitty had come in wearing her dachshund apron. Her cheeks were flushed and there was spray paint on her hair. 'Mr von Hassendorf, why don't you stop and have some supper with us? I can put another fisherman's pie in the microwave.'

Kitty was oblivious to the smell of burning coming from the open door. Sylvia went into the kitchen where the milk pan had boiled dry. She turned off the gas and stuck the saucepan under the tap. A plume of steam misted the neon strip and then billowed across the ceiling.

The sudden rush of moist air loosened one of the ceiling tiles and she took the end of a broom and prodded it into place. Most of the polystyrene was stained from the leaking roof and she did not like to think what would happen if they had another summer of monsoon rain. The house hadn't been built with climate change in mind.

In the front room Bosco had opened his laptop and was reading off the auction houses where rare Meissen had recently come up for sale.

Sprawled on the sofa, it was hard to know what Armin was thinking. At one point, Kitty thought he had fallen asleep. His big head had begun to nod and his chin dip towards his chest but when he heard the prices quoted for some of the Meissen, he had looked at Bosco from under his heavy lids and his eyes had been as keen as lasers. 'Two hundred thousand dollars for a Scaramouche? Are you sure? Let me take a look at that.'

Kitty heated the fish pies in the microwave and served them with frozen peas. For dessert there were individual pots of crème caramel a month past their sell by date but who was counting?

After Sylvia had left, the men began to talk about things that did not interest Kitty and so she had retired to bed. When they were finished they would let themselves out.

It was rare for her to have male company in the evening. Alfred had not been one for friendships, not one for inviting people to the house for a meal. She hadn't minded. They enjoyed one another's company. She had only one regret and that was letting Alfred talk her into going to bed the night Derrick went out celebrating with his pals. He was reporting to his regiment in the morning and leaving for Malaya soon after. She had been feeling low all day with a nasty cough and had suddenly been overcome with exhaustion. It had been impossible to keep her eyes open. Alfred had insisted she get some rest and she had agreed on the condition that he wake her as soon as Derrick got back. She had fallen instantly into a deep sleep and when Derrick came to say goodbye they'd decided to leave her. She never saw Derrick alive again. Nor could she forgive Alfred for not keeping his promise. It was to remain a flashpoint for any argument in their marriage for the rest of their lives. She blamed herself almost as much. Her body had betrayed her just when she'd needed it most. She could understand why sick people said they felt trapped inside it, that is exactly how she'd felt.

When she went into her front room the next morning she found Armin curled up on her couch. There was an empty bottle of whisky on the table and beer bottles on the floor.

She glanced at him under the blanket. With his beaky nose and heavy jowls he looked rather formidable, she thought, like Goethe's death mask.

She had been about to go into the kitchen when he opened one slit of an eye and said, ‘Coffee, could you make me some please Kitty? I need lots of coffee.’

Later she was to hear him gargling and snorting in the bathroom and making such a noise the sounds carried all the way to Trish's garden. And so much water! When he finally pulled the plug, it flushed the frog out of the drain.

It had been a particularly golden morning with a faint mist rising from the river and she had taken the coffee into the porch and later Armin had joined her. He'd shaved with the electric razor he kept in his briefcase and come in smelling of Imperial Leather, his hair wet from the comb. Kitty thought what an attractive man he was in a dangerous and unpredictable way. They had sat watching the dog walkers and cyclists. A girl had jogged past on tiptoe as though fastidious about the effect of the towpath on her white trainers.

‘Rivers are special,’ Kitty said. ‘They make me feel I'm in touch with something very old and elemental.’

‘There are islands on the Spree that were settled by ancient peoples thousands of years ago. In summer the gardens are full of fruits and flowers.’

‘That sounds lovely. I can see why you miss it. I suppose now that you have your wonderful house you won't bother coming here very often? What an exciting life you lead Mr von Hassendorf.’

‘It's mostly business, not pleasure.’

He had reminded her of the harlequin and she had got up and covered it in bubble wrap and put it in a box for him.

He asked her to hold onto Columbine in spite of her

misgivings. She had never had anything that valuable in her house before. She could make no guarantees for its safety.

'Don't worry about it. It's better here with you than in my suitcase while I'm on the road.'

'As long as I am not liable for it,' she said. 'If anything happens...'

'Nothing's going to happen,' he said with confidence.

He thanked Kitty for letting him spend the night. 'I will pay you in full once my affairs are in order,' he said, snapping the locks of his briefcase. He was gathering himself together now, his eyes no longer focused on the river or Kitty perched on the garden chair, cradling a chipped cup.

Most of her china was cracked, he'd noticed. But it was part of the general deterioration of the house, the genteel poverty he'd heard so much about but never witnessed until now. He found it touching and rather delightful, this piece of old England which had always eluded him until he'd stumbled upon Seething Wells.

He was sipping a double espresso in Café Flora on the Brompton Road and flicking through the pages of *Der Spiegel* when Bosco called him on the mobile.

After their talk last night Bosco had been doing some research into Columbine.

'Your aunt must have documentation. Where she bought it and from whom. I need some kind of provenance.'

'That isn't a problem,' Armin said.

'There's mention of a Columbine that disappeared around 1939. She must have gone into private hands.'

'Sounds like the one,' Armin said brightening.

'There's a Columbine in the Italian Comedy series commissioned by Catherine the Great from the Meissen factory around 1738. If I am correct it is a very rare example. The fact that your Columbine has a green bodice will make it easier. I don't know how many of these are still in existence.'

'I'm making a few contacts of my own and I'll let you

know,' Armin said.

'You don't want this getting out, right?'

'As I told you last night, discretion is my top priority,' Armin said.

There was a pause and then Bosco said, 'And I still get my commission no matter what?'

'Why would I change my mind?'

'Well, a bottle of whisky and some beers can make you say things you regret in the morning.'

'I was perfectly sober.'

'Breaking up a collection can't be easy.'

'Let me worry about that. As soon as I have found a buyer I'll be in touch. Then we can proceed to the next step.'

Chapter Nineteen

'Termites?' Armin repeated the word Patty had just spluttered to him over the phone.

'But I thought you'd got rid of the bastards?'

'So did I, but Rosita's just rung me and said she's found them crawling up the back of the refrigerator when she was cleaning. She's hysterical. I'm hysterical. You know what termites can do. They'll eat everything and turn my beautiful home to honeycomb if I don't stop them. I can't believe it. I've been crying all day and where were you? I left one message after another and you didn't return my calls. I'm going to have to go home.'

'Sure, I understand,' he said.

'You'll come with me? I could do with your support.'

'Patty.....'

'I know, I know.' He heard her heavy sigh. 'Where are you?'

'At the house. I just got in. The plane from London was delayed. When are you planning on leaving?'

'I'm booked on the first flight from Frankfurt tomorrow.'

'I'll join you as soon as I can. I wish I could be with you now.'

'So do I. Don't make it too long. I have my two harlequins as a reminder of our time together but it's not the same.'

After talking to Patty he had sat in the house, drawing

the darkness to him as the street lights had blinked on and the trams had hissed down the avenue of trees. He had propped his feet on the table and eaten the kebab he'd bought on the way in, the pungent smell of lamb and pickle, his smell, overpowering the beeswax polish and Crystal's fragrances in the bathroom. His bag was dumped on the Persian rug in the hall, his coat flung on Karl's bed. Muddy footprints defied the shine of the parquet and made a trail into bathroom and kitchen where he'd taken the bottle of Zinfandel from the refrigerator and poured himself a glass. Karl's vineyard. Karl's house. And now a wine stain on the damask sofa that he concealed with a cushion. He hadn't expected this anger. It had come upon him the moment he had unlocked the door and disabled the alarm. Acrimony that had been in the air and which he had picked up and made his own, stalking the rooms muttering to himself, wild eyed like a raider in search of plunder.

He knew very little about Trudy's past, only that she had spent the war in Berlin working in an underground hospital. But what of these treasures? Had they been buried too, in the garden under a sea of scillas only to be seized upon by the *Sozis* when Trudy had thought it safe to display them? He needed proof of provenance, catalogues, and went into Karl's office and tried the drawers in his desk but they were locked. Only the thick file documenting the house's restoration; Karl and Crystal dressed in overalls and hard hats with the Polish restorers above a half-finished ceiling. Crystal holding aloft a piece of masonry. Karl posed in front of the window of St Anthony, its putty still damp and its leaded lights depicting an English script wrenched from a church many miles from here. On Karl's mahogany desk a backgammon board in amber and ebonised wood gleamed darkly. His cousin had tossed the dice and won decisively.

He finished the wine and went downstairs and

unlocked the gates to the garden that emerged between the high walls of neighbouring gardens, a velvet dampness of spring rain that made him for a moment wistful. A key on the bundle fitted the stable lock and he saw the mask of Caligula leering blindly from the gloom and below him, the rack of champagne left over from the last house warming. He noticed a droplet of oil on the floor. Julia's Trabi was taking an airing.

He found the seat under the trees and was on his second bottle when the *Hof* resounded with the chatter of a car's motor. Julia had been alerted by the blaze of lights from the house, for he had left them on in all the rooms, and he saw her now in the garden. The car puttered behind her and he called out, '*Julchen*, it's me, Armin.'

'Armin? You didn't say you were coming.'

Behind her Sabine was steering the Trabi into the stable.

They went upstairs and he sat with Sabine in the kitchen while Julia walked through the house, turning off the lights.

'It's your house too, isn't it?' Sabine said slyly. 'You should be able to come and go as you please. Surely you don't have to ask permission?' She lit a cigarette and looked at him critically, 'If *Julchen* and I didn't make use of it now and then it would be neglected.'

'That's rubbish,' Julia said, 'Mum and Dad come here a lot. They bring their friends. The house is very much their home.'

'Yeh, sure,' Sabine said. 'But it's not like they're family heirlooms. Most of this stuff was bought at auction from Jews who had no option but to sell.'

Julia dropped the wrappings from the kebab into the waste bin.

'If you're going to eat take away, I'd be obliged if you'd restrict it to the kitchen. It's greasy and Mum and Dad spent a fortune on the upholstery. And most of this stuff was bought during the recession in the thirties. It's got nothing to do with the Jews.'

'Listen to yourself!' Sabine said.

She turned to Armin, 'I've been digging up a few more family secrets.'

'Give it a rest for heaven's sake,' Julia snapped. 'He's not interested. No one is except you.'

He had spoiled their evening, helping himself to their wine, turning on the lights and dumping his things all over the place in an unconscious statement of possession. This sofa, that chair. Mine. They had planned a night together, watching TV from the bed and making love in that unsatisfactory manner he imagined it must be when a man played no part.

He saw them out and locked the doors after them. Then he switched on the TV and, putting his feet on the table, fiddled back and forth with the remote control, the sight of an audience of animated pensioners clapping in time to the gyrations of a leather clad pop star who was at least fifty, making him suddenly burst out laughing at the folly of it all. The late night channels were better.

He was watching a soft porn movie when Sabine phoned him to a background noise of blaring music. They were in a club and she was inviting him to join them. 'Where are you?' he asked and she gave him the address. It was in Orienberg, at a gallery in one of the yards, up two flights of stairs, a peephole in the door. 'Ask for Naomi,' she said. He got to his feet and stumbled over the empty bottles, clutching onto the side of the armchair and feeling his way into the hall. 'Ignore *Julchen*,' she said, 'the tankard's important. Crossed swords in underglaze blue and painted with chinoiserie in gold. It came from *Schloss* Reibnitz. It's practically a ruin and was bought by an artist's collective for one mark in 1997. They're repairing it floor by floor. I'll take you there if you like.'

‘Ask for Naomi,’ he mumbled, reaching for his coat.

Sabine laughed. ‘Forget it grandpa. Get some sleep. I'll pick you up tomorrow at ten.’

* * * * *

Julia had decided to forgive him for disrupting her weekend, ringing the bell that Sunday morning with an armful of fresh bread rolls; sunflower and linseed, rye and white, split open and lined with slivers of salami and cheese that melted on the tongue. He had woken with a thumping headache, forgetting that champagne did not agree with him, and had stuck his head under the shower and shaken off droplets like a shaggy dog. His body was still tanned but the skin hung slack about his belly and his sexual organs looked shrunken between thighs still primed for action. He had been unable to summon the energy or the imagination for an erection and had gazed ruefully at himself in the full length mirror before pulling on one of Karl’s robes. It was too short and too tight. Karl was a member of a gym and took regular cycling holidays with Crystal all over Europe.

On bare feet he had padded through the house and had been about to return the harlequin to the shelf when a key had sounded in the lock.

He took the figurine from the bubble wrap and, opening the vitrine, placed it among the others just as Sabine appeared in the hall.

After breakfast she suggested they visit the *Schloss* and they had gone downstairs and got into the Trabi, Armin being consigned to the back seat while Sabine sat up front and gave Julia directions.

They were soon in the countryside, the browns and greys of winter trammelled by snow but released now to the fresh green of sown crops. He saw a large bird hovering above a field and cobblestones on a road. Forests speared a leaden sky, enclosed them and then relinquished them to the flat sandy landscape. Houses, in his eyes no more than hovels, made him wonder if funds were still destined to reach these outposts. They remained unchallenged as far as he could see. There was no mountain range to rebuff the surging cold. The wind came straight from Siberia.

The *Schloss* stood outside the village, a crumbling fancy with bulbous casements and a turret. Scaffolding stood above the door. The rooms were partitioned with swathes of muslin and screens to form the ateliers of the commune of artists who lived there. They wore sweaters and heavy coats to combat the draughts that whistled through the broken windows. Upstairs was a ballroom with gilt mirrors cloudy as chalcedony where a woman in red velvet posed for a man at his easel. Charcoal sketches were pinned on the wall and fluttered like captive birds. Sabine popped her head around doors, smiled in greeting, knew many by name.

Julia looked in horror at the loops of electric cable, the haphazard arrangements of lives. 'A fire trap,' she declared with a shudder and went off.

Armin had forgotten why he had been brought here. Was it to offer investment?

Sabine said, 'Every year they raise funds by holding a ball. They light candles all over the place and some of Berlin's best cabaret artists perform for nothing.'

He had stood rattling the change in his pocket and looking about him at dust and decay. Once an immaculate servant girl would have served potato soup from a china tureen to a table of whiskered men and women in high necked gowns.

He was at a loss why they had come all this way to stand among these rattling panels and barely secure floorboards. He had almost put his foot through one earlier. A lifesize papier-mâché horse with an erect penis painted in the colours of the German flag caught his eye. Sabine said, 'A fantastic dildo, don't you think?' and skipped downstairs to a kitchen tiled with old Delft. She switched on the kettle and took coffee from the well-appointed cupboards. He was surprised that anything functioned. Later he was to go to the bathroom and find it immaculate, its brass taps gleaming and fluffy towels on a heated rack.

'The tankard belonged to Baron von Reibnitz,' Sabine said.

Through the window he saw Julia bundled up against the cold, striding by the lakeside.

'It was in a household inventory I found dated 1759. The tankard has a signed enamel for Fromery in Berlin and Meissen.'

'Why are you telling me this?' he asked. His head was throbbing and he swallowed another two paracetamol with a gulp of coffee.

'It should be returned to its rightful owner. There's a niece.'

'It belonged to my aunt,' he said.

Sabine shrugged. 'Okay, if that's your opinion.'

'What other opinion should I have?' he asked testily. 'If everyone gave back what they had acquired by what you imagine are dubious means then half the museums in the western world would be empty. There'd be no Nefertiti at Charlottenburg, no Mona Lisa in the Louvre. It would be impossible.'

Sabina had raked her hair with her fingers, leaving it in dark brown tufts above a wide forehead, her thick eyebrows like cuneiform; an old face, he'd thought, not in the way Patti's was, but knowing.

'I can go further back than 1759. The Baron acquired it from a dealer acting for a shipping merchant in Danzig. He lost one of his ships off Majorca to English pirates and went bankrupt. It then passed to the Baron. I've seen a photograph of it. Unbelievably, a picture of the last Baron von Reibnitz and his family and behind them on a dresser, voila! The tankard.'

Julia had come back, her clothes scented with rain. Had they finished and could they now leave this dreadful death trap of a building?

He remembered too late that he had promised to call Patty before she boarded the plane at Frankfurt. She would be halfway to Miami by now, the two harlequins nestling in her luggage and worth, at a guess, over three hundred thousand dollars.

And the tankard. 'How much is it worth?' he'd asked when they had stopped for meringues in a village café. The Oder was not far from here, its grey supine shape mirroring a sky leaden with snow. He had thought of asking Julia to make a detour and then decided not. There was a Russian graveyard on the slope if he remembered rightly. But what did he want with such history?

'A million euros at least,' Sabina whispered while Julia was choosing cheesecake.

'At least?' Armin repeated.

'Old porcelain is a limited resource, Armin,' Sabine said mockingly.

Julia drove to the Oder, almost as an afterthought. The visit to the *Schloss* and the talk about the tankard a sop to Sabine's curiosity but the main event was here, parked above the turbulent water, quickened by snow melt. And Armin having to relive the day in 1945 when he had arrived on the bank with Karl and their mothers. No they had not waded through the current under fire from Russian snipers, that was Patty's story. Sorry to disappoint. They had crossed the bridge in the relative comfort of a crowded train.

A snow flurry sent them back into the car and as they approached the outskirts of the city he asked Julia to drop him off on a street where he'd seen a beer wholesaler. Sabine's badgering and a restless night had left him weary. Once the Trabi was out of sight, he hailed a taxi and went back to the house.

He fell asleep on Karl's bed and it was dark when he awoke. He was hungry and went onto the street for a kebab. The owner was getting to recognise him now. He went back and ate his meal in front of the TV, a *Krimi* this time about drugs and betrayal among Hamburg's moneyed set. He was pondering Crystal's similarity to the female protagonist, a peculiarly held together type of woman local to Baden Baden and aging operetta singers, when his phone rang.

'The termites have got into the foundations again, as if you cared.'

'Patty, honey, I was about to call you.'

'Oh, go fuck yourself Armin.'

'I thought you might be sleeping. I didn't want to disturb you.'

'You expect me to believe that? What's with you, Armin? I thought we had a relationship. I thought we had a commitment.'

'We do....'

'Don't give me all that bullshit.'

'You got back okay? No problem with customs?'

'As if you care. As if it's any of your business.'

'I want to make it my business.'

'I'm going to have to move into a motel for I don't know how long. If you want us to be together then do something about it. I could come to Berlin and stay in the house. You promised to take me places, the museums, the galleries and all those interesting clubs. Didn't you have a *Schloss* somewhere?

She spoke as if he had mislaid it in a fit of absent mindedness. 'That's in Poland now,' he said.

'And those beautiful beaches you keep talking about? Kilometres of white sand where you can find amber?'

'The bulldozers got their first. It's all gone, Patty.'

He heard her sigh. 'I don't think you really care about anything, not deep down. There's a wall around your heart Armin and I don't know why. Someone just built it up stone by stone. Well, call me if you change your mind. I might still be in the mood to give it another try. I thought we had something special.'

She had rung off before he could reply and he'd stared blankly at the TV where the Crystal look alike had fired a gun at her young lover and now the cops were bursting in.

He tried calling Patty but her phone was diverted to voicemail. Either she was asleep or she'd decided to let him stew. He went into the stable and selected a burgundy this time, uncorking it and leaving it to breathe while he dialled Karl's number. He paced the room and was by the vitrine when he heard his cousin's voice, a little breathless for he'd come downstairs to take the call. Armin got the impression that he'd been expecting someone else, a woman perhaps. Some little masseuse he'd got tucked away. Hadn't he insinuated as much when they were at the hotel? Hungarian or Romanian, he couldn't remember. But for a second Karl had sounded disappointed.

'Look, about Patty. I've spoken to her and she'd like to meet you.'

'I'm sure we can arrange something.'

'Thing is, she's taking the *Kur* at Baden Baden and is in the middle of a course of treatment. She can only make this weekend.'

'Didn't Crystal tell you she's invited Herr Doktor Schiller, the art historian this weekend? He's been badgering her to see the Meissen.'

'I don't know when Patty will be free after this. She's got termites in the house and has to fly back once her treatment's finished. I have no idea about her future plans or when she'll be in Berlin again. I know how much Crystal wanted to meet her. They've got a lot in common.'

'I suppose Crystal could put him off. It sounds a bit of a bore and I don't expect a week or two will make any difference. I'll talk to her and see what we can arrange.'

'I'm sure the Herr Doktor will understand. It's not as if the Meissen's going anywhere,' Armin said.

'No, but we don't like letting people down,' Karl retorted before ringing off.

The proximity of the Meissen, brought into sharp focus by his conversation with Karl as though it were only possible to see it clearly in relation to his cousin's acquisitiveness, had sent him to the vitrine. He had taken out each figurine in turn, inspecting the harlequins in their grotesque poses, in scarlet, black, citrine, and lilac enamel, gilded on buckle and cuff. Pierrot and Pantaloon, another with gold buttons, a plucked cherry between his fingers; the greeting harlequin, the scowling, the drunkard. Then the shepherds and shepherdesses with their restrained ardour and sidelong glances. Give him a fluffy kitten any day. He appraised Kitty's copies again and could see no obvious flaw although he knew that even the most rudimentary glance from a Herr Doktor would be enough to expose them as fake. He experienced again a sense of elation at the dangerous waters he was treading. If Crystal decided that a fawning art historian was more important to her than impressing a Palm Beach widow, then he was sunk.

The next morning Sabine called and invited him to her studio.

'Give me an hour,' he said.

He made a cursory inspection of the rooms and rubbed at the stain on the sofa with some success before covering it with the cushion. He'd already stripped the bed and bundled the linen on the floor as Crystal had requested. She had shown him the coded canvas bags for the laundry when he had come the first time, unlocking cupboards to expose the starched bleached smell of stacked sheets and pillowcases, some of them with Trudy's monogram on the lacy corners. The damask and embroidered tablecloths and matching napkins. Another cupboard had been filled with glasses from champagne flutes to brandy schooners, 'the best bohemian crystal,' Karl had qualified with a waggish finger. Did he know that red glass was made with gold?

Sabine had given him instructions and he'd walked the two kilometres, first along the Spree from which on that chill morning the wind blew sharp in his nostrils and then across a patch of reclaimed land, new trees, flower beds, a couple of benches, until he reached the post war block. Sabine had converted part of the communal laundry into her studio, an enterprise that she shared with two other artists, both painters. She was alone when he arrived and he quickly realised that a viewing of her work, most of which looked unfinished although he was too polite to say so, was not the real reason for her invitation. He made some complimentary noises about what appeared to be a collection of badly welded junk but then who was he to judge? He had just held a thirty centimetre Meissen Scaramouch worth two hundred thousand euros in his hand.

'Can I trust you Armin?'

He had followed her up the stairs, admiring the firmness of her behind and her long athletic legs. He could tell that she was conscious of her effect on him, a luscious fruit just out of reach. She had a habit of forking back her hair with her slim fingers and leaning back in her chair to draw attention to her breasts prominent under a navy sweater.

'Depends what you mean,' he'd said when they were in the café next door.

'Not to tell *Julchen* or those control freaks she calls mummy and daddy. She's completely dependent on them.

Anything you say will get back to them eventually, believe me.'

'Do they know about you?'

'Oh, sure,' Sabine said. 'Julia wets herself every time she thinks about our little love nest being exposed.'

The waitress had come over and they'd ordered coffee and he'd asked for a pastry.

'Do you know where Karl keeps the papers relating to the stuff in the house? There must be receipts, records of purchase?'

'Julia will know. I'll ask her. Listen, Armin I know the tankard was stolen. I'm convinced of it. Trudy was travelling all over the place and she had an eye. She must have visited the farms near the *Schloss* and heard rumours about what had been there once. The place was already a ruin, the Reibnitz family were all killed by the Russians. I think she was tipped off about the tankard. Maybe a grateful farmer whom she'd helped with his state insurance. Anyway someone had it and she got it. But then what to do with it? Remember by then everything had been catalogued by the *Sozis* and she knew when she died they'd find it and it would go the same way as the rest. That's when she decided to hide it. And where better than her allotment where no one would look? I can imagine her trimming her beans and then taking the tankard out of the box to admire it when no one was looking.'

'Where do I come in?' he asked.

'I told you that there is a niece. I'm going back to the *Schloss* to talk to people in the village. They might know something. Look I love Julia and I don't want to hurt her.'

'What's this got to do with me?'

'I think the niece should know what happened to her family heirloom. If she's still alive, that is. I think she should have it back.'

'That's your business,' he said gruffly. 'It's a wild goose chase and I don't have the time.'

Chapter Twenty

Adele and Sylvia helped Kitty clear the cupboards after Jason rang to tell her that the furniture was going to be collected that very afternoon and taken to the auction rooms at Guildford.

'He could have given you more notice,' Adele had protested on hearing the news. She had appeared on the path, a flurry of lilac and magenta with her big rings clicking on gnarled fingers that drew attention to her tremor. She was going through a bad patch and it was affecting her neck and making her head bob like Zebedee. She refused to see a doctor. Medication turned her into a zombie.

She was no use at all when it came to removing Kitty's best china from the Welsh dresser; the two Clarice Cliff plates and the dainty art deco tea service with its wavy edged cups and saucers painted in the sappy greens and yellows reminiscent of springtime on the ait.

Sylvia had gazed at the snowy pear blossom outside the kitchen window and feeling the familiar dip in her mood had hurried over to Adele who was juggling one of the precious cups. 'Here, let me do that, dear. Why don't you help Kitty with the boxes in the front room?'

It wasn't true that Jason hadn't given Kitty notice. Once the valuer had made his assessment Kitty had been expected to start removing her things from the furniture going to auction. But the idea of life beyond Seething Wells was something Kitty refused to consider and not even the sight of her pots of enamel and sable brushes tumbling onto the floor each time she opened a cupboard was enough to jolt her into action.

The writing desk remained crammed with old letters, cards and photograph albums. Kitty had found one with snaps of Elsie's trip to Australia during the war. Her father had been the ship's doctor and there were pictures of a slim and delicate young woman on deck with the captain in his white uniform. Looking happy, with her large luminous eyes. Kitty wondered if there had been a shipboard romance. Elsie had never mentioned it, but then nobody of her type ever did. Only the upper classes flaunted their depraved lives.

Should she leave the album for Jason? In the end she had taken it upstairs and added it to the bundle on top of the Klug, only removing it when the Indian boys had turned up without warning and loaded half a dozen crates into their van.

Kitty had run her hands over the backs of the kidney shaped chairs which she had protected from the ravishes of paint and solutions by covering the seats with linen dish cloths and decided she would substitute them with ones from the garden. The table would stay. The valuer had peered at the cheap pine trestle and declared it fit only for firewood.

When they ran out of boxes, Sylvia had used the Klug crates that Bosco had been gradually emptying after stumbling over Kitty's, 'neat little off licence,' the night he'd carried Armin upstairs.

Since then, Bosco had been helping himself whenever he popped into Seething Wells. But where was he when Kitty needed him? Who was going to make sure they didn't take her Parian statues by mistake? Kitty couldn't face it. As soon as the van appeared in the drive she was off down the towpath where she would stay until the whole ghastly business was over.

It was Sylvia who told her that Bosco had gone to Switzerland.

'It was very much last minute. I thought he'd told you?'

'Not a word,' Kitty said.

Why hadn't Bosco mentioned it when he'd come to collect Columbine earlier in the week? Kitty had been reluctant to hand over the figurine for she had promised Mr von Hassendorf to take good care of it and there had been no mention of passing on the responsibility to Bosco. 'You can talk to him if you don't believe me,' Bosco had said, offering her his mobile phone. But after some hesitation Kitty had decided not to bother. She trusted Bosco. She had known him since he was a teenager when he'd come to visit her with Vida. Besides, she was secretly relieved to be rid of the Meissen. The thought of someone breaking into the house and stealing it had given her sleepless nights.

Bosco had been in unusually good humour when he'd called. He'd brought his camera along and had photographed Columbine on Kitty's table. Did Kitty know how much she was worth? Kitty had put her hands to her ears and cried, 'Don't tell me. I don't want to know!'

And the delightful little Columbine with her elbow crooked as if she were about to perform a dance. Would putting a price on her head make her any more desirable than she already was?'

'For some people, definitely,' Bosco had replied gleefully when Kitty had asked.

Armin had phoned while Bosco was packing up and he had gone swaggering down the path with the phone clamped to his ear, a tall man, Kitty hadn't realised how tall until Bosco had pulled himself up to his full height. And when he suddenly laughed in that extraordinarily loud guffaw, he had frightened the magpie off the lawn and sent the squirrels scurrying into the lilac.

The next morning she had received a parcel with lifesize photographs of the original Columbine and a cheap reproduction figurine that according to Bosco's note, 'will require the usual adjustments.' Could Kitty prepare one as soon as possible? Armin had four other figurines from the Italian Comedy series that he wanted copied and he would be providing details later.

* * * * *

After the auctioneer's van had driven off, Adele went up the towpath to collect Kitty from her seat under the black poplar. Kitty didn't say a word when she saw the empty room. She walked straight into the kitchen and closed the door. Adele told Sylvia that Kitty was taking it very badly and she was going to have to keep an eye on her. She didn't think Kitty could be trusted with the gas and microwave in her present state of mind.

It wasn't only Kitty's kitchen appliances that needed watching. Sylvia had had to store the jars of inflammable liquids on the windowsill now that most of the cupboard space was gone. The garage and shed were already stacked to the rafters. On the other ledge were the fillers; the kaolin, barytes and titanium dioxide powder, marble flour and plaster of paris. The remainder of the glaze mediums and solvents had been put into two empty Klug crates. Sylvia consoled herself with the thought that if there was a leakage it would at least be spotted quickly.

When Kitty came in with the tea tray she automatically skirted the space where the French cabinet had once stood. Elsie's furniture had protected those areas from the ravages of incontinent Yorkies and the carpet emerged now in shades of grey and eau de nil like a small patch of ocean under a cloud pattern. Oblongs of wallpaper printed with tea roses and forget-me-nots were still vibrant where the pictures had been taken down.

Adele had gazed at the room with the river's reflection dancing on the ceiling and said it was like being on a boat that was about to slip its moorings and carry them gently downstream. 'Like the Lady of Shallot,' she had added dreamily.

Not wishing to be reminded of how tenuous her hold was on dry land, Kitty had retorted blithely, 'Nothing is forever, remember that. Nothing.'

Refusing to show how deeply she'd been affected by it. What was the next step in this relentless process of letting go?

Kitty had noticed a faint greenness in her friend's complexion where her face powder had loosened, the caking of pan stick in her nostrils and the smudged mascara eyes and had said that Adele should take herself home. Sylvia had already left, muttering something about a church function but Adele had wanted to stay and keep Kitty company.

'We're both exhausted and you've done more than enough. I'm very lucky to have such a wonderful friend,' Kitty had said and then gone into the kitchen for she couldn't bear emotional leave takings. She needed to be alone and was relieved when Adele had taken her advice and gone off to catch her bus.

She was dragging the plastic chairs in from the garden when Bosco rang to ask if his parcel had arrived.

'It came this morning,' she said. 'Sylvia says you've gone to Switzerland?'

Bosco laughed and sensing that he did not want to talk about it Kitty was about to change the subject when Bosco said, 'Listen Kitty, don't be modest about your fee for making a Columbine.'

'It's only a little china repair.'

'It's much more than that. You're helping Armin free up his assets.'

'Oh? So how much do you think I should ask?'

'Five grand. Half up front and the rest on delivery.'

Kitty was too stunned to reply.

'Don't undersell yourself Kitty. Armin's a very rich guy. He has a huge house in Berlin and a castle somewhere in Poland. Five grand means nothing to him. His girlfriend spends that on a pair of shoes and a bag. You've got to stand up to him, okay?'

Bosco had still been in a buoyant frame of mind when he'd rung Kitty. Earlier that morning he had passed through Swiss customs with no trouble, the Meissen Columbine bubble wrapped, boxed and tucked into his hand luggage before being deposited in the safe at his hotel in Lugano.

After a shower he had telephoned Armin in Berlin to confirm arrangements. Armin had found a private collector willing to buy Columbine and like Armin did not want dealers involved. The transaction would be completed with the utmost discretion.

'Do you think you can trust him?' Bosco had asked. He had worked for his father in Macau before the triads had squeezed him out and his death some months later in mysterious circumstances (he had been found floating face down in the murky waters of the Pearl River) had made Bosco deeply suspicious of strangers waving large wads of cash.

'I've done my homework, don't worry,' Armin said. 'A man called Pierre representing my buyer will call at your hotel at seven this evening. As soon as he arrives, telephone me and I will speak to him. He is a world expert on Meissen and I have no worries about him or of the quality of my collection. I have sent him images of the other figurines from the *Commedia* series which I am also planning to sell. Columbine is just a *Vorspeise.* a taster for what is to come.'

Bosco was unaware that Armin often reverted to culinary terms when he was feeling tense and his subsequent reminiscence of a memorable meal in the hills above Lugano, 'The simplest you could imagine; *Pfefferling*e from the local forest cooked in butter and fresh parsley, nothing fancy, but quite delicious,' had momentarily made Bosco wonder if the real reason for his flying visit was to sample the local *Pane del Nonna* at the Grand Café Al Porto.

'And my fee?' Bosco steered the subject back to business.

'Once the banker's draft is in my possession, you'll get your five percent.'

There had been voices in the background, German voices, Bosco thought and Armin had abruptly rung off.

Bosco celebrated with a double cheeseburger and fries at the local MacDonald's and after a brief saunter along the lakeside returned to his hotel. He collected Columbine from the safe and, after informing the clerk at reception that he was to direct his visitor to the bar, ordered a Cinzano lemonade and settled himself in one of the leather club chairs to wait.

He had not drunk Cinzano since Macau and was suddenly overcome by a wave of homesickness, the combination of a sultry evening and the villas under the palms in their pastel coloured washes evoking memories of his childhood on the Praya de Camoens. He made eye contact with the handsome young man behind the bar and pointed at his empty glass, the promising look he received in return raising the prospect of consolation should his mysterious visitor fail to materialise.

But at one minute past seven a man in his mid-fifties appeared at his table and, after introducing himself as Pierre, accepted an offer of a drink before Bosco called Armin.

Armin took the call in the house in Berlin, his eyes fixed on the painted ceiling where cupids in a riotous scene played peek-a-boo amongst the foliage. It was in stark contrast to the tightly buttoned Crystal stalking the corridor behind him. Patty was late. Karl had already made an appearance in a Harris tweed jacket with elbow patches, blue jeans and a checked shirt, no tie. Weekends in Berlin were strictly casual and Armin had been told to let Patty know that a walk to the lake was planned for Sunday weather permitting, and to leave the finery at home.

Armin said, 'Yes, this is von Hassendorf. You are Pierre? You have met my representative?'

Crystal came in and placed a glass of wine on the table, her expression quizzical. 'Patty?' she mouthed. Armin shook his head.

Pierre introduced himself. He was a renowned expert on early European porcelain and was keen to see the Kaendler. It was very unusual for anything of this quality to come on the market. He was intrigued. Might he ask how Armin had come by it?

Armin said, 'More of that later. It's a once in a lifetime opportunity for you but I have other interested parties. I need a quick decision and at the right price.'

Armin then asked to speak to Bosco. He sounded excited. Armin said, 'He's okay, show him the stuff. I'll catch up with you tomorrow,' and rang off.

Karl appeared in the doorway and glanced at his watch. 'Was that Patty?'

'No, it was an investor in the brewery. Don't worry, Patty will be here soon.'

'She's half an hour late,' Karl persisted, coming into the room and going over to the window. He moved aside the heavy curtains and peered out, hoping to spot Patty's taxi. New shops and restaurants were opening every month on this popular stretch of road. He'd been gratified by the sight of so much scaffolding going up when he took a walk down the cobbled back streets. The relegation of personal responsibility to a state that had had neither the wit nor the money to carry out more than rudimentary repairs had brought about a rapid decline to what had once been a prosperous suburb. All that was changing now. The monstrous parliament building erected by the DDR near the opera represented everything Karl despised about the communist regime; a statement of power like a great concrete boot that crushed everything in its path. He shuddered. Thank God it was destined for demolition once they'd got rid of the asbestos.

It had been a condition of Trudy going into the nursing home that she put the house in his name. No one had forced her to do it and he knew that Trudy would be proud of what he had achieved. Everything was where it belonged except for one ebony wood cabinet that he'd had transported to Bremen to house Trudy's collection of fifteenth century apothecary jars. It was too dark and heavy for Crystal's taste but he had insisted. The cellars still bulged with treasures but he simply had no room. Julia would have the pick of them when she married.

Almost everything had been lost in the war, the small *Schloss* now in Polish hands, the patrician house in Gdansk which had been heavily restored by Stalin before being converted into flats. Karl didn't mourn the loss, he was a pragmatist and understood that sentiment should not stand in the way of progress. But this house had an emotional pull. It was his past and his future all rolled into one. He vowed never to give it up.

'Patty's gone back to Florida. They've found termites in the house.'

Karl had heard Armin on his mobile in the corridor, catching here and there a word in English and unaware that it was a strictly one way conversation. Armin had phoned the Baden Baden number knowing that Gilda was away and then pretended he was talking to Patty. He hadn't realised he could still be so creative. Crystal who was a better linguist than Karl and had been eavesdropping from the kitchen told him later that she thought the termites were just an excuse and that the relationship appeared to have hit a rocky patch.

Karl said, ‘We put off Herr Doktor Schiller because of you.’

Armin said, ‘I have no influence over termites. Patty's freaked. She's exhausted and she apologises for not letting you know sooner.’

‘Well, we'd better eat,’ Crystal said, looking helplessly at Karl.

She had been anticipating getting the measure of Armin's new woman. She couldn't be any worse than Angela who had rarely attended family gatherings.

Armin had told Crystal that she was living on a boat and working in a supermarket. Crystal would never have admitted to such a humiliating end but Armin didn't seem to care. He had a way of challenging you with those cool blue eyes and then blanking you out. It was impossible to know what he was really thinking.

But she blamed him for ruining their evening. He ought to have kept in touch with Patty and warned them. Now it would be months before the Herr Doktor had another free weekend.

And where had Armin been staying? He had told her that business had kept him in Germany all week but when she'd gone to check on the bed upstairs, it had not been slept in.

Crystal gazed gloomily at Patty's empty chair. It was going to be a long evening and she did not relish the prospect of picking at her dinner while the two men tucked in. Food was not an accompaniment to good conversation, it was the focal point of the evening for them. The cousins ate with the single mindedness of survivors who vowed never to be hungry again.

She had ordered a typical German menu from a local restaurant; Kassler, sauerkraut, red cabbage, potato dumplings. Armin had said that Patty had a particular fondness for *Spaetzle* and Crystal had especially asked for the egg noodles to make her feel welcome. For dessert there was *Rote Gruetze* served with vanilla sauce and American ice cream.

Crystal by contrast had lost her appetite. She sipped her wine and gazed thoughtfully at the two Delft plates on the wall in front of her before turning her attention to the Heroldt tankard.

She had brought it out of the vault in expectation of the art historian's visit and was wondering whether to leave it in the vitrine until they could arrange another appointment. Porcelain needed careful handling and too much toing and froing might damage it. She was waiting for it to be valued before contacting the insurers. If the premium was too high she would suggest to Karl that they put it up for auction. It did not have the sentimental value of the other pieces. They could not be sure that it had belonged to Trudy.

She thought Armin looked more preoccupied than usual and not only with his food. His mind travelled to places where she was excluded. Once it had upset her not to be part of his world. Of the two cousins she had preferred Armin. His unpredictability had challenged and excited her. There had been a recklessness about him as though nothing mattered, not deep down. And she had so wanted him to care about her, had longed for it once before she'd learned better. He had no real understanding of how to behave and that is why he always failed. Karl had been dull and predictable by comparison. But of course she had chosen the right one. Armin would never have given her this life, these things. Everything was a game to him. She'd asked him once what really was important to him and she was still waiting for an answer. Oh, he'd mentioned family, business, the usual stuff, but that wasn't the truth. You could give Armin everything you had and he would never be grateful. She had offered herself, years ago when they'd gone to the coast and got separated from their group. She had just started going out with Karl and she'd been prepared to give him up for Armin. But he had walked off up the beach to look for amber and left her there. He was still searching but she didn't care. There were moments when she'd wanted to hurt him badly, moments of pure hatred but now all that was left was contempt.

Chapter Twenty-One

The jar of gherkins stood on the table, limpid green as the Spree. Armin tugged at the cucumber by its tiny stalk and placed it on the chopping board. He sliced sour dough bread and larded it with goose fat and onion and then added a sprinkling of paprika. Others he smeared with liver sausage, *Mettwurst, Teewurst*, and the hard *Harzerkaese* embedded with caraway seed that had the texture of compacted muslin and smelled of sweat. He would warn them that it was not for the faint hearted, this cheese, *der Harzer.* Finally he had garnished the platters with the gherkins, cutting them lengthwise and fanning them out like the feathers in a bird's wing. There was also potato salad bejewelled with green peas and tiny cubes of apple. From the white cartons he took slices of blueberry and apricot cheesecake that was five centimetres thick and decorated with kiwifruit, then *Amerikaner, Schweinsohren*, the thick cream gateaux with their flaky chocolate and morello cherries, *Sandkuchen* and fruit tarts with colours as flamboyant as costume jewellery.

The table had been cleared, the oilcloth with its globs of congealed glue and paint, folded and put away and a fresh cloth embroidered with flowers and trimmed with lace now covered the scars from Kitty's cutting tools.

'Kitty, the glasses!'

Kitty fluttered her hands to her face in mock absent mindedness for she knew very well that the polished flutes had been put for safekeeping in her bedroom.

The champagne cork popped and hit the ceiling,

loosening a puff of plaster dust before bouncing into the porch.

'I do adore champagne. I do love a party!' Adele cried, grabbing a glass from the tray.

Armin had bought the food from KDW on the Ku-damm after depositing the banker's draft with his bank in Berlin. He'd packed the cartons in his suitcase as carefully as if they were precious Meissen.

Two nights ago he had celebrated with Bosco over cocktails at the casino in Lugano before heading for the tables. 'Money to burn,' Bosco had said, his jacket still damp from the boat's spray on the lake. He had not been tempted to raise the stakes. 'You can't beat the system,' he had said but Armin had ignored him. He had finished his drink and walked off towards the plush low lit casino, the head waiter appearing at his elbow being heard to say, 'Ah Signor von Hassendorf, we have not seen you for quite some time. Welcome.'

The next morning a taxi had driven them to Malpensa. Armin had slept for most of the journey from Lugano, his large head sunk upon his chest as the lake had come briefly into view before they'd hit the motorway.

Over there, somewhere on that blue green water Bosco had completed the transaction. Columbine in exchange for a banker's draft for two hundred and fifty thousand Swiss francs. A boat had taken him to a private landing stage where Pierre had come down to meet him. Later Bosco would tell Armin he had not been able to see the villa for the flank of Lombardy poplars that shielded it, only the crenelations of a Tuscan tower. Columbine had been taken to the house and Bosco had waited in the boat, gripping onto its side as the swell rocked it. A grey veil of rain had descended from the mountains and the man who had brought him in the boat had offered him an umbrella.

Bosco had become increasingly agitated with the passing of time. He knew the ruthlessness of men when large sums of money were involved. He had huddled under the umbrella, his hands trembling as the minutes had ticked by.

It had felt like hours before Pierre had returned with the banker's draft.

'I thought they'd tricked us. I thought they would take me to the middle of the lake and....' Bosco had rolled his eyes when he'd met Armin on dry land later.

'You have the money?'

Bosco had reached for his inside pocket and handed Armin the envelope.

'He got a bargain,' Armin murmured, folding the draft into his wallet after inspecting it. 'But a taster is the most important part of the meal. It stimulates the appetite for the main course.'

He wrote Bosco a cheque for five thousand pounds. He also took care of all his expenses. Bosco put the money into his wallet and went back to his hotel where he fell onto the bed in a state of nervous collapse. He'd had visions of being murdered on the boat and thrown into the lake. And Armin not batting an eyelid.

* * * * *

Only Milly tried *der Harzer* at Kitty's table and after one bite she had spat it out in the bushes. The German's cruel joke, she'd thought, and looked round to see if he was watching. Adele had come over and whispered that she'd just talked to Bosco on the phone and he'd told her that Mr von Hassendorf had sold the little Columbine for hundreds and thousands of pounds.

'It's supposed to be a secret,' Bosco had said when she'd called him at home. He was still recovering from his ordeal on Lake Lugano and wasn't coming to the party.

'How much, Bosco? You can tell me.'

'Two hundred and fifty thousand,' Bosco had said breathlessly, 'but don't tell a soul. I was taken in a private boat across the lake to this magnificent villa to collect the banker's draft.'

'How thrilling! It's like something out of James Bond,' Adele said.

'Promise you'll keep it to yourself. I don't want to upset Armin.'

Last night Bosco had dreamt he'd been killed in an air crash and Vida had searched the Alps looking for his body.

In the front room Armin was raising his glass. 'To Kitty. To all of you. I couldn't have done it without you.'

Sylvia glanced at Kitty. 'Has he coughed up yet?'

She was bristling with indignation on Kitty's behalf for nothing had been mentioned about payment and there was Adele telling everyone that Mr von Hassendorf had sold the Columbine for two hundred and fifty thousand pounds.

'You've got to be tough with him Kitty! If you won't, then I will.'

Sylvia had folded her arms under her breasts, a diamond and amethyst brooch glittering on the lapel of her navy suit. She didn't wear it very often, it was too dressy, but she had decided to give it an airing after Kitty had phoned to say, 'Mr von Hassendorf's back and he's invited us to a party!'

'And what exactly are we celebrating?' she demanded now. 'It's you that matters Kitty, not helping the rich get richer.'

Armin had come into the porch, silvery grey with a hint of blue, is how Kitty pictured him when she closed her eyes. He was a force of nature like the river that meandered behind him. She crossed the lawn and passed the pear tree. Tiny bobbles of fruit thrust forth between the brown petals. It would be a bumper year Kitty thought and then caught her breath. No need to chase off the parakeets with a flapping tea towel. It would all be over by then.

She was at the door, ‘I believe you owe me some money Mr von Hassendorf? Five thousand pounds I think?’

It was Bosco who had put it into her head. It was an exorbitant amount for so little work. She would have told Armin to forget it if Sylvia hadn't been behind her, listening to every word.

But Armin didn't flinch. He gazed at her with his distant blue eyes and said, ‘That's one of the reasons why I'm here today. You'll take cash? I prefer not to get the tax man involved.’

He went to his briefcase and, matching up the numbers on the code, opened it and drew out an envelope.

Kitty said, ‘That's very generous of you Mr von Hassendorf. I will use the money to have the roof repaired. The squirrels have eaten great holes in it and the rain comes pouring through.’

Armin said, ‘Your Columbine will join the others in my vitrine. Now, I have one more request.’

In the front room the platters had been pushed to one side to make space for the sheaf of photographs.

‘Four figures from the *Commedia dell'arte*. The Doctor, Scaramouch, Pantaloon and Mezzetino. All very rare.’

The figurines with their dynamic shapes and colours cast vivid patterns across the table. Kitty was baffled why Armin would want to sell these. And if he was prepared to substitute copies that in her opinion were nothing better than fairground tat, then what *did* he value in that grand house of his?

Bosco was already on the case, ‘sourcing good imitations,’ Armin informed them. Kitty's job was to tweak where necessary and add authentic touches such as a flower strewn pedestal, gilded buttons, a bow on a slipper, ‘anything that will make these figurines look like they never left my vitrine.’

Armin's mobile had started to jangle. 'I have to go, ladies. A business appointment. I'll be in touch. Enjoy the rest of your afternoon.'

Sylvia followed him to the door. 'All this food. We won't eat it you know. It will all go to waste.'

Armin surveyed the table where some of the platters had not been touched and said into his mobile, 'Patty, *Schatz*? I'll call you back.'

He packed cartons with *Wurst* and cheese then scooped up the gherkins and dropped them into the jar. Sylvia put cling film over a plate of pastries and carried it to Armin's car. It was not the BMW, she noticed, but a silver Mercedes. Armin had hired it that morning at the airport.

She rapped on the window. 'When do you need the figurines by?'

Armin said, 'As soon as possible.'

'It will be a rushed job,' Sylvia warned.

The window had glided shut but she guessed that even if she had managed to get Armin to listen, it would have made no difference.

Armin parked by the tennis courts at Ham House where only a few weeks ago he had spent the night stretched out on the front seat of VJ's BMW. He'd had nothing but his overcoat to keep him warm and had woken at dawn shivering with cold. When he'd gone out to relieve himself he'd seen a fox like a red vapour trail dissolve into the bushes ahead of him. Later he would wonder if it had been an illusion. He had seen some strange phenomena sleeping out under the stars. Whenever he heard that another Starfighter had crashed, he'd take off somewhere, anywhere. It was the only way he knew of preserving his sanity. And yet nothing had happened to him. It was as if he'd done a deal with Death. Or maybe the quota had been filled. He ran a finger down the scar that bisected his face from temple to jaw and speed dialled Patty's number.

Patty sounded bored. The contractors were working on the house and she had moved in with Sigi Merryck until they were finished.

'How long are you going to be there?'

'A month, six weeks. Sigi's throwing a party for me, she thinks I need cheering up.'

Warning bells sounded in Armin's head. Patty was a very attractive woman and he didn't want her finding solace among the golf club crowd. Some of those octogenarians had been given a new lease of life since Viagra.

'Let's take a trip,' he said. 'How about a cruise to St Petersburg? What do you think?'

'As long as it doesn't include East Prussia,' Patty said. 'I never want to go back there again.'

'You don't have to.'

'I went begging from farm to farm in friggin Latvia! When I dropped the eggs my mother nearly strangled me!'

'We won't go near your mother, I promise,' Armin said and she gave a grim little laugh. He knew Patty's mother had been dead for twenty years.

He had to be careful not to hurt Patty. It was never his intention but he couldn't help falling short of expectations sometimes. His mind buzzed with ideas but not all of them would come to fruition.

He thought about the brewery on his way to Ealing. He would be meeting VJ and the nephews tomorrow and pondered how to incorporate it into his plans for WTD. With his stock rising he could afford to think bigger.

All he needed was a few more weeks and after that it was *alles Wurst* to him. Three million euros for the four outstanding Meissen. That was his asking price and, if he knew anything about obsessive behaviour, then he was pretty sure his collector wouldn't be able to resist. The Meissen plugged a hole in a needy soul. He'd spoken to Pierre that morning and told him that Bosco would deliver them as he had done previously, only this time there was to be no humiliating inspection in an hotel lobby. 'The figurines have been in my family for generations and there is no question about their provenance,' he'd said flatly.

He glided up to the kerb and parked outside the deli. Through the window he saw Sonja bent over the counter reading a book and was suddenly as moonstruck as a teenager. Sonja drew on some element in himself that made it impossible for him to keep away. He did not think he had seen anything as exquisite as the ball of her bare shoulder in the white sleeveless blouse.

She must have noticed him getting out of the car for she didn't bother to look up when he came in.

'How's the beer doing? The Klug?'

She blinked as if she had just realised he was there. 'The beer? You will have to ask Pavel, I have been away, I don't know,' she said returning to her book.

He went over to the drinks section but couldn't find it.

No wonder the shop was empty when she showed such contempt for her customers. That's how it was under the communists where everyone was told they were equal. She needed to learn what mattered and that it was service with a smile that made the difference between profit and loss. He moved along the aisle, a distinguished looking man in a checked sports jacket that had the sheen of new wool. A blue silk handkerchief peeped from his top pocket for he had dressed to please, his hair cut at a smart barbers in *Mitte* while he'd waited for the airport bus. They had shaved him and invigorated his cheeks with cologne. His skin was like hers, they both tanned quickly. They were of the same type he and Sonja, one tawny cord entwined with another.

'I'll bring you a couple more cases. I said it would sell. It's a great beer at a competitive price.' He took out his notebook and scribbled himself a reminder and then put on his reading glasses and studied the labels on the jars. He could tell at a glance that they were not of German quality, the gherkins in particular had a greyish skin and would be soft to the bite. There was nothing better than a crisp Spree gherkin. *Knackig und frisch*. He continued down the aisle, absorbed now in the presentation of food in the familiar and yet indecipherable Polish script that led him to undiscovered towns beyond Gdansk. He only had to point at the tins of fish in their creamy and tomato sauces, the *Rollmops* and *Bratheringe,* the eels and sprats to make the connection. She would deny it vehemently of course that there were any similarities between them.

The impression he had formed did not match the reality. Distance had refined the coarseness of her features; the blob of a nose that was like a dumpling and the surliness of her mouth. He was disappointed. But then she turned and he saw the sensuous glide of her cheekbone and relaxed. No, his memory had not deceived him.

'I would like to invite you to a picnic,' he said. 'You will close the shop for an hour and we will have a picnic on the common.' He stuck out his chest, dismissing all thought of rejection.

'We will drive there,' he said indicating the Mercedes gleaming in the sunshine. 'I have specialities I know you will enjoy.'

'I can't leave the shop.' she said, but he could tell from the sound of her voice that she wasn't sure.

'You are entitled to a break,' he said, flicking over the closed sign and opening the door. 'It is all prepared especially for you. All you have to do is eat.'

She hesitated and then shook her head. 'Pavel will come and I have to be here.'

'Is Pavel your boss?'

'No, he just works here.'

'Well then, it's settled,' he said.

He found somewhere to park close by and they carried the food onto the common under a chestnut tree. He spread a blanket on the grass and peeled off the cling film and set his gift before her, the *Mettwurst* and *Teewurst* on triangles of sour dough bread, goose fat with onion and paprika that he had first sampled in the seventies on a holiday in the Burgenland. She plucked a diamond of liver sausage from the plate and took a bite.

He opened the champagne and sent the cork soaring into the tree where it loosened the pink blossom and scattered petals onto their heads. The champagne frothed over the rim of her glass and he heard a sound he thought he would never hear. It was of Sonja giggling.

It was at the picnic that Armin knew he wanted to take her to Berlin. Not now, but when he had sold the Kaendler and was flush with money, then he would ask her.

He was in good shape for a man of his age but he knew Sonja would need some persuading to go away with him. It wasn't about sex. He wanted to share with her his memories of a place where he had lived until the war had uprooted him.

But it would be difficult persuading her unless he could offer her a good time. An expensive hotel. The best restaurants.

He asked her why she had come to England.

'To learn English of course,' she said as if it wasn't obvious. 'I studied law but to be a success you must have good English.'

She had sucked at a cigarette and blown smoke into the leaves above her head.

'I was at university in Cracow where my grandparents live. They brought me up since I was a small child. My parents were in Warsaw. They were lecturers at the university and had no time for me.'

‘You must have missed them,’ he said.

Sonja shrugged. ‘They visited at holidays. She was my step grandmother. My grandmother died and my grandfather married again after the war.’

She had got to her feet and was brushing at imaginary crumbs on her blouse. She noticed him struggling to stand and offered to help but he refused her hand and clutching at an overhanging branch managed to pull himself up.

She went ahead with the empty bottle and glasses and they stashed the food in the boot where Kitty's Columbine lay in the box that he would be taking to Berlin in a few days time.

‘You have been to Berlin?’ he asked but she didn't answer, the sirens of a police car roaring across the street had drowned him out.

Chapter Twenty-Two

The next morning Armin drove to Ealing Broadway and picked up VJ and his nephews. VJ had arranged a preliminary meeting with Edgar at the brewery and was hoping to move on to the next stage.

Armin was shocked when he saw VJ. He had lost weight and there were mauve circles under his eyes. The last results had been inconclusive and they had called him back for more tests.

'It's the suspense, man, it's killing me,' he said and Armin saw his lip curl in that old Elvis way, for it had been VJs calling card once. Here's Elvis.

'You'll be okay,' Armin said. 'If it was serious...'

'I'd be dead, right?'

'You'd be in the hospital,' Armin corrected.

Neel leaned towards him from the back seat and whispered into his ear, 'That's what he's saying. You don't know the NHS, man.'

Edgar had come out at the sound of their car and had led them up a flight of rickety stairs to his office on the first floor. He introduced a friend, JP Da Souza, a man of about sixty with dyed black hair who had recently arrived from Mauritius. Armin guessed that JP had been invited to advise Edgar and make sure VJ's wily nephews didn't tie him in knots.

JP had interests in hotels and Armin told him that he was currently re-organising his business in the US and planned to go global next year. Funds currently in Switzerland would be used to finance WTA in the next phase of its development. 'I intend to become a substantial shareholder in Klug. I believe it has potential. An English beer with a clever German name. I see it having worldwide appeal like San Miguel, Tsingtao, Kingfisher.'

The nephews fiddled with their Blackberries and yawned. Nothing was going to be decided in a hurry and VJ contemplating his imminent CAT scan had been in no mood to push the proceedings along. Talk had drifted to domestic matters. An uncle's death had created bad feeling among some of Edgar's family members and it looked as if Edgar might have to travel to Mauritius to sort out the fishing rights on one of the properties. Everything would be delayed as a result.

The meeting came to an end and Armin drove VJ and the nephews back to Wembley. 'I've heard he's over extended himself,' Sam said when the subject of JP Da Souza came up. 'There was a fire in one of his hotels and now there's talk about builders cutting corners. I don't think he's in any position to dictate to us how to run a business.'

Neel said, 'Why bother with a brewery, man? Buy the land and develop it instead. You can't lose on real estate. Houses, apartments, that's where the money is.'

Perhaps it was the sight of VJ subdued by the thought of more tests that was bringing Armin's own situation into sharper focus. In the past few months he had found himself being driven by an urgency bordering on panic that what he had undertaken would not be finished in time. In time for what, he did not know. But he had woken in the early hours with his heart thumping and his body bathed in sweat.

Back at his hotel, he poured a couple of fingers of Asbach Uralt into a tumbler and went over to the window. He was on the fifteenth floor and the park with its budding trees and expanse of fresh grass reminded him of how much he had missed the north European spring.

He took a gulp of brandy and phoned Lugano.

Pierre sounded breathless. He had been at the lakeside and had had to come up to the terrace where he had left his mobile.

'Have you reached a decision?' Armin asked.

'That's not for me to decide, I only advise,' Pierre replied.

It was difficult to gauge the mood while Pierre was still trying to catch his breath but Armin thought he detected a coolness that hadn't been there the last time they'd spoken.

'Your client is getting a bargain. If these ever came up at one of the big auction houses I would expect them to go for double.'

'I think you are exaggerating your case,' Pierre said. 'Similar items have come onto the market before.'

'And you know what they went for?'

Armin had no idea but he knew how to bluff. 'I think you'll find that my price compares favourably.'

'Three million is rather more than my client wants to pay,' Pierre said.

'This is a once in a lifetime opportunity Pierre and I would advise your client to think hard before I change my mind. These figurines are family heirlooms.'

He felt shaky and dropped onto the bed. 'Nothing this good will be available again. Your collector knows that, you know it, I know it. Three million euros is a generous offer.'

'It's a lot of money.'

'Then your client must come to a decision. Either he wants them or he doesn't. I have an interested party in New York who's willing to pay three million fifty.'

'I don't see how that makes a lot of difference,' Pierre replied a little offhandedly.

'US dollars.' Armin said.

He waited for Pierre to digest the fact and then added,

'I am giving you first refusal because I would prefer the Meissen to stay in Europe.'

'And you have provenance?'

'That is part of our understanding. The full amount to be paid by banker's draft upon delivery of the Meissen with provenance. But I will need your decision by the end of the week.'

After speaking to Pierre he had needed an escape and decided to see some of his old customers from his Deli World and House of Chocolate days. He might even take a few orders. He'd been hearing complaints that the new reps weren't doing their job properly. They preferred to work online or for companies where the commission was higher. Armin was the last of his kind. Who else understood that tastes in Harlesden differed from those in Hampstead and St John's Wood was not Alperton?

And he had something else to show them this time. Klug, plucked from the crate he'd stashed in the boot for impromptu tastings over the counter and at the back of the shop.

'Kloog,' Armin says, flicking back the stopper and pouring the beaded liquid into a glass. 'German quality brewed right here in Hounslow and at half the price.'

In the course of the afternoon he sold forty cases for prompt delivery and another three hundred subject to a five percent discount as well as a range of chocolate and delicatessen. His success with Columbine was starting to have a knock on effect, boosting his confidence and reminding him of what he did best. Clinching the deal. Things were looking up.

He drove to Edgware to a café that had a fax machine, and after a Turkish coffee and a rum baba, sent through his orders to Deli World and House of Chocolate. They neglected their most loyal customer base at their peril, he scrawled on the sheet and if their reps couldn't be bothered then he was doing it for them. He asked for his commission to be paid into his old bank account.

He ordered another coffee and celebrated with a shot of brandy from the flask he kept in his briefcase. He considered paying a visit to the club off Curzon Street where he'd been a member once. In the good times before the glycol scandal and his divorce. They did a very good steak tartar, as he remembered.

He rang Neel while he made up his mind and they spoke about the brewery and then VJ.

'When are the tests?' Armin asked

'Tomorrow,' Neel said, 'He's fucking worried about it. He thinks it's the end.'

'He's going to be okay,' Armin said with conviction.

There was a pause but he felt that Neel had taken some comfort from his words. 'You'll keep me informed?'

'Sure,' Neel said.' 'Is there anything else?'

'I'd like you to do some deliveries for me.'

He gave Neel the addresses of the Klug customers and added, 'I think we're onto a winner and we must make sure we get the brewery. I'm ready to invest in it, I can't say how much but it will be substantial. I am expecting monies from Switzerland shortly. Make that clear to VJ, okay?'

'It's what VJ wants, it's what we all want.'

'Good. Has VJ mentioned WTA to you?'

Neel couldn't remember hearing about it.

'World Trade Agency. I'll be looking for someone to represent me in the South East Asia arena.'

'That's huge!' Neel laughed.

'It will be,' Armin said meaningfully. 'But in the meantime, could you top up the Klug at Seething Wells? Another fifty cases should do it.'

* * * * *

Neel telephoned Kitty before he set out for Seething Wells the next morning but he'd picked a bad time. Kitty had just opened the door to Jason and was far too bewildered by his appearance on her step to take in what Neel was telling her.

'A delivery of Klug?' she'd repeated, pronouncing it Neel's way so that it rhymed with plug. 'I've never heard of it, I'm sorry. You've got the wrong number.'

Jason had come ostensibly to check that the furniture for auction had been collected but even Kitty who took most people on trust knew that wasn't the real reason for his visit. Jason had little idea of what Elsie kept in the house, he'd hardly come near when she was alive.

She had left him with the inventory and gone into the kitchen to put on the kettle, her balance unsteady in that woozy preliminary to a giddy attack. She had gripped the draining board and waited for it to pass. Nothing about this world was fixed, no foundations deep enough. Kitty's own Andreas fault bucked and spun and then subsided. Sometimes after a turn there followed a moment of lucidity. She had been wondering what to do with Mr von Hassendorf's five thousand pounds and now she knew.

She returned a little shakily with the fondant fancies that were as vivid as a sunset, and put them on the table.

'I was thinking of bidding for a few of Elsie's things,' she'd said.

'So you've found somewhere else to live?'

'Why would you think that?'

'Obviously if you want to buy the furniture you've got to have somewhere to put it.'

'Oh, but they'll come back here with me where they belong,' Kitty said.

Jason had gone very red. She'd touched a nerve, she could see that and it made her suddenly reckless.

'I've come into some money.'

'Enough to buy this place?' Jason asked, yanking his tie to give his thick neck airspace. He folded his arms across his barrel chest. Were all rugby players bullies, Kitty wondered?

'Won the lottery have we, Kitty? Or has one of those chipped vases of yours turned out to be a rare piece of Ming?'

'You may scoff, Jason, but I read recently about a couple who had been using a Sung wine jar for an umbrella stand. They sold it for five hundred thousand pounds.'

'Not much chance of that here,' Jason said, gazing at the stacks of chipped china. 'I'd advise you to hold onto your money. You're going to need it when you move. Face the facts Kitty, you can't stay here. The place is a death trap. It's jerry built and will have to come down. Let's have a sensible discussion about it and come up with some alternatives.'

Kitty leaned towards him, 'What alternatives could there possibly be? This is my home. This is where I belong.'

'If you're planning to take up your option of first refusal on the house, you've got a fortnight to put in your offer,' Jason said aggrievedly.

'First refusal?'

'Yes. If you decide you want the house then you have another three months after signing contracts to come up with the asking price.'

'But that's seven hundred thousand pounds!'

'I know. If not, the house will be put on the open market. It won't be a problem selling this place. River view. It's a cinch.'

Kitty crumbled her cake and moved it despondently about her plate. It was one thing to discuss in abstract what was going to happen for in these circumstances she was quite capable of mentally removing herself from the picture and putting another Kitty, her *doppelgänger,* in her place. But when Jason produced his blue folder which was crammed with information on sheltered housing projects and brochures on sunshine homes and retirement flats, all sheathed in plastic with accompanying lists of useful telephone numbers then Kitty suddenly found herself merging with the other and facing it alone.

'Take a good look,' Jason said, 'Once you find something you like, phone us and we'll drive you there one Sunday. You don't have to decide right away but it's better to be prepared.'

'On Sunday? But that's out of the question. I have an important commission from a client and I have no time to go anywhere until it's finished.'

Jason gave Kitty's front room a disparaging look. The place was even more cluttered now that Elsie's furniture was gone. China was stacked against the walls, a hotchpotch of bowls and mismatched plates and cups, vases, jugs and pots and an assortment of figurines most of which required attention. On the window sills were tins and bottles, no doubt some of them highly inflammable. It was a miracle the house hadn't gone up in flames already. Jason suppressed his irritation. In two weeks it would be all change at Seething Wells and he couldn't wait. Once Kitty was gone, everything would be dumped on the skip and any china that wasn't chipped or cracked donated to Cancer Research.

On the way out he'd noticed the photographs of four figurines on Kitty's table. They at least had their arms and legs in tact although they weren't his kind of thing. Marion had a weakness for themed china plates and he'd developed a particular fondness for the bird series she'd begun collecting once they'd decided against having children.

'They are famous works by Meissen,' Kitty said, noticing his interest. 'Figurines from the *Commedia dell'arte* series fashioned by Kaendler, a German master of porcelain sculpture in the eighteenth century.'

'I wouldn't give you tuppence for them,' Jason said, 'It's like modern artists who can't draw so they stuff animals and fish instead. It's all a con as far as I'm concerned.'

Kitty thought about that word after Jason had left. She had become a con artist too, fashioning the figurines to resemble the originals. Not that anyone with the slightest knowledge of Meissen would take her efforts as anything but fakes. In the display cabinet perhaps, in a dim light, they might give a creditable representation.

Jason had sucked all her energy and she sank onto the bed exhausted. She didn't want to have to think about the future, not at her age, not at any age. She had always held onto her belief in the authority of life and it was not in her nature to suddenly start making decisions. She dropped Jason's fat blue file behind a Parian figure of the Three Graces and closed her eyes. Something would turn up, it always did.

She was roused some time later by an insistent ringing on the porch bell and peering out of the kitchen window, her mind still tangled by visions of hope and retribution, she had thought for an instant that it was an avenging angel; Sam's arms spread wide like wings, his body clothed head to toe in white Adidas reflected in the pebbled glass. A symbol of deliverance that was to remain with Kitty long after the nephews had carried the crates upstairs and driven off on an unearthly wave of thumping music.

She had gone to her table and arranged her tools, meticulous as a surgeon. Upstairs the Klug bottles winked in the sunlight and cast their reflection across the walls. As shadows deepened they began to resemble a small army lined up in battle formation, their spring tops glinting like helmets. The floor braced itself and then gradually began to buckle under the weight. The joists were spongy after the last flood and water had become trapped in a skein of plaster. It swelled gently, voluptuously, mimicking the glide of the river.

Chapter Twenty-Three

Armin came closest to quitting after Pierre phoned him with a change of tactics. He wanted to see the figurines, photographs were not enough, and until he had handled them and confirmed their authenticity there was to be no deal. Bosco was to bring the pieces to Lugano and only after they'd been verified would they discuss terms. Pierre had been adamant. His client was still interested but there were too many fakes on the market for the Meissen to be taken on trust. Pierre had his reputation to think of.

Armin had said he would see what he could do but in his heart he had wondered if it was worth the hassle. He was weary and wanted it over and done with. Later he would phone Pierre and tell him that either they made a deal for that weekend or the whole thing was off. He was prepared to negotiate the price and would arrange for the figurines to be delivered to the hotel in Paradiso as before, with provenance, but it had to be this weekend.

'Why the haste?' Pierre had asked suspiciously.

'I'm going home. Back to the US. I've got termites in the house,' was Armin's reply.

Memories of his life poolside with Florida's poster paint sunrises had suddenly looked attractive. He couldn't get used to Europe's fickle spring, blowing hot and cold. Besides, the longer he stayed footloose the more chance there was of losing Patty.

'What did she think about him coming home?' he

asked when he'd rung her. Forget about the house. He would organise it so that Karl took care of it. He was missing her.

'But what about your business interests?' Patty had sounded bewildered.

'Nothing that can't be done from Florida thanks to e-mail and the phone.'

'And you really trust that cousin of yours? He sounds pretty nasty to me. Anything could happen while you're away. Are you really sure this is a good idea Armin?'

He wondered who Patty had started seeing.

'I've been telling everyone about your wonderful house. The pictures, the furniture, the Meissen. I had someone call by yesterday who knows about these things and he told me my little figures are worth a fortune. But I can't keep them. I don't think you realise how valuable they are. You've got to take them back.'

'You want me to come and fetch them?'

Was that what Patty was insinuating? That he should pick up his things and leave?

'What about the cruise?' he said.

Patty was ambivalent and when he pressed her she admitted that she was considering a trip to Bermuda with some friends from the golf club. St Petersburg was too cold and the language gave her the creeps. 'My aunt died of starvation in the labour camp and I was the one who found her.'

Something had happened but Armin was too stressed to ask any further questions

'We'll think about it, okay?'

'Yes, *Schatzi*, we'll sleep on it. Love you.'

He drove to Ealing and waited for Sonja to close up the shop. He lurked like an amateur detective, visible from the road in his silver Mercedes. She came out with a young man he didn't recognise. His hair bristled on his bullet head and he had the stocky vigour of a recent arrival from Poland. Armin watched for signs of intimacy between them, a hand pressed into the small of her back, the shielding of his body to protect the match she had put to her cigarette. She was not worth it, he told himself, but he could not take his eyes off her.

Suddenly the man walked up the road and Sonja went the other way without looking back. Armin felt the pain of her indifference.

He parked the car and followed her into a small park. He had been visiting some of his customers in the area, he told her when he caught her up.

'You are a very busy man,' she replied without sarcasm.

She looked tired. Her skin was sallow and there were pimples on her cheek. They walked without speaking while he tried to catch his breath.

'I have to go back to Poland,' she said slowing down. 'My grandfather is very sick. My brother is trying to arrange a flight for me but it is so expensive.'

He said, 'Let me lend you the money.'

'I could not possibly.'

'If you need a ticket I'll lend you the money.'

They walked past the beds of red and yellow tulips, so perfect he thought with their cups of sleek petals. Too much sun and they splayed out, exposing their sooty hearts.

'You can pay me back, it's a loan.'

He took one of his business cards from his wallet and gave it to her.

Armin von Hassendorf CEO World Trade Agency, Palm Beach, Florida, USA.

'I've been in the same situation. I know what it's like. Call me,' he said.

But she didn't call and the next day he decided to cut his losses and go to Berlin. It was earlier than planned but there was nothing for him here. He was still in two minds about the Meissen. Something about pushing his luck too far. Again he considered putting an end to the charade. He'd made his point, if that was his intention. But he hadn't meant to damage the Spanish Lovers. He had taken it out of the vitrine to look at it more closely and suddenly the hand was on the floor. He could still remember the sensation of the porcelain snapping like a pretzel stick. A dry, gratifying sound. Clean as a whistle. And his initial panic before he'd acted to save the situation. He hadn't felt so alive for a long time.

When he arrived he booked into the Marriott and fell asleep fully clothed on the bed. He woke with a dry mouth and a feeling of disaffection that he couldn't shake off. Like a stray dog it followed him onto the tram to *Mitte,* a poor skeletal thing that not even the sparkling spring light and sumptuous array of cakes in the Opera café could rid him of completely.

He had hoped that a walk would clear his head and after a while he managed to put some distance between himself and his dogged pursuer. As long as he kept moving he was okay. He left the centre behind and continued on a road with no particular landmark although the feel of the place was familiar to him. He turned into the backstreets with their scribbled khaki walls; blocks of post war flats built with no time or money for aesthetics. Just house the population as quickly and efficiently with what was available. Everyone equal. Except that was a lie. A goddamn lie, he thought irritably and recovered some of his old spark.

He reached a small square with a long strip of grass and a church at its northern tip and realised with amazement that it was here that he had been baptised in 1935. The seedling grass lent a gentle blur as though the building was floating upon a strip of water.

There was a kindergarten nearby and he could see clearly the scar from the incendiary bombs that had destroyed the houses where the kindergarten now stood. Some of the buildings stopped abruptly, cut off like limb amputations.

He recognised this place now. First the church which interestingly did not invite him to explore and then the bombsite at the other end of the square where some poplar trees had taken root (he estimated they must be as old as himself) on what had been his grandparents' apartment. Gone of course, for it had taken a direct hit a few weeks before the end of the war. In its place a communal garden had been organised with a few shrubs and a bench where two drunks lolled. They eyed him blearily and one of them called out and asked if he was from around here.

'No, but my grandparents on my mother's side lived just there,' he said, indicating the bench. 'They moved to the country before it was bombed.'

A couple of W*essies*, came to look at it now and then, one of them told him. Armin was alerted by that word.

'*Wessies*?'

'You can always recognise 'em. They think they own everything around here. A man and his wife. Smart car.'

Trees sprouting from the rubble. An old drunk pissing into the bushes.

He found a bar on the next corner and ordered a coffee and after a couple of chasers he rang Julia to tell her he was in town and ask whether he could stop by and collect the key. He got Sabine instead.

'She's gone with mummy and daddy to the opera. *Die Fledermaus*.'

'I was hoping to stay at the house this weekend,' he said.

'They've got friends from Bremen there. Full house. Sorry. What will you do?'

'I'll stay at the Marriott instead.'

'You need to book in advance, Armin. Your house is turning into an hotel.'

He grimaced and rang off.

The drunks had gone, leaving behind a plastic bag stuffed with empty tins. The air stank and he went under the trees and peered through the branches, trying to remember the apartment; the distinctive smell of freshly ground coffee, potato salad, the *Wieners* bobbing about in the pan of simmering water that he'd had to watch and make sure the skins didn't split. His grandparents had owned the house, four floors given over to flats and them in the high ceilinged apartment on top. He remembered the doors and their thick brass handles. The large carved *Schraenke*. Everything solid and overpowering like Berlin itself. Built to command awe and submission.

The house was gone but the land remained. Tree strewn and divided neatly into flower beds of pansies and forget-me-nots. A note tacked onto one of the poplars proclaimed it an open space for the people, an old socialist prerogative that carried no weight now. Someday soon it would be bulldozed and the block rebuilt. Was this part of the deal Karl had struck with Trudy? The land and the house in return for two years in a nursing home reserved for the socialist elite?

He went back to his hotel and sat in the bar, drinking steadily as the Spree turned from silver to black. He thought about the river and its meanderings through mirrors of water, the reed beds and lakes with willow and birch that were part of the great northern plain. It wasn't a bad life, selling pickled gherkins to passing trade in the tourist punts.

The streets were quiet and the trams snaking over the bridge suggested a journey undisclosed. Earlier, he had attempted to view the baroque chapel in the park grounds opposite the hotel. It was rarely opened to the public and he'd slipped in on the tail end of a tour group only to be recognised as not one of them and ordered to leave. This was for special permits only the guide had told him in his thick Saxon accent and he was clearly not one of them, not one of the old guard but a despised *Wessie.* Armin began to think it really was time he got out for good.

He was still sober when Sabine appeared in the foyer, a tall tawny figure, hugging a parcel to her breast as if it were a stray puppy. She saw him and came over.

He offered her a drink but she rejected it nervously. She had something to show him. Where was his room? What floor? She was already walking away and he got down gingerly from his stool and lumbered after her, pulling himself to his full height and concentrating on the figure ahead of him. Things were a little blurred but he managed to negotiate the various obstacles. Sabine was already in the lift, her finger on the hold button.

'You have something to show me?' he repeated and she pressed that same finger to her lips, her eyes half closed as though in a dream.

He gave her the swipe card and she opened the door and fixed the lights. He wished he hadn't drunk so much. He lowered himself onto the bed and asked her to make him a coffee, indicating the kettle and sachets of granules on the side. 'No milk.'

'What is it?' he said, 'This something?' And attempted a leer. 'Have you come to seduce me?'

Sabine snorted. 'Is that what you think this is about? Idiot!'

She shoved the drink into his hand. 'Sober up for god's sake.'

He sipped the scalding coffee while she drew the curtains, twitching the nets like an old *Tante* and checking the terrace before turning to him. He could see that she was bursting to tell. There was a triumphant gleam in her eye but she was fighting to control herself, to keep command of the situation and introduce it to him coolly. Cloak and dagger stuff. A hotel room, curtains drawn. Straight out of a cheap spy story. He by contrast was beginning to experience the first pangs of anticlimax, the dip in mood that brought reality a little too close. His cousin and the plot of land. As though the house was not enough.

'You should get away while you can,' he said casually. 'Karl and Crystal, they stick together. You won't break them.'

Sabine said, 'That's why I had to do it.'

The Heroldt tankard stood on the table, its silver lid gleaming under the lamp.

'I went to the house this evening and took it,' she said triumphantly.

'Bravo!' Armin said.

Sabine gave him a frosty stare. 'It's not funny.'

He leaned back on the bed, his head on the pillows.

'Take whatever you like. Help yourself. It's none of my business.'

He may have dropped off for suddenly Sabine was shaking him by the shoulders.

'You don't care a damn about anything. That's what Julia says. You never came near for years, only when you thought there was something in it for you, that you were going to inherit, that's when you suddenly took an interest. If you weren't so transparent you'd be despicable.'

'I find that rich coming from you,' he said.

'You think I want to keep this thing?'

'Why else break into the house? Deceive your whatever you call her, your lover, I don't know. You think they won't find out?'

'You are going to help me,' she said firmly.

'Help a thief? Be your fence, is that the idea? You'll offer me a percentage and my lovely relatives will know nothing about it'

'Shut up!' she said.

'Take it back before they realise it's gone. Do yourself a favour, do Julia a favour. It's hard enough for her as it is. They don't know about you, her little secret.'

He could see that she was more vulnerable than she wanted to appear. He said, 'How do you know I won't tell them? That tankard is part of my inheritance too.'

But the word was bitter on his tongue and he brought his hand down heavily on the bed. How had she managed to get into the house?

With Julia's key? Well, that was very clever but surely it was giving the game away unless of course she could throw suspicion on the Hubschmidts and that was pretty unlikely. Those old socialists would take any opportunity to grass up their neighbours but stealing was altogether different

Sabine said, 'I left the doors unlocked to make it look like a burglary.'

'That will fool no one,' he said.

'If it's only the tankard that's gone then maybe they won't pursue it. Too many awkward questions if they go to the police, you know?'

He was wide awake now. 'Can you get me papers on the Meissen? Their history, previous ownership that sort of thing. Provenance on the Italian Comedy series. Do you know where the files are kept?'

'Julia has copies at home. It's no big deal. It's not as if they are a secret.'

'Make copies for me and leave them down at reception. You do that and I'll take care of the tankard.'

'I can trust you?'

'You'll have to wait and see,' he said, looking at her through lowered lids. 'So you've left the house unsecured? Doors unbolted and inviting anyone in off the street.'

'Do you go trying strangers' doors?' Sabine asked, 'Anyway, they'll be back soon.'

A smile slowly crossed her face, 'They won't believe it. It will be a nightmare for them.'

'But Julia will know. She'll know it was you,' he said but couldn't be sure if she'd heard him for she had already closed the door behind her.

He thought he saw her at the bottom of the bridge, just a fancy but the long legs and that determined walk were like hers and how he wished for such a fearless woman in his old age, a tigress to fight his battles for him. He was slow of pace and urgent in his heart, the Spree like grease hardly moving and beyond the great spread of the lake a church spire was illuminated against the night. He crossed cobbles and passed the wine cellar with its vaulted ceiling where a jazz band was playing *Tiger Rag.* Laughter broke the low hum of voices, the clarinet snatched by the breeze and travelling with him, past the gothic brick and lemon coloured town houses, the new trees protected in their triangular supports. He had been a traditional jazz fan as a young man, he and Angela slumped on the floor necking to the Dutch Swing College Band in some smoky club. He shivered but was not cold.

The house was unsecured just as Sabine had said, the great doors giving as he turned the handle and entered the yard where the etched glass panelling leading to the garden had the opacity of milk. A TV from one of the neighbouring tenements blasted out the frenetic commentary from a soccer match. He climbed the winding staircase passing St Anthony's leaded lights on the landing. Another flight of shallow steps and he was on parquet. Ear to the door he listened for any giveaway sound before covering the handle with his handkerchief and letting himself in.

The familiar chemical smell was mixed with bathroom fragrances. Somewhere a clock ticked. He felt his way to the front room, a little shaky on his feet for he had done a lot of walking that day and wasn't used to it. His footsteps were muted by the rug as he went to the vitrine. Its doors were flung wide and inviting inspection like a woman offering herself without compromise. The street cast yellow ribbons of light on the ceiling and it was enough for him to find them, opalescent as pearls, and to place them without haste between the folds of bubble wrap in the empty pastry carton he had brought for the purpose. Scaramouche, Mezzitino, the Capitano and Pantaloon swaddled like pupae in their cocoons. He nestled them gently in the plastic bag and left.

Chapter Twenty-Four

Bosco was waiting for Armin when he arrived in Lugano the following evening. He had taken the next available flight after Armin had called him on the mobile at Seething Wells where he had been helping Kitty with the colour matching. 'I have a good eye,' he had informed Armin. 'Never mind that,' had come the reply.

They had met in the Hotel Eden at Paradiso after an early thunderstorm had polished the town and set its reflection sparkling in the lake. Bosco had gone onto the balcony and breathed in the moist air, the mountain tops gleaming with fresh snow. 'Unseasonably cool for May,' had been Armin's only comment as he had placed the Meissen in the room safe.

He had hired one of the conference rooms for the next day. It was equipped with powerpoint and a projector, neither of which they would be needing. 'Just a table and two chairs will be necessary,' he had said to the manager, but Bosco was to find pads, pencils, laptops, spring water and a coffee machine when he turned up early to await Pierre's arrival.

In the meantime they still had the evening to get through and Armin suggested a *grotto* above Lugano where they could enjoy a meal and panoramic views. The risotto and polenta were to be recommended.

Over a glass of *prosecco* he told Bosco that he liked simple food where the flavours were allowed to come through without being smothered in elaborate sauces. Bosco recalled a memorable dish of chicken rice in a roadside restaurant in Malacca, 'plastic chopsticks and chicken bones on the floor. But the real thing,' he had enthused.

He was struggling to keep his mind from straying to thoughts of the Meissen.

Was Armin really planning to sell off all his family heirlooms?

'Do you have a problem with that?' Armin had asked.

'I have nothing to sell. It's my problem. Nothing personal,' Bosco had replied hurriedly.

'Family's not everything,' Armin said darkly.

'Only if you have one,' Bosco said.

Armin eyed him over the top of his glass. 'Your father was murdered?'

'That's what my mother tells me.'

'And you're scarred by it for the rest of your life. See what I mean about family?'

Armin asked for two portions of tiramisu with vanilla ice cream on the side.

'I was eight and riding my bike down a country road when the Amies came out of the sky, two P51 Mustangs. This was 1945. One of them came at me with guns blazing and I dived into a ditch. The bike fell on top of me. One of the bullets ricocheted off the pedal, that's how close it was. Then they flew north to the station and took pot shots at the people waiting on the platform.'

Bosco said, 'That was close.'

Armin dug thoughtfully into his cake. "I guess I was born under a lucky star.'

They went onto the terrace for coffee and cognac, sitting under a vine with the lights of Lugano twinkling below. It reminded Bosco of Rio, the promontory before them shaped like the Sugar Loaf above the sweep of the lake. He told Armin that he had a friend in Sao Paulo and that it was his dream to visit Brazil and take Vida with him. He blamed the climate and the insularity of the English for making her ill.

They smoked their cigars in silence and then said goodnight. Armin would be keeping a discrete distance while Bosco was dealing with Pierre in the conference room but if there was a problem he could be contacted on his mobile, he said.

The provenance of the Italian Comedy figurines had been couriered to him shortly before he left Berlin but he had not spoken to Sabine. He guessed she was still reeling from the news that four of the prize Meissen had disappeared with the tankard. Something she hadn't expected, he'd thought drily. The Heroldt was in the safe deposit box at the hotel in Berlin and he would get around to thinking about that once he had sold on the Meissen. One step at a time he told himself. At least he could count on Sabine to keep her mouth shut. It had been a stupid idea taking the tankard although he had to admit her intentions were honourable. And it had worked to his advantage. Sometimes you didn't need to do anything for things to fall into place.

He stretched out on the bed. By this time tomorrow he'd be a rich man. All he had to do was to stay in the hotel and wait for Bosco's call. Earlier he had given him a cheque for ten thousand pounds with the promise to double it once the money was safely in his account. Bosco was a simple soul and not one to show initiative. The money would get him to South America which was what he wanted. Again Armin congratulated himself on his good fortune. Others with more guile would have demanded more, much more.

* * * * *

Bosco hadn't been able to contain himself when Armin had given him the cheque but when he tried calling Vida to tell her the good news there had been no answer and he guessed she had gone to bed. His mother tended to retire early, curled up in the foetal position in the bed she'd had shipped to England when they'd left the Far East for good. She had never looked for anyone else to share its soft expanse and over the years the mattress had moulded to fit her shape. It was a gruesome reminder to Bosco of the body he had found embedded in Pearl River silt when he was a young boy growing up in Macau. Perhaps he could persuade Vida to let him buy her a new bed now that he had the money.

With no response from Vida, he had dialled Kitty's number.

'Ten thousand pounds!' she'd exclaimed when he told her about the cheque, 'My goodness, Mr von Hassendorf has money to burn.'

'Money doesn't mean anything to these people,' Bosco said. 'So be sure to ask a good price for the reproductions, Kitty.'

He had caught her at her table making latex moulds for a flower strewn pedestal. She worked best at night under her neon strip with only the foxes and owls for company. A disco boat had floated past earlier, all lights flashing, the murmur of voices and screams carried downriver on a thumping beat that had set off the Canada geese on the banks. But once that had passed, the silence had descended like a velvet curtain, deep and sumptuous with the press of the lilac bursting against the window in thick florets and the river hardly stirring. But Kitty only had to peer out and there was life in the TVs in the houses on the ait and the ever circling planes above Heathrow; no sound though, life with the mute button on.

It had made Kitty think of death and of her own death in particular.

She had mentioned it to Adele that afternoon about her ashes being scattered on the water, right here, by the landing stage. The wooden platform had dissolved into the river years ago but the concrete steps were still there.

Kitty had shown it to Adele, taking her past the drain where she had seen the mitten crabs and Adele had exclaimed, 'Well I never and I've never noticed it before! A proper landing stage. That will add value to the house. Mooring rights are like gold dust.'

And all Kitty's intentions of not thinking about the future had come to an abrupt end right then.

But there was something so artless about Adele that Kitty couldn't be angry with her. It was healthy to discuss these things, not hide them away in the hope they would disappear like poor Freddy. Kitty had no idea where Jason had taken his remains but he had muttered something about contaminating the water supply and now there was a bald patch by the verbena where nothing seemed to grow. How many Yorkies over the decades had been interred in the pet cemetery was anyone's guess but Kitty wondered if special conditions applied for burial grounds and whether this might prevent Jason from redeveloping the site. Clutching at straws. That was Kitty. And not concentrating on the task in hand which meant she was behind schedule with the replacements.

Not that it mattered now but Armin had been too preoccupied with completing the biggest deal of his life to give much thought to Kitty. He had no idea how long it would be before the theft of the Meissen became common knowledge but what he knew about Karl suggested he would do his utmost to keep it out of the press. Too many skeletons, he thought, too many questions. He, of course would be on the other side of the Atlantic before fingers were pointed in his direction. Once he was back with Patty he could turn his attention to what really mattered. With millions in the bank there would be no problem raising money to fund WTA or of buying a large stake in the brewery. He felt confident about Klug. He liked the name as well as the taste. Klug, the beer for clever people. Like him. He savoured the thought for a moment and made a note to phone VJ once the Swiss transaction was brought to a satisfactory conclusion.

In the morning he took a taxi to the Al Porto café in town to await Bosco's call. On his way down to Lugano he had seen a large dark figure standing on the hotel terrace that overlooked the car park where Pierre was expected in an hour from now. Clearly Bosco was taking no chances at missing him. Later he would hear that Bosco had had nightmares about dropping the figurines before he could clinch the deal.

Armin ordered cappuccino and a croissant and leafed through the local newspapers. At nine thirty Bosco rang to say that Pierre was on his way up to the conference room where he was already sitting with the boxes. 'I'm bloody petrified, I can tell you.'

Armin could hear his voice trembling.

'Have coffee together. Have a preliminary chat. No point in rushing it. Remember, you're holding all the trump cards,' was Armin's response.

'I'm going to drop one, I just know it,' Bosco said.

'Leave Pierre to handle the Meissen. If he damages any of the figurines his insurance will have to pay. Any problem, just phone me.'

When his mobile rang almost immediately he thought for a moment that Bosco had lost his nerve and was pulling out. He was not expecting a woman's voice, a soft enquiry that took him so much by surprise that for a moment he was dumbstruck.

'It's Sonja. I am in Berlin tomorrow. You said I should give you a call.'

'Yes. Sure,' he said.

'My grandfather has had a stroke. He can't speak and he is paralysed down his right side. He can't eat.'

'Can't eat?'

'Not proper food. Only liquids.'

'I'm sorry,' Armin said.

'I will have to go back to Poland. There is nobody but me to look after him.'

'Nobody?' His phone indicated that he had an incoming call. 'I see. Look Sonja, I'll phone you back? I'm in the middle of an important meeting.'

He heard her hasty apology and then switched to the other line. Bosco sounded flustered. Something not quite right about the figurines. 'I don't know but he's not happy.'

'Nail him down. Get something specific.'

'I've tried,' Bosco replied hotly, 'but I get the impression he thinks they're, well, not the real thing.'

'What does he mean real thing? He wants flesh and blood? A lifesize harlequin that maybe cries blood tears like a Madonna. What does he mean real?'

'I mean fakes,' Bosco said weakly.

'Fakes?' For a moment Armin wondered if by some strange alchemy Kitty's copies had been transported to the conference room of the Hotel Eden. Could they have?

'Rubbish. They can't be. They're from the vitrine in my house. I took them myself. Kaendler circa 1740. Crossed swords on underglaze blue. Can't he see it damn it, tell him to use his eyes!'

'He's not convinced,' Bosco said flatly.

'Where is he? Let me speak to him.'

'He's outside on the phone to his client. I'm sorry Armin, but he almost laughed in my face. The bloody things are reproductions.'

'Impossible,' Armin thundered.

He was attracting the attention of people in the café and lowered his voice. 'I can't believe what I'm hearing. He's trying to cheat us. He wants us to lower the price; it's a game and you can tell him we aren't falling for it.'

Bosco was in tears. 'What do you want me to do?'

'Put the stuff back in the boxes. Tell that conniving sonofabitch we're not for sale and we're going somewhere else. Call his bluff. Once he sees we're serious, say New York, tell him a buyer in New York is begging for them, wants to pay another fifty thousand. Put pressure on him, show him you mean business. Break him.'

'And if he doesn't?'

'Doesn't what?' Armin was on the street now, blinking into the hard light coming off the lake. He was beginning to regret getting Bosco involved.

'Come to his senses,' Bosco said, 'I get the impression he isn't bluffing. Talk to him yourself, he's here.'

'Pierre?' Armin said, 'My associate sounds a little confused. He tells me you don't believe our Kaendler are the genuine article?' He attempted to make light of it but he had a sinking feeling in the pit of his stomach when Pierre replied curtly, 'That's correct. They are not genuine.'

'But they come from my collection! They are from the collection in my house in Berlin. How can they be different? You took Columbine. Your client loved her. What's the difference?'

'About two hundred and fifty years and the hand of a great master,' Pierre said brusquely. 'I'm sorry. I am sure you did not intend to deceive but I can assure you that the figurines are copies, probably made in the last couple of years at the Meissen factory. You can buy them in the shop. They are Meissen, but they are certainly not Kaendler.'

Bosco was waiting for Armin outside the hotel. He looked shrunken and Armin couldn't help but see a reflection of himself in the figure shambling towards him; his brain still trying to come to terms with what Pierre had just said but not able to grasp it and Bosco blubbering as his own hopes dissipated like the fine spray coming off the hotel fountain. How was it possible that four Kaendler could turn into fakes overnight? Armin's suspicions settled briefly on Bosco but it was obvious that the man was as devastated as he was.

'The only way to find out is to get a second opinion,' Armin said.

There was nothing more that Bosco could do and he told him to go home. 'But not a word about this, do you hear? This is unfinished business. I have my reputation to think of and I am sure this little misunderstanding can be quickly resolved.'

He drank two vodka martinis at a nearby bar and then went into one of the antique shops near the lake that catered, from the look of its baroque furniture and excess of gilding, to those second wives currently gossiping over their *Bellinis* at the nearby lido. He placed the figurines on the glass topped counter under the playful eye of two alabaster cherubs and longed suddenly for another drink. The dealer examined them carefully, asked how much he had paid for them to which Armin demurred. 'They're not for sale,' he said.

On the street the light reflected in a passing windscreen temporarily blinded him and when he became accustomed to the gloom again he could see that the dealer was not impressed. Even a cursory glance had told him that these were not eighteenth century Meissen. The pigments were modern day equivalents of those used in Kaendler's time. Attractive reproductions of Meissen's quality, but nothing more. Worth perhaps a thousand Swiss francs apiece.

'You must be mistaken,' Armin said. 'You wouldn't recognise a genuine Kaendler if it was staring you in the face. All this tat you palm off as Louis Quinze. I shall get a second opinion.'

But there was a tearing in his gut, a recognisable loss of self as though he were being ripped skyward by the thrust of a force beyond his control, the roar in his ears and then the distant speck of metal falling. The suck of his parachute and then the rush of the open sky. He packed away the figurines and left the shop.

He went back to his hotel room and taking the bottle of Asbach Uralt from his briefcase drank steadily until shadows fell and the lights on the mountainside began to twinkle with such vivacity that it made him feel sick. Staggering onto the veranda he dared their trembling eyes to follow him to where the palms rattled like bones in the dark pit of the garden below. He wanted suddenly to drop into their callous hearts and have done with it. He flung one leg over the rail and the palms reached up to him as he swayed unsteadily on the narrow ledge. There was no urgency now, no ejector seat to propel him into the merciless blue sky. He saw a woman look up still clutching the rose she had just plucked. She murmured something and the rose fell. Then the manager with placating hands came hurrying to confront him, chin tipped at Armin's dusty shoes, followed by others clutching their throats in expectation or in horror that he would jump. A woman in white linen gave a little scream and averted her gaze. His mobile bleeped from the bed. Pierre calling to tell him he'd made a mistake? He swung his leg back over the rail. *'Die Vorstellung ist zu Ende,'* he shouted and gave a bow.

Before he'd had time to check his mobile, the manager and two members of staff came bursting into the room. One of them picked up the empty bottle and the manager's conciliatory tone turned to anger. He demanded Armin pack his bag and leave immediately.

Armin held out his phone. He had put his reading glasses somewhere. All he needed was someone to read the text. 'Here!' he said thrusting the mobile into the manager's hand, 'This will explain everything!'

The manager went over to the window and read, 'Welcome to Switzerland. Using your mobile abroad is cheaper than you think. Phone this number for details.'

Chapter Twenty-Five

Kitty saw the clouds welling up behind the chestnuts, a dark plum backdrop and the sun in the west gilding the trees. A rainbow appeared that quite startled her by its luminescence. ‘God pulling out all the stops,’ she said to Adele as she joined her in the porch. It had been hot all morning but now the river was gently ruffled by the stirring air.

Adele said she was going upstairs to secure the windows. Kitty said why bother, the rain when it came would find its way whether the windows were open or not. It was the roof that needed attention. She should have called Lee earlier to finish the job but now it was too late.

Three figurines from the Italian Comedy were finished and sat on the top shelf out of harm's way along with Kitty's Parian cupid and the Japanese teapot painted with birds and cherry blossom on the softest shade of grey porcelain.

She heard the creaking of the floorboards overhead as Adele moved from room to room. Kitty rarely went there but that morning the heat had sent her up to ventilate the rooms. It had become unbearable downstairs after she had used the oven to bake the glaze medium. Pantaloon was giving her problems and she'd had to be very careful with the bedacryl. Then had come the question of whether to bake or air dry. She had been considering her options when the weather and Adele had decided it for her, the wisp of cloud behind Adele's head as she'd appeared on the path heralding the storm to come. So Kitty had heated the oven rather than risk an afternoon of wet.

Adele had brought lemon slices and the intriguing news that Bosco was back, ‘and very upset about something although he won’t say what.’

They had sat in the porch doing what they liked best; speculating on events that they could make as pliable as plasticine. Had something happened to Vida? Or that boyfriend of his? Or was this to do with Mr von Hassendorf and his precious figurines?

Adele had got very little out of Bosco but then he tended to see a disaster where other people saw a hiccup. It had to do with his Portuguese soul, Adele had told Kitty once, the *fado* being an expression of melancholy in song that typified Bosco's take on life. Kitty said that she had never heard him sing and Adele had replied that wasn't the point. Bosco carried the worries of the world on his shoulders and should not be taken seriously.

So was there a problem or not?

‘We will have to wait and see,’ Adele had replied, licking her fingers and winking at Kitty. She adored intrigue.

But Kitty had to get on and Adele for all her good intentions was limited in what she could do to help. After she'd washed up the cups Kitty had sent her into the shed to look for the jar of titanium dioxide stored there and then Kitty had become absorbed in her work and forgotten all about Adele.

It was only after a disturbing call from Armin that Kitty had gone looking for her.

‘Mr von Hassendorf isn't making any sense,’ she said, wandering into the shed to find her friend staring out at her with blood dripping onto the floor.

‘The jar toppled off the shelf and caught my hand,’

Adele said helplessly.

'Not a serious cut,' Kitty commented after she had bathed it under the tap in the kitchen. 'But it might need a stitch or two.'

'Eight hours in A&E?'

Adele had shuddered. 'Stick a plaster on it for me would you darling? We've seen worse haven't we?'

And Adele told Kitty about her mother's four babies, all aborted at home and left squirming on the grate, 'perfectly formed and fighting for life. Oh dear, why do I have to think about this now? So many horrible thoughts. The past isn't a refuge Kitty, it's a bloody place.'

Kitty had put three sugars in Adele's tea and added a shot of whisky, the last drop in the bottle of Red Grouse, for Mr von Hassendorf had left her practically dry after the evening he and Bosco had sat up half the night talking. 'I think he was drunk,' Kitty said, 'just now when he phoned. He asked me if I had the originals of the Italian Comedy. Pantaloon, the Doctor and so on. Of course I haven't. I told him he had them in his house but I don't think he believed me. 'What house?' he said. 'I don't have a house.'

He had insisted Kitty check her reproductions just in case there had been a mix up and she had taken them down and examined them and it was quite obvious that they were not Kaendler. All Kitty had seen were the flaws. The uneven application of paint and a hairline crack on Pantaloon's head appearing as if by magic when she was sure......

The light had been especially vindictive at that angle and she had winced at the glittering brightness of the river and its diamond reflections. Everything around her had looked in a state of decay and when she had gone to pick up the phone, (Mr von Hassendorf rambling to himself all the while in German) the carpet had been as damp as moss beneath her slippers.

'Definitely not Meissen,' she had said firmly. 'You

have kept them with you in your house, Mr von Hassendorf.'

And then Kitty had heard his cynical laugh before he'd said, 'My house? Well where would that be? I have no house. *Es ist alles Futsch*. Castles in the air. I have no Meissen, no painted ceiling. Do you understand, Kitty? My house is my cousin's house, it's all our houses, yours, mine. In my house there are many rooms.... '

The phone had suddenly gone dead and in the silence Kitty had remembered Adele in the shed and gone to look for her.

Something bad has happened, they had decided.

'And Mr von Hassendorf definitely said he had no Meissen?' Adele's bandaged finger rose and fell involuntarily.

'No Meissen and no house,' Kitty said and was reminded of what she had been trying so hard to ignore since getting up this morning.

The deadline for her option to buy Seething Wells expired today.

* * * * *

Armin's call to Kitty had been a last desperate attempt to make some sense of a situation that was to continue to baffle him until he reached Berlin. Only after hearing Kitty's spirited denial of there being, 'any funny business,' and her incredulity that, 'somehow the originals could have ended up in my house, but how, Mr von Hassendorf when you yourself decided to bring us photographs to work from?' Only then did Armin begin to look closer to home for an explanation.

He arrived in Berlin unshaven and suffering from a hellish hangover and went straight to the Marriott. After being unceremoniously removed from the hotel in Lugano he took the precaution of hanging the *do not disturb* sign on the door before swallowing codeine for his headache and retreating under the covers to sleep it off.

Time was when he would have woken none the worse for wear from his excesses, his capacity for keeping sober when others keeled over having been useful in his old rep days when eyeballing big men on exhibition stands up and down the country, glass in hand, had been an asset. He had won a lucrative contract to supply an hotel chain with Sweet Dream chocolates after sharing a bottle of single malt with the then CEO. A deal that had lasted until the good man had died of cirrhosis of the liver some five years later.

Now Armin had surpassed even himself and ten hours later he stood under a hot shower and contemplated a paunch that had filled somewhat since coming to Europe. But hell, eating and drinking were stress related and seeing the biggest deal of his life snatched from under his nose had consequences. Three million euros evaporating before his eyes like the morning mist on Lake Lugano.

He had tried phoning Patty but got only the answer phone and had sat on the bed, face in hands and gazed at his bruised feet and snagged nails. It seemed a long time since Ming had cupped his heels in her small hands and fondled cream into the tiny crevices of his toes.

His head hurt when he moved but he took another couple of codeine and went downstairs, hair damp from the comb and attractive in its steely streaks, and needing all his concentration to put one foot in front of the other.

The young man at reception recognised him when he asked for his key to the deposit box. Armin took the tankard upstairs and examined it closely but it looked no different in its execution from the Italian Comedy figurines. There was the same lustre, the same delicacy of painting. He studied the silver lid with its chase work, but had no idea what he was looking for. A Heroldt tankard similar to the one in the Smithsonian in Washington? He would have to take Sabine's word for it.

He was surprised to find it still light when he flicked open the blinds. He took a moment to adjust to it after the twilight of his hotel room. The Spree moved lugubriously between its banks with no indication of the sylvan paradise that awaited the traveller further upstream; the islets with their vegetable gardens and slavic gables, the gherkins for sale on the stoop. He had an appetite for something sour to sharpen his juices and went downstairs and ordered herrings in a cream sauce that came with small yellow potatoes, ripe with the earthy taste he remembered as a child. The ground was all sand around here. In Trudy's allotment he had watered the beans and watched as it had been sucked into the soil. A thirst impossible to slake.

He had walked out into the twilight intending to get some air but was drawn like a homing pigeon by some electromagnetic impulse to the house. Lights in all the rooms and voices coming from behind the great doors. He had followed a couple into the cobbled yard beyond which the glass panels reflected a gathering of friends dressed for an event more formal than drinks under the lantern lit trees. A prelude to something, he guessed and quietly burped, the herrings tart in his mouth. He was thirsty and went over to the bar where a pert young woman offered him a glass of champagne. 'Just water,' he said.

He looked for Karl and thought he recognised him amid a knot of people further down the path. All Karl and Crystal's friends exuded a sense of satisfaction with their lives, the knowledge that they had done well from the opportunities offered to them. The women wore silver threaded dresses, frills of chiffon, their bodies sleek, their hair groomed. They could be transported to Palm Beach with no difficulty. He had concluded long ago that it was similar status and interests that bound people together not language or nationality. He guessed the blond by the stable would have no problem communicating her trouble with the iron wedge to Sigi Merryck back home. Home. He had thought this was where he belonged but his family had decided otherwise. They must have seen him as a lost cause the moment he'd left Germany to start a new life in England.

He cradled the glass of spring water and moved into the yard and then up the stairs. It had struck him that for a man who had only recently been the subject of a million dollar heist, Karl was being very lax about security. Doors opened to him and he was soon treading parquet and then the carpet, the familiar chemical smell quickening his pulse as if her were an interloper here, a thief come to help himself to the contents on the shelves.

He was in the front room when a sound made him turn. Crystal had come in and was clutching her throat in contrived surprise. She had seen him in the garden and detaching herself from her group had followed him into the house. Crystal on tiptoe. It was the way she conducted her life, noiselessly, and then springing her surprises.

'Armin? We didn't expect you. You never said you were coming.'

'A sudden business decision,' he said.

He did not want to look at the vitrine too closely but his first impression was that nothing had been disturbed, the figurines displayed in all their distorted coyness and flamboyance. The harlequins, shepherdesses, Pantaloon. He was sure that he had seen the miserly old fool on the shelf. Couldn't be. He was hallucinating.

Crystal was wearing blue and it brought out the depth of her eyes, the slightly glazed look of contact lenses which had intrigued him once.

She had taken the seat on the damask sofa and was levering one shoe off with her toe. 'We have tickets for the Berliner Philharmonic. Karl's friend knows Simon Rattle, a wonderful conductor. You've heard about our burglary?'

Her voice was soft. It was her best feature. He had never found her beautiful, that broad Russian face and the watchful expression that seemed to be waiting for a chance to dig, to explore the tiny wounds she could inflict. She laughed and there was gold in her teeth. 'Don't look so shocked, Armin. It's not so bad.'

'They took much?' he asked, finishing his water.

'The Heroldt tankard. That was a blow. A terrible loss. I don't like to think how much it was worth. And not insured.'

Armin went into the kitchen and filled his glass from the tap. When he returned he shot another glance at the vitrine. It *was* Pantaloon.

'They had a key. Not from Frau Hubschmidt. But they let themselves in and went leaving all doors open. It was a horrible shock coming back to find our house defiled by strangers.'

'So what did they take?'

'As well as the tankard, as if that wasn't enough?'

She paused and he had the feeling that she was playing with him, making him sweat.

'Four figurines from the *Commedia dell'arte,'* she said. ' Il Capitano...'

Armin listed the others in his head; the Doctor, Mezzetino, Pantaloon.

'Must have been a terrible blow,' he murmured.

'It could have been a disaster. But after the key disappeared, remember, at Easter time how we spent the day looking for it everywhere? It never came to light and that got me worried. I couldn't sleep for thinking that someone had the key to our cabinet and one day they might come back. I felt it very strongly. I have intuition about these things. So I had all the Meissen shipped to Bremen. We have a large ebony display cabinet there and it shows them off quite well.'

'But what are these here?' Armin indicated the vitrine.

'The shelves looked so empty that I bought a collection from the shop at Meissen. They were very obliging and they've clearly fulfilled their purpose. The thieves took them thinking they were the genuine article. So I bought another set. They are very easy to replace.'

Armin got up to prowl the room.

'Any idea who took them?'

'We are still trying to find out. We decided to take the matter into our own hands. The police are hopeless.'

He gazed at paintings and furniture and then at the ceiling where the cupids cavorted beneath a powder blue sky, the gilded tracery of vines snagging their plump ankles. He saw a small breast bared in a wisp of gossamer.

He told Crystal that his business in Berlin was over and he was going back to America.

'I don't feel German anymore,' he said.

'But your roots are here,' she protested. 'And you will always be welcome to stay in the house. Next time you come bring Patty with you. Karl and I are sorry we missed her the last time.'

His gaze was arrested by the painting attributed to Kaspar Friedrich of a snow scene which he realised now contained the hazy form of a man huddled under a tree. He hadn't noticed him before. A mere shadow in the hoary atmosphere.

He couldn't stand the cold, he murmured. Florida had thinned his blood.

Crystal said she thought he had made a good life for himself and he had glanced at her, tight in her smart costume with some sparkly piece of jewellery at her throat and wrist, the abundant chestnut hair and the gaze that could not conceal her suspicion of him.

'You were always too reckless for me,' she said and he thought he detected a sense of frustration as though she wished it had been otherwise.

He went downstairs and slipping through the big doors and onto the street experienced a feeling of intense relief. It was as if he had been sentenced to jail and arriving at the prison gate had found all the prisoners gone and the gates flung wide open.

He was thirsty but he decided to forego a drink. He walked past the cellar restaurant where the jazz band was taking five and was arrested by someone calling his name. He saw Julia hurrying towards him across the cobbled square.

'What are you doing here? When did you arrive in Berlin?'

'This morning.'

'You heard the tankard's been stolen? Well, I know who took it. Sabine.'

'And the Meissen? Doesn't sound like her sort of thing.'

'Who else then? All that socialist conscience crap. But you can't go on trying to make amends by giving everything back.'

'I know. But she feels very strongly about it,' he said.

'Sabine feels strongly about herself. It will make her feel better, that's all.'

He asked Julia if she had spoken to Sabine but she told him she was in Japan organizing an exhibition of her work. A woman had come to her studio and offered her gallery space in Tokyo.

She looked helplessly at Armin. 'They interrogated the Hubschmidts but they deny they did anything wrong. I'm the only one with a spare set of keys and now they suspect me.'

'Their own daughter?'

'That I colluded with someone.'

'Then tell them about Sabine,' he said abruptly. 'Let

them know how you feel about her.'

He was tired and his head ached. 'If you explain maybe they'll understand.'

He was anxious to get back to his hotel and began to move away from her, touching her gently on the shoulder before walking onto the bridge.

Julia remained there for a while, thinking about what he had said but he wasn't sure she had the courage to tell them. Deception ran deep in this family.

Chapter Twenty-Six

Armin left Berlin that evening, picking up his hire car at the hotel with the idea of stopping for the night in a guest house somewhere on the road, his destination as yet undecided. But east. Of the direction he was certain. First the village where his grandparents had spent the last years of the war and then a brief visit to Frankfurt/Oder where he, Karl and their mothers had stopped briefly before being pushed further west by the advancing Russians. He had left Danzig in 1944. Gdansk, he corrected himself. It had been part of Poland for over fifty years and he had to get used to it. Even his German was old fashioned. At the airport he had asked about *der Flugplatz* and been corrected by a young man who had told him that *der Flughafen* was the more common term now. Aerodrome or airport. Armin had murmured grumpily that they both meant the same thing so what was the problem?

And thought projection, wishful thinking, what was it that brought his mobile to life just as he was about to head out of town? The call that he might have ignored if the traffic light hadn't blinked red and in those few seconds he'd fished the phone out of his briefcase on the seat next to him and heard Sonja's message on voicemail. He had forgotten that she was in Berlin. She told him she was at the *Hauptbahnhof* and about to board a train to Zoppot. Her grandfather had been taken to a clinic there. She was sorry that they hadn't managed to meet up.

Armin nodded ruefully and drove out of the city and

was soon on one of the tree lined roads created by Napoleon or so Karl had told him on that other journey when the details of Trudy's Will had yet to be disclosed and Armin had still believed he had everything to play for.

He found a guesthouse in a village with a small *Schloss* set in parkland at its southern tip and woke after a good night's sleep to birdsong and the rustle of deer tugging at the foliage outside his window. It had rained in the night and he inhaled the sweet scent of earth and lime flowers and felt for a brief moment that he had come home. He recalled that the other *Schloss* where Sabine had taken him could not be far from here. She had mentioned that the previous owners of the tankard had lived there and that a relative might still be alive.

He had brought the tankard upstairs, still cushioned in the box that Sabine had made for it, in the hope that it would inspire his journey. But Armin did not have the energy. And for a man who had been pursuing profit for most of his life nor did the promise of easy money grab him with the fervour he might have expected. Give it a day or two and he was sure to see it differently.

In the meantime he intended to do a little sightseeing and let the realisation slowly take hold that he was in possession of a small fortune (several hundred thousand euros, if Sabine was right about the Heroldt) and was a rich man if he invested wisely and ignored the skewed idea she had of returning the tankard to its rightful owner.

The first cherries were in the shops and he bought half a kilo and ate them in the *Schlosspark*, the juice spilling down his chin and staining his shirt. But they lacked flavour. He remembered the trees lining the dirt road to his grandparents' village, the twisted moss scarred trunks and the abundance of small yellow fruit specked brown and split by a late frost that had given them an unforgettable sour sweetness.

He phoned Neel when he stopped at a petrol station for a curry sausage and fries. Breakfast at the guesthouse had been healthy but inadequate, plenty of yoghurt but the muesli had tasted like bird fodder. Even the rolls had been more air than substance, their crusts pappy from the damp. Patty would have enjoyed the ambience. He had paced between the parked trucks, good luck charms dangling in the cabins, naked pinups, bits of crochet placed fastidiously on the passenger seat knitted by girlfriends or mothers.

How was VJ?

'He's in the clear,' Neel said, 'no tumour, but his prostrate is enlarged and they're going to treat it.'

'Good news,' Armin said. 'What have you got for me on Klug?'

Sam had delivered another fifty cases to Seething Wells but Kitty had been most unhappy about it. There was no space left in the top room and he'd had to leave half the crates in what had once been Kitty's kitchen. Business was slow. Many shopkeepers still had old stock and were reluctant to place a new order until the backlog had been cleared. Neel blamed the weather.

'They don't drink as much when it's pissing down, man.'

'I'll talk to Kitty,' Armin replied.' 'Any news on the brewery?'

'Edgar's gone to Mauritius to sort out his family problems.'

'So it's on hold till he gets back.' Armin could not disguise his relief.

It was this damned hangover he told himself. It was proving impossible to shake off and was sapping all his energy. He went back to his car and drove until he found a clearing amongst giant firs that had darkened the road for kilometres and given the illusion that he had not moved. He parked and struck out into the forest. It had a primeval look, abandoned to itself, the floor littered with fallen trees, their roots embedded in impacted sand and exposed to the sky. He ducked beneath branches that scratched his face and hands, intent now on foraging for the first blueberries, a few mushrooms although it was too early in the season for mushrooms. His stomach rumbled but he did not know how to satisfy his hunger.

He went back to the car and fell asleep and dreamed about Kitty. When he woke he telephoned her.

The signal was faint and he had difficulty hearing her voice. 'I apologise for the inconvenience, ' he said. 'The beer will be gone by next week. I will see to it personally and pay you for your trouble. You have been very patient, Kitty.'

He thought of mentioning the figurines but needed a better signal if he was going to explain properly so he decided to wait until he saw her.

* * * * *

Kitty had been in the kitchen, emptying a bucket from the dripping ceiling when Armin had rung. She had recognised his voice but not much else, what with the rain drumming on the roof and the lightning crashing about like a sack full of cutlery. A thunder clap had put paid to any hope of conversation and when Kitty had tried to phone back the line was dead. And the electricity off. Snuffed out by the storm or the squirrels in the roof. They had been gnawing and romping for days and making such a nuisance of themselves with their high pitched quarrels. Such voracious little creatures, she ought to have got rid of them years ago. But she only had to watch them scampering across her lawn and reaching on tip toe for the peanuts in the bird feeder for her heart to melt. They were such handsome little creatures with their white waistcoats and tails like sable brushes.

The best thing to do in circumstances like this was to get on with the job in hand and wait for the storm to pass.

Pantaloon was on the table in front of her and she thought he had a peevish look as though he couldn't quite understand how he had become the butt of so many jokes. It made her think of Alfred. Not that people had laughed at him except when he had gone on a bit about the spirit world.

They had been happy except in the last years when he had failed to recognise her and she'd had to face the fact that for Alfred their life together had become a blank page. Only when she mentioned Derrick did she notice a flicker of recognition cross his face but even that was to disappear as his Alzheimer's advanced. All the love shared. All the tears. Was there no accumulation of it somewhere, no expression of it made tangible?

Another lightning flash, so close she heard it crackle and then came the thunder bolt that shook the house to its foundations. Rain blurred the windows and turned the landscape the uniform grey of the river. Indeed Kitty had peered out after the last crash at a wall of water as if the river was rising like a tsunami and about to engulf her.

Two bad storms in so many days. Adele had phoned Kitty after the first rumble of thunder and offered her sanctuary in Teddington.

'Are you sure you'll be all right, Kitty darling?' I don't like you being in that leaky old house on your own. Not after yesterday's downpour. Are you sure it's safe? Are you sure you wouldn't rather ride it out over here? Gordon's away. You could have his room.'

But Kitty said she had to get on. 'Mr von Hassendorf's Pantaloon, remember? He'll be needing it shortly. And I'll be perfectly fine. I don't mind being alone.'

'Alone but quite happy,' she'd thought heating up the kettle just before the power went. Kitty had suddenly forgotten about her friends.

After yesterday, she had the stack of pots and buckets

ready in the kitchen. She knew just where to place them under the neon strip and in various corners where the polystyrene tiles were most discoloured. Several of them were already hanging by a thread and with the next downpour she would have to be on her guard. No point in trying to glue them back until they had dried out. She dragged the hip bath into the centre of the kitchen and listened to the drops' timpani. Storms in her experience lasted at most an hour.

She went back to work. She was at her most content at her table surrounded by her china. So many bits, some of them really rather good, awaiting repair or collection. She would make a point of ringing the young woman about her Chelsea plate once the line was reconnected. She would tell her that it didn't matter if there was a hairline crack, it was still a beautiful object and it was the sentiment behind it that was important. There were a dozen pieces of china on her shelves that were reminders of events in her life. The Worcester cup and saucer given to her by the china class on her seventy fifth birthday, Alfred's Staffordshire mug, the Parian cherub asleep on a tasselled pillow that she had bought after Derrick was killed.

She had intended to take it to Malaya and place it on his grave but Alfred had been against the idea and then the toe had got knocked off and the poor little cherub had slept on through the years until quite suddenly two weeks ago Kitty had been sorting out her china when she'd discovered the missing piece inside a ceramic pot. How odd that she should have put it there and then forgotten about it! It was another of those odd instances she had begun to notice recently, as though she were winding down or up, she wasn't sure. But she had taken the cherub off her dressing table and bonded the toe to the foot there and then.

It had grown so dark that Kitty gave up trying to finish Pantaloon. Outside the steaming windows the Peace roses were quite battered, their petals collapsed in a soggy mess. The lilac branches scratched the glass, whipped into a fury by the wind. The house creaked and groaned. There was a cascade pouring from the roof but Kitty couldn't be bothered to go into the kitchen and empty the overflowing containers. Let the house have its way, she would see to it when the storm had passed. It seemed so futile, this constant patching when nature would triumph in the end. The house was nothing more than sand and water and if these storms continued it would save Jason the bother of having it pulled down.

Kitty had been happy here in her own world and was grateful to Elsie for giving her such a wonderful home. She'd been very lucky, all things considering. She thought there might be a little tea left in the pot and covering Pantaloon with a square of muslin was making her way into the porch when the giddy attack sent her lurching against the door. She crumpled against the wall and lay crouched there, waiting for it to pass. But this was a bad one and did not stop after one or two violent spins. She lay on the floor and closed her eyes.

Her doctor had explained it as an imbalance of fluid in the inner ear, unpleasant but not life threatening. She had pills for it in her dressing table. There was nothing else she could do but give in to it. She surrendered herself, frozen by a world suddenly at a tilt.

The carpet oozed the faint doggy smell of Elsie's Yorkies and the spills from the jars and pots of her repair materials. Araldite, kaolin, ammonia, and now her vomit. The rain hammered on the roof and cascaded through the light fixtures.

Kitty felt as if she were being sucked into the vortex of the storm.

She heard rumblings in the ceiling above her, the squirrels, she thought, leaping across the rafters of their flooded home. And then a tearing noise as though cloth were being savagely ripped. Her last thought was of the swans and the sawing of their wings as they soared above her beloved river and then the ceiling opened and the Klug crates came crashing down on her head.

* * * * *

Armin tried phoning Kitty when he reached the coast but the line was dead.

'Don't bother about the Meissen, there's been a change of plan,' he wanted to tell her. He was going to write her a cheque for forty thousand pounds to thank her for all her trouble. He could afford to be generous now that he had decided to keep the tankard. He had seen a colour plate of the Heroldt owned by the Smithsonian Institute but thought that his example had more intricate chasing, the gilded chinoiserie an extra feature that was sure to attract the eye of the connoisseur. He would take it to one of the big auction houses once he reached New York.

His mood had lifted and he was beginning to have a renewed appetite for life. He had never been one to let things get on top of him; he found it difficult to bear a grudge. Let Karl keep his properties if that is what made him happy. Besides, what would he have done with such a house? Always the problems with security and the fear that he might knock a Bustelli off the shelf or smear tomato ketchup on the Caspar Frederick? Where could he enjoy his kebab or smoked eel in front of the TV without first protecting the table's veneer and spreading newspapers across the carpet? The more he thought about it the more he was convinced that he'd had a lucky escape. The house would have chained him for the rest of his life, forcing him to live in a fortress in an area that still resented the arrival of wealthy *Wessies* waving the deeds of houses they'd been forced to abandon decades earlier after the Wall went up.

Armin could not see himself as either landlord or

family curator. The idea of sliding about the floors in felt sandals to protect the parquet was ludicrous. And so much stuff bored him, like the art galleries and museums that Angela had taken him to and which had always induced in him the urge to lie down on the nearest bench and fall asleep.

Trudy had given him her legacy. It was her sweet tooth.

* * * * *

The little seaside resort of Ahlbeck was primped and shining on that summer's afternoon when after a long drive he decided to accept its invitation and stay. He had gazed at the white beach with its *Strandkoerbe* facing the sun like giant hermit crabs and chosen a guesthouse behind the dunes, a substantial turn of the century building with a pale yellow wash and the name Trudy scrolled in large gothic script beneath the gables. How could he refuse? It amused him to think that he had come home and that Trudy would enjoy the irony that her house was his, at least for a few days.

Over strudel and coffee he had studied the map of the coastline and Zoppot had leapt out at him. The photograph on Karl's desk of Trudy and *Oma* languorous as cats in the warm sunshine had been taken on the promenade at Zoppot, the swastika flying high and triumphant behind them. It must have been the summer of 1939 just before the outbreak of war. Holidaymakers enjoying the sun and the band playing.

After a stroll along the front he had gone back to *Haus Trudy* and telephoned Sonja.

‘I'm not far away,’ he said when she answered. ‘What are your plans?’

She was visiting her grandfather every day but there was no change in his condition. She sounded grave but also a little bored, he’d thought.

'Are you managing to get out, have a look round?'

She had taken the train to various resorts along the coast and then hired a car. He could not quite understand how she had ended up being her grandfather's sole carer. Where were her parents? he wondered.

'Do you think you will be returning to London?'

She didn't know. He could tell that she was becoming tired of his questions and he said, 'Well, it was nice talking to you Sonja.'

He was about to put down the phone when she said that she was driving to Berlin the following day. He thought about it but he did not want to travel far or be too close to Karl.

He told her where he was staying and she said she might look him up. It was a long drive to Berlin.

'You're welcome to stop off here. There's a coffee shop close by and they do an excellent cheesecake.'

She said she would call him in the morning.

He slept and in the evening wandered down to the pier and ordered the seafood platter in a restaurant overlooking the sea and watched the moon laminate the waves and cast shadow across the *Strandkoerbe*. Once he would have gone swimming. He'd been fearless as a boy, Karl had been no match for him, standing on the water's edge while he had struck out for the horizon and come back to laugh in his face. They had been close before their mothers had fallen out, he could not remember the details, but it must have been acrimonious for there were no more Sunday visits. That is where the grudge had started he supposed, passed on from mother to son. What did he care? Now the sea looked forbidding in its blackness, its golden treasure swept away by Russian bulldozers. He thought suddenly of Sonja and wondered casually if she would phone him, an old man grateful for any attention from a young women. Not so old, he reminded himself, but the last few months had taken its toll.

Back in his room he had checked the time and then telephoned Patty. She had sounded pleased to hear his voice.

'Lots to sort out,' he said wearily when she had asked why he hadn't called earlier. 'Some confusion over the Meissen being genuine or not. I'd get the two figurines checked out just in case.'

'You mean they might not be the real thing?'

Patty lowered her voice. 'Is that why you let me have them?'

'I didn't know then. I gave them to you in good faith,' he said taken aback by her aggressive tone. 'I've just found out Trudy had copies made...' It was easier to lie. Who said the truth was straight forward?

Patty was taking the news as a personal insult.

'I'm not saying they are fakes,' he insisted. He couldn't remember whether he had given them to Patty before or after he had pocketed the key and sent Crystal scurrying off to replace the originals with copies.

But did it really matter?

'Well of course it matters! I've been telling everyone that they are eighteenth century Kandle.....'

'Kaendler,' he corrected.

'That they are old and very valuable. You told me they used to belong to Catherine the Great, for God's sake!'

'That's what I thought. And it may still be the case. As I said, check them out.'

'I don't want to check them out,' Patty said angrily, 'I took your word Armin. I believed you. I thought wow, here's an expression of your regard for me, of your love. But if you can deceive me with the Kandle ...'

'Kaendler...'

'If you can lie to me about that then what else are you hiding from me? How can I trust you?'

'Sure you can.'

'No, it doesn't follow at all.'

'Okay Patty. I don't own the house, Karl owns it. He and Crystal together. It all went to them and I got nothing. But you liked the Meissen so I gave them to you even though they weren't mine to give. You can contact Karl if you like and give them back. He doesn't know you've got them but that's okay. He probably hasn't even missed them. But you can do the right thing if you want, fake or not, I'm fucked if I care.'

That night he slept like a log.

The next morning while he was enjoying crusty rolls and local honey, Sonja phoned and they agreed to meet in Bansin about twenty kilometres from where he was staying. He planned to show her the smokeries along the beach on the crescent between the sea and dunes but it didn't turn out that way. He arrived early but was disappointed. Only a few of the smokeries remained and he didn't enjoy the experience of eating smoked eel, standing at a gritty table with plastic cutlery and sipping beer from a paper cup. The eel was fatty and tasted as if it was farmed. The smoked herring was no better. He noticed that the local McDonalds was heaving.

And they had flattened the sand dunes, extending the rows of guesthouses where once had been an expanse of beach and the wide open sea. No chance of finding amber on these well-trodden shores. But further east, maybe. Up there deep into Poland and then Russia where the Scandinavian firs dropped their warm resin into the cool Baltic and the waves licked it into globules hard as toffee.

Sonja wore amber, conscious or not that it was he who had given it to her that afternoon in Richmond Park. A cloudy droplet, sanded smooth by millennia in the ocean, it now dangled on a gold chain about her neck. She was to stroke it occasionally as they sat in the small café on the seafront. She had put on a little weight that made her chin fleshy and her cheeks fuller but he thought it suited her. She had looked quite gaunt the last time he had seen her. There were bright red streaks in her hair. He had noticed the fashion in young Berliners too, this penchant for dayglo colours of mauve, orange, green worn with dusty black clothes. Sonja wore blue jeans and the faded denim jacket with the grubby sheepskin collar that wasn't real sheepskin. He experienced the familiar mix of disappointment and anticipation, rejecting her one minute only to be enchanted the next. He wondered if she knew the power she had over him. Sometimes he suspected she did when he experienced the sudden dip of her eyes, that knowing look he recognised in women who knew they were in control.

But he didn't care. He enjoyed being with her, even her silences were replete with promises she just might express.

He told her that he was leaving in the morning and it appeared to settle something in her mind, for she began to tell him about herself in the way two strangers might share their most intimate secrets on a train journey that would eventually take them to different destinations.

He was puzzled that she had never mentioned her parents.

'They were academics, communists. They worked for the country and I was an individual. I think they loved me but they had no time for me.'

'So your grandfather brought you up?'

'He and my step grandmother. He was an anti-communist,' Sonja added with a smile, 'He was subversive. He knew what it was like before the war when life had been good for him. He was not from Cracow. He and my grandmother were born in eastern Poland, what is now Belarus. One day they were told to leave, take what they could and get out. The house and land were divided up and given to the Russians. A present from Hitler to Stalin. Many Poles fled the country, they went to France, London, but my grandparents stayed.'

Always the shifting of boundaries, he thought, the unresolved differences that simmered beneath the surface. At least in America they had no history. 'No personal history,' he corrected. 'You can buy a house, change your name.'

'That is the idea,' Sonja said.

'And your parents?'

'I was born when my mother was forty five,' Sonja said wryly. 'Oh, they are still alive but they have been destroyed by what has happened. Their ideals, their beliefs have no importance now. They sit with their old friends and discuss the past, that's all they have. My mother lost her own mother when she was young. She had Jewish blood and was shot by the Germans. Someone reported her, someone with a grudge. My father was away and when he came home he found her and her sister dead on the lawn in front of the house.'

Sonja stirred the sugar with her spoon. 'It's history.'

'Our history,' he said sombrely.

She had taken the menu card. She was hungry and he said, 'Not here.'

He had noticed another smokery further up the beach with a cocked tin pot chimney blowing out the tarry salty smell of his childhood. There was a small café attached with clean tables. He took her there and they had a fish platter, golden smoked with the tang of sea salt and beechwood and a side dish of yellow potatoes.

If she were here longer he would suggest a trip up the coast where there was an expanse of white sand, fine as chalk with glints of amber trapped in the waves. But even as he spoke he felt his own enthusiasm waning.

'You are a romantic,' she laughed.

No one had said that to him before and he was touched.

'There's no room for sentiment in business,' he said.

They walked back to where she had left the car and as

they passed the guest house he asked her to wait. He went upstairs, a little out of breath from the effort or maybe it was the intoxicating effect that Sonja had on him. He could not explain it beyond a recognition, some connection with the past that awakened in him the desire to nurture and protect. He took the box and carried it down to the street where she was waiting.

He gave her the tankard. ‘It's rare and worth a lot of money.’ he said.

‘Then I can't take it,’ she replied handing it back to him.

‘I insist. It's of no use to me but it is to you. Sell it for the future. Buy yourself a ticket to America and continue your studies. Be sure to get a good degree. I have all I want here. Do some good with it. Take it.’

She accepted it without further protestations. She could see by his face that he would be offended if she kept on resisting.

‘I'll keep in touch. I'll ring you and let you know how I get on,’ she said, looking at him in bewilderment.

‘Be sure and do that,’ he said.

He waited until she had driven away and then he went back to *Haus Trudy* and packed his bag. He had a momentary pang of regret, not for the loss of the Heroldt but that the smoked herring he had ordered for her had not been quite as good as he'd expected. Sonja hadn't complained but he didn't like to think she'd gone away, a dissatisfied customer.

It made him think about the standards he'd set himself and whether he'd been deluded in believing that German quality was best. It was a while since he'd sampled a Spreewalder gherkin and here he was not a few hundred kilometres from the source. He started the car but his mind was already travelling to the Spree and the islets bejewelled by rambling vines that fed on the limpid green water. A small house and jars of gherkins for sale on the stoop. He would offer tasters to tourists passing in the punts. Pickled marrow, onions, but above all cucumbers. He didn't feel hungry. He was full of hope.

Chapter Twenty-Seven

So many people turned up for Kitty's funeral that it was standing room only for those who arrived late. Adele recognised about half of them, the china class of course and people along Water Lane who were acquaintances rather than friends. The newcomers now occupying the large houses were very different from the original owners who had settled there after the war. Then the men had still worn their blazers emblazoned with the badge of their regiment and the women in their pinnies had always been eager for a chat over a cup of tea.

'Waste not want not,' Adele had been taught but as she remarked to Sylvia in the church hall after the service, 'Can you imagine Trish or any of her sort coming to Kitty with a chipped plate or asking her to bond the handle back on a cup? It's the end of an era. It's a throwaway society now. The world has changed.'

They drew comfort from the knowledge that Kitty had died exactly where she would have wanted and nor did they question whether it was true that she had been clutching a tube of Araldite when the walker on the towpath had found her. No one was going to object to a little poetic licence when remembering Kitty's final moments.

Doreen was seen talking to Marion and Jason over the plate of cocktail sausages and warm white wine but the rest of the china class kept their distance. Jason could not have hoped for a more satisfactory resolution to his problems but Milly said she thought he looked rather sheepish and that he had averted his eyes when she'd stared at him.

Bosco had sent a telegram from Sao Paulo where he had gone with Vida and met up with his friend Jao. He had tried contacting Armin but the mobile number he had was not registering. Doreen could not help blurting out that as far as she was concerned, Mr von Hassendorf had to take his share of the responsibility for what had happened to Kitty. Wasn't the weight of the beer the real reason for the ceiling collapsing?

Sylvia said it was the volume of water collecting in the roof during the storm that had done most of the damage. And the squirrels had played a part too, gnawing at the fabric of the house for the last thirty years until everything was a fine mesh. First Elsie and then Kitty had threatened to do something about them but never had.

Adele liked the idea of nature taking its course and she knew Kitty would have too. The elements and God's creatures uniting to bring about Kitty's timely end. Adele was quite sure Kitty would not have wanted it any other way.

She was found buried under the silt by a Jack Russell. A Yorkie would have been more appropriate, Adele thought but it didn't matter. The main thing was that Kitty hadn't realised what had hit her. Here one second, gone the next. It was just a shame that Adele's idea of floating Kitty downstream on a skiff like the Lady of Shallot was given short shrift by the Council on grounds of health and safety, but it happened in Adele's imagination without a hitch. Her darling Kitty with Derrick's framed photograph on her breast and wearing something floaty. Elgar playing in the background. Adele wept when she thought about it.

On a summer's evening the china class gathered at Seething Wells for the last time. They parked in the drive and walked across the back lawn, past the pet cemetery now overgrown with bindweed that clung to the verbena and cloaked it in a trail of vines and white trumpet flowers. The moles had been busy and Milly told Molly to watch her footing. They passed the shed where later they would find some of their own cups, vases, plates and figurines among the stacks that Kitty had put to one side when something more urgent had come up.

Molly was to be reunited with a creamware centrepiece that she had brought to the class in 1989 and never quite understood how it could have disappeared. And the chipped Worcester and Derby, the Staffordshire and Royal Doulton, the classical Parian figures, the bold ceramics from the fifties and sixties, the cheap china animals from car boots and bring and buys, all of them piled from floor to ceiling and as Doreen dryly commented, 'not one of them without a flaw of some kind.'

Into the front garden they went and down to the river that was riding high between its banks for the flood was coming from beyond Oxford and was now a yellowish brown as it surged past. The road was closed until low tide.

Already the grass was knee high and some of the pots had been blown over in the storms and their contents scattered. Sylvia had righted a wire mesh bowl of pansies and made a note to take them with her before she left.

Behind them the exposed damp beams of the house steamed in the late sun as if on fire. Part of the roof was exposed and there was a gaping hole in the porch where the ceiling had come down, swilled by the torrent of underground streams that had converged and burst through the floor, sweeping everything before them. Kitty had been directly under the crashing wood and plaster.

'I believe she was thinking happy thoughts,' Adele said after surveying the damage.

They had descended the worn concrete steps of the

landing stage and there they had scattered Kitty's ashes, taking turns to shake the dust into the fast flowing water.

A new moon was visible above the chestnuts and the stillness was agitated by the pipistrelle and the churring of the grebes.

Adele shivered and pulled her cardigan close about her shoulders. In a way it was the best of endings. Kitty would never have survived anywhere else. Seething Wells was her home to the very last.

'I'm afraid I must leave you,' Doreen said. She wanted to be back before dark.

They agreed that they would try and keep up the china class and Doreen suggested drawing up a rota for when they could visit each other's houses. Adele wasn't sure how she would get to Godalming but she'd find out about buses and Sylvia didn't see a problem although she'd had another odd turn recently with her foot refusing to move off the clutch. No point in mentioning that but she was wondering if it was time she gave up driving.

The light was fading fast and Adele remained in the drive, waving them off until they had disappeared. Seething Wells was beached like the hulk of an old ship on a sandbank sinking gently into the gloom.

Soon the house would be bulldozed, the ground flattened, the trees uprooted and the squirrels shooed from their dreys. But the river would always be there.